A Time to Heal

SONEAKQUA J. WHITE

Published in the United States by
Pen2Pad Ink Publishing.
www.pen2padink.org

Requests to publish work from this book or to contact the author should be sent to: sjw@atthetablecounseling.com

Soneakqua J. White retains the rights to all images

Revised interior 1/18/2019

*In memory of my uncle Robert
and cousins Monique and Edward.
The truth might have saved you all.*

The Reunion

One day they'll know
I'm leaving a paper trail
Who the mother really is
Why she should go to hell

Who will tell
How long will it take?
She's evil on Earth
Filled with hate

Christian…whatever
Lies upon lies
She doesn't know Jesus
I hope she fries!

THAT POEM HAUNTED me as I got ready for the reunion. I couldn't get it off my mind. Ever since the day I read it I knew what it could mean, but I didn't want to believe it. It made me question even the obvious reasons why I had doubts about going to this event in the first place. But, I felt drawn to the family. Sure, I was invited but that didn't mean I should go. Part of me was saying I most certainly shouldn't because of my license. It was actually against my professional ethics to hang out with clients. I could get into a lot of trouble for things like this yet I still had the urge to go. So, I decided to take the risk.

I couldn't stay long though because I needed to meet my mother at three o'clock. I couldn't wait to see her! She was finally ready to tell me what had been on her mind over the past several months. She was acting so strange and I was worried about her.

She didn't even want me to pick her up from the airport. I thought that was really odd, but she had been acting strange for months, like I said. I had been praying that this visit would be what we needed for her to get to know me as an adult instead of her little girl. Don't get me wrong… I enjoyed being her baby and always have. I was just hoping maybe she would be able to accept me as an adult as well and to not be afraid to treat me as one. I know the friend thing doesn't work that well when you're trying to raise a child but once the children become adults, I think it's okay to be friends.

I grabbed the address to the park and ran out the door. Being new to the city, I still needed directions to get to most places. I was hoping they would have some good food because I was hungry! I had previously told the Cameron's I probably wouldn't make the reunion due to work related reasons and they seemed to understand. Hopefully they wouldn't mind me just showing up after I said I couldn't. Oh well… it would only be for a few minutes anyway. I did want to meet Amber. After all I had been through with the family, I was really glad they were reuniting and wanted to congratulate them all for putting aside their differences to pull this off. They were thinking of the family as a whole instead of themselves individually. Even though they still had a long way to go, they had worked hard to make this day possible.

I hopped in the car and headed on over. The reunion was supposed to start at noon but I waited an extra hour because I knew it wouldn't start on time. Family reunions never do. Somebody always had to go to the store because they forgot this or that or to get one last thing. Plus, there was no point in getting there early if the food wasn't ready! I hated to have to eat and run but that was exactly what I planned to do. My mother was the most important thing on my schedule for the day and besides, I wasn't supposed to be fraternizing with clients anyway.

By the time I got there the Cameron family reunion was in full swing! There were dominos to the left, bid whist to the right, food in the back, drinks to the side, adults over there and kids everywhere! This day had been a long time coming. The

Cameron's hadn't been together as a complete family in over seventeen years and most of them had barely spoken to one another during that time.

"It's hot out here!" A little girl shouted as she ran by.

"If you would sit your little busy body down somewhere you wouldn't be hot."

Aubrey thought to herself, "boy is she wrong. Even if that child sits down she is still gonna be hot". The sun was blinding Aubrey as she searched desperately to find her sunglasses. The heat felt like 4pm in Texas in August! There were clouds in the sky, but not the gray ones that brought the rain. They were the pretty fluffy ones. The ones that invited you to lay in the yard, on your back, and make pictures out of them. It was actually an unseasonably warm day in Collinsberg, IA. But, she figured it was as good a day as any to get this reunion over with.

"You alright, baby?" Arlene asked her youngest daughter.

"Sure. I'm okay. I was just thinking" she answered.

"I'm so glad you here and I shol' wanted Dr. Payce to be here to meet you. Wasn't for her, we prolly wouldn'ta been able to do nun a dis."

"She's not coming?" Aubrey asked, but it wasn't really a question. It sounded more like a demand.

"Naw. She said somethin' 'bout it being 'gainst the law or somethin' like dat."

"What?" Randall interjected as he walked into the conversation.

"Not against the law" he said. "It would be against her professional ethics. She can't have a relationship with her clients outside the office. If she came and hung out with us it would be more like she's our friend rather than our counselor" he explained.

"Oh… Yeah… Right" Arlene said.

Randall had hoped the same thing. He wanted his sister to meet Dr. Payce as well because he felt like she had brought them all back together. She had helped them all so much and he felt a sense of connection to her. He wasn't too disappointed though because she had agreed to be the mediator in the family meeting they were scheduled to have before his baby sister went back home.

All of Arlene Cameron's children were in attendance for the reunion. The whole clan was back together again. Arlene wasn't sure if she would ever see that again after the way things went down over thirty years ago. Her eldest daughter Sally Agnes, whom they called Aggie, was there with her four children. Aggie wasn't all that excited to be there, but she was there. She made a promise and refused to go back on it. As she looked around, everyone appeared to be having a good time, but she couldn't seem to relax. She could have cared less about seeing the majority of her family members, but she was happy that her baby sister, Amber, had come. Aggie was certainly looking forward to getting to know Amber again. Even though that was true, Aggie secretly thought Amber was a fool for coming back to have anything to do with this family.

"Can you believe Amber is here?"

"If you ask me, I thought the gal was dead!"

"Well… now why would you go and say a fool thang like dat?"

Randall, Arlene's only son, was listening to the conversation but decided he didn't want to know the answer to that last question. He was so delighted to have his sister back with him that he didn't know what to do with himself! Amber looked the same way she had when she left. Like a little girl. She had beautiful, bronze skin. Her slender but shapely figure made it hard to tell how old she really was. Of course, she wasn't a little girl anymore, but Randall found it hard to look at her as a grown woman. His wife, Brandy, was with him and they both just sat and watched her.

"Why don't you go over there and talk to her, Rand?"

"Because I don't know what to say to her…"

"Well, invite her over here. She looks lonely."

Amber was the only reason Randall agreed to the reunion. It was only, truly a family reunion if she was going to be here. Otherwise, in his eyes, it would have been just a family get-together and he probably wouldn't have come. Having Amber home had been just a dream of his for a long time. Now it was happening.

Molly Bea, the middle girl whom they called Bea, was running around with the kids. Anyone looking in would have thought she was the youngest of Arlene's children. She had the meekest demeanor and she still wore her hair in pony tails! With her smooth, brown skin she looked as young as some of the children she played with. Bea would rather hang out with children than adults any day. That was just her spirit. She was happy to see all of her family in one place at one time because she couldn't remember the last time this happened. Not even for a wedding or a funeral. Of course, the Cameron family had plenty of funerals but not many weddings. There were lots of baby mama's and baby daddy's but very few husbands and wives.

Unfortunately, the Cameron's were not a very close family. But, not without reason. That's what made it easy for them not to see each other very often and not really miss it. Bea would never have said much even if she had missed it. She was never really one to express her feelings. But, today was a good day. She was excited to see Amber, especially. This was an event that desperately needed to happen.

The baby of the family was home! Amber stood in the middle of the park picking her nails. She was amongst the people she'd escaped from and wasn't really comfortable with being around her family after all this time. Of course, she was all smiles on the outside but a nervous wreck on the inside. She wouldn't eat because she felt like anything that went down would eventually come up. Feeling like an outsider among people whom she bore strong resemblance to was freaking her out! They continued introducing themselves to her as she wished she could disappear behind the sunglasses she finally found.

Once she was no longer being blinded by the sun she looked up and noticed Brandy, Randall's wife, looking as if she wanted to invite her over. She hoped the anguish she was experiencing being around her siblings and her mother again, wasn't visible. She didn't leave home on good terms and hadn't seen or spoken to them since. Until a few months ago, when they started contacting her about the family reunion, she really didn't know who was alive and who was dead. Now she was face-to-face with them all. Deep in thought, she hadn't even noticed the commotion going on near the parking lot.

Trying to find a place to park was a nightmare. There were people everywhere! I had only been to other people's family reunions. I didn't have family so it was hard for me to believe all these people were related. I was sure some were second and third cousins but there were still so many of them. They were all different shades and hues. Some light skinned some dark some medium brown. I had been to reunions before but this one was different. Probably because I had never been to a reunion with my clients!

As I opened my car door and was about to put my left foot on the ground, a man approached me. I didn't know who he was from Adam but I'm sure he thought I was related to him. He was wearing plaid shorts, a white wife beater and tri-colored striped socks. The left sock was raised to his knee and the right one hovered at mid-calf. The black house shoes on his feet completed his outfit. I was sure they called him 'Uncle Somebody'. But, before he could say anything to me Randall ran up to save me.

"Doc, you made it! Good to see you. What made you change your mind about coming?" he asked.

He called me Doc. I thought that was really cute.

"To tell you the truth Randall, I really don't know" I said.

"Well, come on up and meet Amber."

"Okay, but I can't stay long. I just wanted to drop by."

As we approached the family I recognized Arlene, Aggie and Bea but there was someone else there with them. It had to be Amber. As we neared the huddle she turned her back toward us and started to walk off, but Randall called to her before she could move away.

"Amber...I want you to meet Dr. Sasha Payce" he announced.

My mother's face was the last thing I saw...

PART 1

The Backstory

CHAPTER 1

The Move

TYSON JUAREZ WAS the man of my dreams but I would never admit that to anyone except myself and God. I'd admitted it to myself because I don't like lying and only to God because He knows my thoughts before I do. Tyson was gorgeous. His African-American mother and Puerto Rican father had blended splendidly to give him the hue of a honey nut cheerio! At 6'2, 215lbs, Tyson was lean but cut. His broad shoulders and nearly bald head almost gave me fits whenever I caught a glimpse of him. And although he smiled rarely, when he did it was bright enough to light up the entire office. At least it did for me. But in a season where light-skinned brothers were not in style, none of the other ladies found him attractive. Goodie for me!

I'd been attracted to Tyson since the first day of the quarterly business convention. We were introduced for no other reason than because I happened to be near him and another associate, who were both uninterested in what was going on as far as the speaker was concerned. I had seen Tyson almost every week at work but never spoke to him. My admiration of him had only been from a distance. You see, Tyson was an executive at the firm. I didn't want to risk rejection and embarrassment and I most definitely didn't want to compromise his position with the company. At least, those were the things I told myself so I could justify not pursuing him. As the corporate Psychologist with the company, no one really wanted to be pursued by me anyway. Anyone I was talking to was presumed to be crazy...or so they thought. I was conveniently placed in a fast paced, stress inducing management firm for those employees who were having difficulty handling their workload and personal life. Secretly, I hoped Tyson would have a break- down of some sort so I would have a legitimate reason to talk to him. Wrong, huh? I'm

Dr. Sasha Wade Payce, by the way…

The next month, after the convention, I decided to join his division in the firm. They were working on a new pilot program for the community and needed some diversity from within the company. I believed in Tyson's vision and wanted to be involved. Of course, I encountered difficulty with this decision. Could I keep my eyes off him during team meetings? Whenever he noticed my stare he'd give a polite smile and I'd divert my gaze. Would I be able to concentrate I enjoyed the work so much but needed to find a way to keep my focus on what I was truly there to do. As usual, I prayed.

Lord…it's me Sasha. You know how much I enjoy what I'm doing at work. I'm doing it for the right reasons, but I need your help. You already know how I feel about Tyson but I don't want that to get in the way of my service. I would much rather be involved in the work that's going to benefit the community and your people more than I want to pursue a relationship with him. He doesn't even know I'm alive anyway. He's very professional. I love that about him! But, I need to be able to focus. I don't want him to know how I feel about him, but I know that if I continue to stare at him and hang on his every word, it won't be long before he figures it out. Help me to get control of my emotions and desires before they lead me to do something I'll regret.

I continued to pray similar prayers for a while. I did receive some relief, but it didn't last long because I didn't completely mean what I said. Sure, I believed in the work and was doing it for the good of the community, but I wanted Tyson too! I couldn't deny that and it didn't help when others in the division began to take my thoughts and desires to a new level.

"Sasha", Marcy said "have you ever thought about dating Tyson? I think you two would make a good couple. He's a cutie."

"No", I lied. "Besides, I think he's more interested in someone else."

Marcy didn't quite buy that but she left it alone all the same. I was so disappointed in myself for lying but I just couldn't risk being found out. I couldn't figure out why she would ask me that. Had she noticed the stares? Was she fishing or was she making an honest observation? Either way, I wasn't biting.

I continued to admire Tyson more and more until the day I made the ultimate slip of the tongue. I expressed an eyebrow raising comment to a close associate named Andrea and immediately regretted it. Letting someone know I had feelings for Tyson that weren't strictly business related was a mistake. Adamantly, I attempted to recant and make Andrea think that what my comment sounded like was not what she thought it meant. Andrea was a known blabbermouth but I was in no way prepared for what she would do with this tiny bit of information.

After a team meeting one Friday, Andrea asked Tyson for a copy of a report she needed. He told her it wouldn't be a problem but that she would have to come to his office to get it. I was waiting for her and when it became obvious she wasn't coming back any time soon, I went to find her. Walking down the hall I called her name without a response. Finally reaching the door, I felt an eerie quietness. Tyson looked from Andrea to me with a rather interesting smirk on his face. It kind of looked as if he was both embarrassed and intrigued at the same time. Andrea invited me to come into the office, which I declined due to the odd way they were both acting. After she got what she had come for she and I both left the building. Upon reaching the parking garage she informed me of what I had walked into. I could have killed her!

"Sasha, all I told him was that you thought he was nice" Andrea reported.

"I cannot believe you would do that, Andrea! You knew I didn't want him to know anything. How could you talk to him about me?" I questioned.

"Are you mad at me?" She asked that question with a smile on her face so I knew she wasn't really interested in my answer. She knew that even if I was mad I would get over it.

She and I had become really good friends. We were almost like sisters.

"I don't know what to feel right now. I just can't believe you did that. Just please don't say anything else to him. Just tell me what he said" I begged. Andrea looked at me with slight embarrassment and sadness in her eyes.

"He said he was flattered but he was already seeing someone" she said. For some reason, I felt like Andrea was only telling me half of his comment.

"Andrea, please tell me everything he said. You owe me that much since you opened your big mouth" I pleaded.

She looked at me with an even deeper sadness than before. "He also said you not his type. He says you too light and too thick for him."

I just left without saying another word. How was I ever going to face him again? Now he knew I existed, but he didn't find me attractive. I didn't know what to do but I knew who I needed. *Lord, it's me again…*

Thank God this incident happened on a Friday. That would give me two days to figure out a game plan. I called my mother to get some advice and began looking in the paper and all the websites for new jobs. I continually prayed for guidance and comfort through this painful situation and on Monday morning I turned in my resignation. I wasn't sure if I had heard from God or not, but I was leaving. Lord, help me. I'd had one phone interview and accepted the position on the spot. I do realize that leaving my job so abruptly was a super drastic move. But, I also knew that I would be unable to continue to counsel in an environment I was no longer comfortable in. A friend of mine let me know of an older therapist wanting to retire from her practice and I jumped at the chance!

CHAPTER 2

Arlene

AFTER GETTING SETTLED into a little town in Iowa called Collinsberg, I began my private practice. Making the decision to move out of the state was done in haste. I was running and I knew it but it felt better than staying where I was and being humiliated daily. My career needed a fresh start and I could do it here. I always wanted to offer Christian counseling services and now I had my chance.

Collinsberg-the small town with big dreams. Everything you could think of in walking distance. It's inviting neighborhoods were much needed when I arrived. Driving down my street I saw husbands mowing the lawns, wives working in their flower gardens, boys riding on their bikes or skateboards and little girls playing hopscotch on the sidewalk. Kids were actually playing outside instead of staring at social media! And the best part of all is that these are African-American families being described!

My office was a quick ten-minute drive from my house! The previous owner left most of the furniture and all her clients! When my first one walked in the door I was pleasantly surprised. I had checked my intake information and the client I was to see had stated she was seventy-one years old during her phone interview. This woman didn't look a day over fifty! She was dressed from head to toe. She looked like she was either on her way or had just come back from Sunday morning service. It was Monday. She was a nice-looking woman with dark brown skin and almond shaped eyes. Although I could tell it was a wig, her hair was beautiful. She took really good care of herself. I almost wanted to ask for ID again so I check her date of birth. But, my office manager had already done that and my better judgment prevailed. If I wanted her to trust me I would have to model that behavior. One thing was for sure. I had no idea, when I invited her in, of how meeting this one woman was going to change my life in a way I never imagined.

"Good morning Ms. Cameron. I'm Dr. Payce" I greeted. She said good morning, gave me a slight head nod, tipping her hat downward without touching it, and took the seat being offered to her. "Ms. Cameron, as I told you over the phone, I believe that counseling does not ask us to stop praying. It simply gives you someone to walk with you through the process until the answers to your prayers have manifested. I like to begin every session with prayer. Are there any pressing concerns you would like to have incorporated into the prayer?" She said she had none and so I began.

Lord, we are coming to you giving you thanks for everything you have done, are doing and will do. We honor your name simply because you are the most high. We give you glory because you are the only one who deserves it and we praise you because you are worthy. I am here with Ms. Arlene Cameron. She has come to me to receive help with some difficulties in her life. Lord, I am coming to you because you are the source. You are the deliverer and the healer. I ask that you would lead and guide us throughout this session. We need you. We are requesting your presence. Fill this room and our hearts, oh God. Open our minds to receive what you have for us. Empty us of our fears and fill us with your spirit. Allow only your will to be done.

When I opened my eyes, Ms. Cameron was staring at me blankly.

"What's on your mind right now, Ms. Cameron?" I asked.

"I'm sorry baby," she said, "I'm just not used to prayin' in the doctor's office." I told her I understood and that if she was uncomfortable she had the right to leave at any time. She said she didn't want to leave and that prayer was exactly what she needed. She went on to talk about several things that had happened over her life. By the end of the session she finally got to what had forced her to seek counseling.

"Dr. Payce" she said, "I got three girls and a boy. I don't really have a good relationship with none of my children and I don't know why. I thank they all upset at me for some reason. I don't even know where my baby girl is. She left when she was seventeen and I ain't seen hide nor hair of her since" she admitted.

I sensed that she wasn't being honest about why her children were upset with her. She knew. It would just be a matter of her owning up to it. Silently, I prayed and asked God to soften her heart. I asked her to tell me a little bit about the circumstances surrounding her youngest daughter leaving. She began to cry and fought her way through a horrid story of her part in driving her daughter away from the family. She admitted she had allowed the other children to mistreat her and that she used her and stole from her as well. As she described the painful events I began to feel sorry for her and her children. I ended the session with another prayer for peace and scheduled her to come back the next week. The courage it took for someone to admit such personal things in a first session was incredible. No one does that without help. *Thank you Lord!*

After visiting with Ms. Cameron, I called my mother. I just had to tell someone about this woman's story.

"Hey Ma, how are you? You got a minute? I just have something on my mind that I wanted to tell you about" I said.

My mom, Aubrey Payce, was the most wonderful mom anyone could have. She was always praying for me and she was always there to listen when I needed her. The most difficult thing about moving to Collinsberg was leaving my mom. She had a lot of friends in our town but I was her only family. I could tell it was painful for her but I wasn't entirely sure why I had sensed such hesitance in her. I knew it would be hard for us to be that far away from each other but there was something else about the pain I'd seen in her eyes when I told her I was going to leave. However, she always encouraged me to do what was right for me.

"I always have time for my little sugar lump" she said. "What's going on?"

I began to tell her about my client, without using any names of course. I told her what this woman had done to her daughter. As I continued the story, I could only hear my mother breath or sigh, but she was no longer verbal. I asked her if she was alright and if the story was depressing her. She said she was fine but I knew she wasn't telling me the truth. I changed the subject of the conversation anyway because I wanted to end the phone call on a happier note.

"Thanks for listening mom. I'll call you this weekend. Keep praying for me because you know I need it. I love you. Goodnight."

When I hung up the phone, I began to wonder what was going on with her. I never really knew her to be sad about much. But, I always had a feeling she was keeping things from me. Maybe the story I shared about my client and her family really bothered her. I knew she wasn't truthful with me on the phone and that worried me. I had never known her to lie to me either. I decided to give her some time and maybe she'd let me in.

CHAPTER 3

Epiphany

WHEN MS. CAMERON showed up for her second session, we began with prayer as we had done before. This time she appeared to be a lot more relaxed. She began talking about the guilt and shame she carried for what she'd done to her daughter. I didn't need the details of what happened but I had the feeling she needed to tell someone. She started at the beginning.

"I don't really thank I wanted no chil'en and I end up with fo' " she admitted. "My baby girl was the center of her daddy attention from the day she came in the world. I was married to him and I start hatin' 'em both fo' the love he gave her. He love her mo' than me! She was the onliest one he had, see. I already had three befo' her so she wasn't nothin' special to me. Just talkin' 'bout this let me see 'xactly how selfish I was but I didn't see it and didn't care back then. The mo' he cared fo' her the less I cared fo' her. I start treatin' her different but not in a good way. I leave her in that bed 'til he come home then pick her up and meet him at the do' like I been lovin' on her all day. That was a way for me to get his attention. So long as I had his child I had him. Least that's what I thought."

Ms. Cameron paused and looked at me as if she were sizing me up. I gave her a warm smile to let her know I was listening and I wasn't judging her. She began to speak again.

"Well, he figured out what I was doin'. He got sick of my actin' and he decided he was gon' leave me and take his daughter" she stated. "Well, I was gon' show him. I fought to keep her even though I really coulda cared less 'bout her. When he got tired of fightin' and puttin' her in the middle, he stopped. He left without her so I set my mind on makin' him pay for leavin' me alone wit fo' chil'en. I called the child welfare people and told 'em he touched my older chil'en and dat was the reason I wouldn't give him his own girl. He got picked up on three counts of molestation of a minor. I made the kids lie in court. They wasn't never hurt but I made 'em thank they was. I even took 'em to dis "doc-inda-box" who helped me. I paid him a lot of money to do it but he came through with flyin' colors. He had them kids so confused they woulda believed fat meat wasn't greasy! People can't stand to see chil'en cry. It didn't hurt dat we got a lady judge with young'ns of her own. So, my husband went to the penitentiary.

"While Riley was locked up, I told my three chil'en dat he beat on me. I told his girl he beat me and her brother and sisters. I got 'em all to hate him. The older chil'en start takin' they anger out on his girl and I let 'em do it. I told 'em the only one he really loved was his own daughter and dat he was only pretendin' to like them. It wasn't true though. He never touched any of us in a bad way. He treated my three like they was his own. True, he had a special place in his heart for his girl but he loved 'em all.

"We treated his daughter so bad dat when she was seventeen she finally got out. She left town I thank. We had no idea where she went. I don't know, to dis day, where she at. But anyway, after she left, the older ones figured out the truth. They found out I told 'em different stories. After talkin' to each other they realized none of 'em was ever touched. When they start thankin' 'bout it, they knowd he didn't do nothing to me neither. They just took me at my word back then I guess 'cause I was they mama. They was supposed to be able to trust me.

"When they found out the truth they told everybody! They went to the police, behind my back, and told 'em I made the whole thang up. My chil'en chose a man who wasn't even they kin over they own mama! They loved him and figured out he felt the same 'bout them. They got him out and all the charges got dropped. It did take some time for all dat to happen but they stuck with it 'til they righted my wrong. They felt guilty for they part in it. They took Riley's side and stopped talkin' to me. He was distraught when they told him what the family done to his girl and that she was gone. He didn't even know where to start looking to find her. He tried but he couldn't get no information. It was like she disappeared. Even if he woulda found her he wasn't gon' tell me where she was. I'm so shame."

Ms. Cameron was exasperated after telling this unbelievable story. It was almost like reading a book or watching a movie. With my human side I wondered who would ever be able to be reconciled from such acts, but I began to talk with her about forgiveness. I thought, her family might not be able to forgive but I know one who will. I explained to her that God would forgive her if she asked for it. She looked at me in amazement which surprised me. She told me she was a Christian and yet she appeared not to know or understand how God could forgive her. I took my Bible off the shelf and turned to Acts 13:38.

"Ms. Cameron would you please read this verse" I requested. She read ***"Therefore, my brothers, I want you to know that through Jesus the forgiveness of sins is proclaimed to you."*** I asked her to meditate on that scripture and think about what it might mean for her.

"I understand forgiveness. I'm just not sure why He would forgive me for the hurt I caused my own family" she said.

"God cannot lie" I said. "He wouldn't tell us anything that wasn't true. His word says that we can be forgiven. He will forgive if you ask. I think what you're having trouble with is forgiving yourself. That concept will take more time but He can help you with that too. You have to begin by asking for his forgiveness, repenting for what you've done and you have to be honest with Him and yourself. He already knows everything. He's waiting for you to ask for His help." I ended the session with another brief prayer and asked Ms. Cameron to focus on forgiveness throughout the week.

After meeting with her I needed to decompress. When I got home, I called my mother again. As I told her some of the details of Ms. Cameron's story, right there on the phone she began to cry. She said she was crying because it was such a horrible story but in my heart I knew there was something deeper than that going on with her. I attempted to probe her for answers but she quickly excused herself and ended the call.

What was going on with my mother? Maybe it was some sort of crisis? I began to feel guilty for leaving her and moving to another state. I had left town for a stupid reason. I was running from embarrassment while my mother was suffering from something much worse. Why wouldn't she tell me? I decided to call her the next day to tell her I was coming home for a visit. I needed to make her sit down and talk to me about what was going on. I couldn't take it anymore. I felt like she needed me yet she wouldn't let me in. Maybe I could call her best friend Constance. At least she could be watching for signs in the event that my mom was in crisis.

A sadness had come over me. Something was bothering my mom and for some reason she felt like she couldn't let me in. I mean, I am a counselor. I listen to people's problems for a living! Maybe she just didn't want to burden me. Sometimes I wished she would. She always tried to protect me. I appreciated her efforts but I didn't need that anymore. I was starting to wonder what she thought she was protecting me from. I'm not protected from anything in a counseling session. People tell me their deepest, darkest secrets. I wondered what secret my mom was hiding that she so desperately felt she needed to keep from me.

Tyson started to run through my thoughts along with my mom. I was in love with him and had no idea how I'd gotten to that point. I mean, we'd never even gone out on a date for goodness sake! How did I develop these kinds of feelings for someone I only looked at and never really talked to? I still thought he was great even though he hurt my feelings. I wondered what he thought about me leaving. Was he sorry for saying what he said? Probably not but I wondered about him all the same. I wanted him to want me. That's all I really thought about when I was alone. Maybe I'm the one that needs counseling. Actually, I'm sure I do! Sometimes I felt so depressed. I often wondered what good I was doing my clients if I was just as in need as they are. I guess the difference between me and some of my clients is that I know where my strength comes from. I sure hoped my mom was praying just as hard as I was.

CHAPTER 4

Aubrey

I T WAS MS. Cameron's eighth session and she appeared to be doing well. She actually had a smile on her face.

"You seem happy today, Ms. Cameron" I commented.

She said, "I been prayin' the last few weeks 'bout forgiveness. I can finally accept the fact that God does forgive if you ask. I know he don't hate me for what I done. I know I got to help others. I know I got to try and find my daughter. I need to tell her what really happened. I owe her that but I'm afred. I forgive myself and I know God forgive me but now I wanna know if my daughter can ever forgive me. Would you help me?" she asked.

"Of course I will help you" I offered. "But, I have to warn you that this will not be easy. If you're going to do this you're going to have to put it all out there. You have to be willing to accept anything she throws at you. You cannot hold back any information and you have to tell her the truth about anything she asks of you."

After Ms. Cameron agreed to do anything necessary to have the opportunity to talk with her daughter, we began. I have a friend, back home, who does private investigation and I decided to give Ms. Cameron her information. I figured it should only take her a few days to find Amber.

I advised Ms. Cameron that she should do some fervent praying before she contacted her daughter. She really didn't know what she would be walking into after all this time. I reminded her that there was a strong possibility that Amber would refuse to speak to her. She could get cursed out! After all, nobody knew what kind of person Amber had turned out to be.

I really wanted someone to talk to after that session because I was very unsure of whether or not I had done the right thing. What if it backfires? What if being refused or ignored by her daughter caused Ms. Cameron to have a setback? My mom was usually the best person to talk to about these things because I thought of her as a counselor in her own right. But, with how she had responded the last two times I spoke to her about this case, I decided I would leave her out of it this time.

As she sat in her favorite chair, Aubrey cried as she thought about the conversation she had with her daughter a few nights ago. The situation Sasha described brought back so many memories of her childhood and what happened to her. She hadn't been honest with Sasha when she told her about her family. She had hoped that she would never have to tell her the ugly, shameful truth. Aubrey was fully aware that her daughter's profession had its hazards. She hated that Sasha had to witness the horrible stories like the one she told her about. This was exactly the kind of thing she had worked so hard to protect her daughter from. Aubrey talked to God out loud.

"How could you have allowed this woman to treat her own children with such cruelty? It wasn't like they asked to be brought into the world and certainly not to be born to her! Children are a blessing from You. They're not ours. You loan them to us and no one has the right to treat anything that belongs to You with malice. I just don't understand why you would let it happen."

The response she got sent chills through her entire body. What she heard was…*I stood in the same place, watching this woman, as I was in when they killed my son. Everything I allow is for a purpose. You will understand why very soon.* Aubrey decided that she wouldn't be asking any more questions any time soon!

She had made major decisions in her life to hide the pain of her past from her only child. She had been even more determined never to inflict that kind of pain on Sasha or to let anyone else do so. She would kill before she would allow her child to be hurt. Aubrey hurt every time her daughter hurt. She didn't want to have any more children because she refused to allow the same things that happened between her siblings to happen between her children. If she had only one child there would be no favorites.

After hearing Sasha talk about the details of her client's situation a second time, Aubrey knew Sasha was counseling with her mother. What she hadn't realized, though, was that her father had been looking for her and that the allegations of abuse were false. Aubrey had run away before the truth was told. She couldn't tell her daughter that she was counseling with a biological relative because if she knew she would have to end the treatment. Aubrey believed that, with God's help, Sasha could help her mother. She decided not to tell her that her client, Ms. Cameron, was her grandmother.

Aubrey had lied to Sasha about her entire family. But, with this new turn of events, it was obvious that eventually she would have to tell her the truth. However, this was not the time. Aubrey felt confident that her secret was safe for the moment. After she ran away she changed her name from Amber Price to Aubrey Payce so no one could find her. She had been successful until now. Her past was about to catch up to her. She had spent so many years trying to protect her daughter, thinking she was doing the right thing, but it was about to backfire. Aubrey just needed this last scene to play out. Through her own daughter, her mother might actually recognize and turn from her evil ways. She could only hope and pray that Sasha didn't find out her secret before that could happen.

Aubrey was pulled out of deep thought by the phone ringing. She didn't recognize the number on the caller ID but she did recognize the area code. She figured it was Sasha calling from a different number in the area so she picked up. "Hello" she answered.

"Amber?" an older woman asked. Aubrey dropped the phone. That name and that voice! She hadn't been called Amber since she was seventeen. She was in shock and wasn't exactly sure who it was, but she was afraid she knew. She picked the receiver up from the floor to tell the caller they had the wrong number.

"Ma'am" Aubrey spoke. "You have the wrong number."

She went to put the receiver back on the hook when she

heard

"Amber, it's me baby. It's yo' mama."

Aubrey put the phone back to her ear and asked "who is this and why do you think you're my mother? My mother is dead" she growled. At least, that was what Aubrey had been telling herself and everyone else since she left home. She had almost forgotten that it wasn't true.

"Amber, it's yo' mama. I know I'm prolly the last person you was 'spectin' nor wanted to hear from. But, I just want you to listen to me. You don't have to say a word and you can hang up the minute I finish. Will you give me just a few minutes of your time? After I say my piece I promise you never have to speak to me again unless you want to" she pleaded. Aubrey thought for a moment in silence and then told the woman, claiming to be her mother, that her request had been granted.

Before Arlene Cameron spoke to her youngest daughter for the first time in thirty-two years, she said a silent prayer. Then, she began her soliloquy with an apology. "Amber, I'm sorry for everythang that happened to you when you was young. It wasn't yo' fault. It was 'bout me. I was selfish. I treated all you chil'en bad but 'specially you. I bet you don't even know why so I'm gon' tell you. I was so jealous of you. I knowd how much yo' father, Riley, loved you. He loved you from the day you was born. He thought the sun rose and set with you. He even named you Amber 'cause that's what color he called the sun and he said, from the day you was born, you was his sunshine. Before you, everythang was fine. He took good care of me and my three and gave me whatever I wanted. When you came thangs changed for the worst. But, it was all in my head. Nothing ain't really change, but I couldn't make him light up like you could. Every time he smiled at you I hated him for it and I hated you too. Yes, I hated my own child 'cause I was selfish.

"Worse den nat, I start hurtin' you when he wasn't around. Some of it you ain't gon' remember but some of it you do. I don't want to go into all what happened to you once you got a little older 'cause I know you remember. But I wanna confess what I did to you when you was a li'l bitty thang. I let you lay in yo' bed 'til yo' daddy got home. Then, I pick you up and meet him at the door like I been takin' care you all day.

"I told yo' brother you was just like one of his sister's dolls but he shouldn't try to take yo' head off or nuttin' like dat. I knowd he would try it. I was already thankin' 'bout what to tell yo' daddy if you got hurt or kilt. I told yo' sisters you was my favorite so they wouldn't like you. I told 'em I thought you was the prettiest and you was gon' be the onliest one of 'em to amount to anythang. After they heard all dat, yo' sister put you in a bag and threw you in the garbage can. I seen her do it and start thankin 'bout what I was gon' say to yo' daddy again. Only thang saved you that time was the fact you was still alive, kicking and screaming when he came home two hours early from work! To this day I don't know what made that man come home early. He tried to leave me and take you with him. He said I was negla...nega...well, dat I wasn't paying you no attention and he was right. But, I convinced him to stay by sayin' the chil'en was only playin' and you needed me and yo' family. He stayed for yo' sake. He didn't want you to grow up by yaself. After dat, I made sho' nobody tried to hurt you 'cause he was on edge. But, even though dat stopped I was still jealous and it was getting on his nerve. He got tired of tryin' to convince me by jumping through my silly hoops. He finally decide to leave and take you with him but I just couldn't let him get away with dat. I figure as long as I had you I was gon' have him.

"I'm sho' you remember the next thang that happened. It was the day the police came got him. What you didn't know was that I already figured out how to make sho' he never got you away from me. I wanted his money and I wanted to git to see him any time I wanted. I knowd he was gon' wanna see you every day if he could. So, dat day in court I told the judge he did nasty, sex thangs to yo' brother and sisters. I told the same thang to the child welfare people. I thought the judge was gon' say he couldn't see the other chil'en but he could see you. That he would have to take you out the house and be watched by me. But, I was wrong. The whole thang got turned round on me. I lied and the charges I put on him got him sent to jail right there on the spot! It turned out dat the lady judge on our case was hurt, as a youngen, by her own daddy who never got punished for what he done to her. She set it up so yo' daddy would pay the price for what happened to her too. Riley couldn't git a fair shot. The chil'en didn't even testify. If they woulda, they'da found out the truth then. But, they went on my word alone. After dat happened, I knowd they was gon' want to talk to my kids. I couldn't let 'em find out I lied. Riley woulda been let go, took you and left town. So, I had to pull off the biggest lie of 'em all. I took the kids to one of them "crazy" doctors. You know the ones dat give out them happy pills? I don't know what he did to 'em but it worked. All three kids said Riley touched 'em. I didn't want him to go to jail but after I lied I couldn't fix it. I was afred of how much trouble I might get in for lyin'.

"Yo' life went all the way wrong after dat. I let the chil'en hate you. I let all us drive you away. You know all dat but what you don't know is dat yo' daddy got out the penitentiary. The chil'en told the truth and got him out. The first thang he did, after he found out you was gone, was start looking for you. I'm so sorry for lettin' you miss out on the good life you shoulda had with him. I carried that guilt over you for a long time. But, with God help and my counselor I know I been forgiven. I can only pray one day you might find it in yo' heart to forgive me too. I know I said I was a Christian when you was comin' up and I know the thangs I did was nowhere near Christ-like. But, I'm changin'. With God help, I am changin'. I want to let you know I'm gettin' a family reunion together and it just won't be right if you ain't there. I don't want to put you in no tight and I understand if I don't see you. I'ma send you the invitation and like I said befo', you won't hear from me again. The ball is in yo' court. I love you, my baby girl. Maybe one day you can see fit to give me a chance to show you like I shoulda done long ago" she ended.

Once Aubrey realized her mother was finished, she placed the phone on the hook without saying a word. She couldn't say anything. It was too overwhelming. Her mother had actually allowed her siblings to make attempts on her life. She lied on her father and then didn't have the guts to save him from prison! Now, after thirty-two years she wanted her to attend a family reunion? What family? If it were not for her belief in God's word, she would have hated this woman. How dare she call her after all this time! On second thought, why had it taken her this long to call and apologize? Maybe Sasha had something to do with it. After all, Aubrey believed this was the woman Sasha had been telling her about. She couldn't decide how to feel. Should she be angry that her mother called or angry that it took her so long to do it? Should she be happy that she apologized? What should she do about this family reunion? She flipped to Ephesians 6:2-3 to see what God had to say about what she was feeling. *"Honor your father and mother- the first commandment with a promise- that it may go well with you and that you may enjoy long life on the earth."* Really God? How do I honor a mother who never valued me?

Aubrey had no problem honoring her father. The mother was something she would have to work on. She didn't want to go against God, but she didn't know if she could ever completely honor her mother. She meditated on that scripture, through tears, and attempted to sleep. But…

Never quite drifting off, she was still in shock over that surprise phone call. How had she found her? She had changed her name, yet her mother called her Amber and not Aubrey. She said she'd send her an invitation. Shoot-it-dang! That meant she had her address! She said she would leave her alone after that initial phone call. Aubrey hoped she meant what she said. She really didn't trust her mother and wanted to get her number changed to make sure but how would she explain this to Sasha? There was just no way around this now. Sasha was going to at least have to know that her grandmother was not dead, as she had told her. She would have to find out about the rest of the family as well. How much longer could she hide this now that her mother knew where she was? Aubrey knew it would hurt Sasha to find out so, she wanted to prolong that reaction for as long as she possibly could.

She had no idea whether or not the woman Sasha had been talking about was still going to therapy. Aubrey had to do some investigating of her own to figure out what was going on with her family. She didn't want to have to admit any of this to Sasha until she had to. She really didn't want anyone to know what she was going through because she had lied to everyone. The only one she could consult was God. With her face to the floor Aubrey began.

Lord, I am in serious trouble. My past has come back to haunt me! My mother just called! I didn't really talk to her but she spoke to me. What does she expect from me? I know she doesn't think I could forgive and forget. I know what You want me to do. I just don't think I can do that right now. I know, I know. Forgiveness. I need your help with this one. I am so confused. I just keep thinking about that phone call. I have never trusted that woman! She has always claimed to be a woman of God and I don't ever remember her even acting like she had a clue about who you really are. I wasn't the only one she mistreated. Look at what she did to my dad. My dad...he searched for me. I never thought about him getting out and coming to find me. Lord, what should I do? I'm conflicted and You are the only one who can get me through this. Show me the right thing to do despite my feelings.

CHAPTER 5

Pastor Warren

I HADN'T BEEN to church since the move and I needed to get there fast! My problem was the uncertainty of finding one I would feel comfortable in right away. My pastor, back home, was the best. But, I had to try because I needed a church home.

I got up early Saturday morning to drive through a couple of neighborhoods and look for churches. I figured if I could find one that was inviting from the outside maybe it would be the same on the inside. While I drove I started to pray.

Lord, lead me to the place you would have me to make my church home. You know how much I need this. I know I can talk to you anytime but I need that family. I have to have the fellowship. Direct me to the place where I can grow.

Just as I finished my quick prayer I noticed a huge church coming up on the right, but I was in the left lane. Aw man, I'm gon' have to turn. I made a quick left so I could turn around and go back, but just as I made the turn there was a beautiful little steeple. I decided to use it as a turnabout, but before I could back up, a handsome man with salt and pepper hair stepped out of the double doors. He waved as if he knew me. I guess I'm gon' have to stop. I couldn't say I didn't see him because my windows were down.

"Good morning" he greeted. "I'm Pastor Warren. Are you lost?"

So, he hadn't mistaken me for someone else. He was waving to invite me to stop.

"Good morning Pastor Warren. I'm Sasha Payce. I'm new in town and was just out exploring. Forgive me for using your parking lot as a turnaround." I apologized, hoping he would let me go so I could get back to that big church on the other corner.

"Well" he said, "I was just coming in to put the finishing touches on my sermon for tomorrow. Do you have a church home yet?" He asked that question like he already knew the answer.

"No sir… not yet."

"Well, park that car right over here and come on in for a tour. My wife's inside and I know she'd love to meet you!"

I couldn't say no to that because he hadn't asked a question. He had ordered me to come inside.

Lord, you are so funny. You knew I was trying to get back to that other church. Not only did you arrange for me to miss the turn, but you lead me straight to this one. You even put the icing on the cake when you had the pastor come out and wave me in! I'm listening…

I parked my car and before I touched the handle my door was open. Pastor Warren was offering me his hand to help me from my car. *How sweet.* We walked through the double doors and I was amazed at what I saw. From the outside the church seemed small, but it was actually a nice size. It could probably seat about two thousand parishioners. This would be the perfect size for me. Not too many but not so small that everyone and their dog would know your business.

As I continued walking through the beautiful edifice, I began to hear *God Is Here* playing in my head. *There is a sweet, anointing in the sanctuary…*This was definitely where I was supposed to be. I felt warm and safe. "Thank you Lord", I said quietly to myself. Or so I thought.

"Did you say thank you Lord?" asked a gorgeous woman popping up from the alter. I hadn't even noticed her. My eyes had been up toward the ceiling since I walked in.

"Yes ma'am, that's what I said."

"Well, when you say that you should shout it! Go ahead. Say it again like you mean it!"

"Thank you Lord!" We both shouted and laughed. Pastor Warren joined in so we all shouted one more time.

"Thank you, Lord!"

"I don't even know what you all are shouting about but I take every opportunity I can to praise Him" Pastor Warren admitted. "I see you've met my wife. She loves the Lord, indeed."

I could tell I was going to love it here. I spent an hour just talking with Pastor and Mrs. Warren. Great couple! I could learn a lot from them. I also found out, while conversing with them, that Mrs. Warren was a therapist. She offered to mentor me in the therapeutic world. She had recently retired from her private practice and started doing grief and marital counseling for the church. She told me to think about it and to let her know. I was definitely considering it. The only reason I didn't say yes immediately was because I didn't want them to think that I was desperate for the relationship. I decided to just keep that between me and God for the moment. I had found my church home and was looking forward to service the next day. I hadn't even heard the man preach and had already decided to join! Even though I was going to drive back past the big church on the corner, there was no reason for me to stop.

CHAPTER 6

Randall

"**D**R. PAYCE, YOU have a new client holding on line #1" Gabrielle, my office manager, informed.

"Thank you, Gabby. Dr. Payce speaking, how may I help you?"

A strong, male voice came through my receiver loud and clear. In his Barry White voice he said "Dr. Payce, my name is Randall Cameron. I found you in the phone book and I would like to come and talk with you if I could" he requested.

I took his information and scheduled an appointment with him. I told him a little bit about my beliefs so he would have the opportunity to back out if he chose to. I answered a few of his questions that the ad had not answered and told him I would see him the following week.

I had Ms. Cameron coming in twenty minutes. I thought that was odd that I had two people with the same last name as clients. Maybe they were related, but I couldn't ask. Today was going to be Ms. Cameron's twelfth and final session so it actually wouldn't matter...

She entered my office with confidence, sat in her favorite chair and asked, "may I offer the prayer today Dr. Payce?" I smiled, gave my approval and bowed my head.

"Lord," Ms. Cameron began "I just want you to know how thankful I am for everything you done for me. I was wrong in the way I treated my chil'en and you forgave me still. You even let me talk to my baby. The one I treated so bad. Thank you, Lord, fo' yo' mercy on me. Thank you for bringing me to Dr. Payce. She has truly blessed my soul. Lord, I do have mo' work to do but I thank I'm on my way. Please help my chil'en Lord. I thank they need you more than me now. I hurt 'em bad and I don't know if I can ever fix that with 'em. Help us Lord, 'cause only you can." Ms. Cameron ended her prayer and looked up at me.

She said "I got aholt of my daughter. I know she was really surprised to hear from me and she was upset but she didn't hang up. She listened. I don't know what she gon' do but I apologized for making her life so hard. I told her I had truly let God come into my life and that I was forgiven. I didn't ask her to forgive me but I told her I hope she give me a chance to be a better mama to her. She hung up the phone without sayin' anything but she didn't cuss me so I'll take dat as a good sign" she chuckled.

"I think you're doing very well Ms. Cameron. You've come a long way since the first day we met. I can tell that you've really allowed God to work in your life. That doesn't mean you won't falter anymore. It just means that now you should know there's nothing He cannot do" I stated. "I feel confident that you will do well on your own now. The point of therapy is not to keep you dependent on me to help you through your trials. You know now that God is not just a resource… He is the source. You have to rely on Him. I'm not saying that I won't be here for you if you feel like you need me but I want you to be able to put your trust in the one with all power."

Before she left Ms. Cameron and I problem-solved to come up with good strategies for her to tackle some of her other issues. She really wanted to make things better with her children as well as some other family members. She had this idea about a family reunion. I told her that I thought it would be a good idea if she reconnected with everyone on a personal level before the reunion. She agreed and told me that, with God, she was going to try and rebuild those broken relationships. Upon her leaving, she gave me a hug and thanked me. She stated that she wished she'd had someone like me before things in her life had gotten so out of control, but that she was thankful for feeling like she has a second chance.

By the end of the day I was so exhausted that I just wanted to shut my brain off. All the talk about broken relationships forced me to think about Tyson. I really don't know why because we never had a relationship. I loved him but he could have cared less about me. When I called Andrea to get the latest scoop at the old job she told me Tyson was dating someone. She said she didn't want to tell me too much so my feelings wouldn't be any more hurt than they already were.

I told her that I already felt like I had been stabbed in the chest and punched in the gut a hundred times. Why did she think I had left town? How much more hurt could I feel? She went on to tell me all about Tyson, Jamie and the behaviors she was observing. She said that Jamie followed Tyson around wherever he went and was never more than a few feet away from him. Jamie sounded more like a stalker than a relationship to me, but maybe that's the kind of person Tyson liked. I had never approached him and this Jamie person seemed to be all over him. Oh, well.

I spent the next several days feeling like my heart had been ripped out and stomped on and the next thing I knew a week had flown by. Back to the office I went. Life did not and could not stop for my broken heart.

"Come in Mr. Cameron. Have a seat. May I offer you some coffee or a soda" I asked.

"A soda? Where are you from?" he asked.

"Oh, I'm from a little town down south. Forgive me. Ya'll call it 'pop' up here, right?" I teased.

"Yeah Doc, I like your style" he complimented. "You kinda remind me of my little sister. You actually look a lot like her too. That's one of the reasons I picked you. It was your picture in the ad. My sister is a major part of why I'm here, along with a butt-load of other issues. I really don't have faith in God, but I do believe He exists. Do you think you can still work with me?" he asked.

"You're just the kind of guy that God loves to work with" I said. "But you have to be willing to do some things that you have never done before. God will do the rest if you allow him to. If you're willing to try it His way we can begin."

Randall didn't say a word. Neither did he get up and walk out so I took that to mean he was willing to try it God's way.

"I always begin with prayer so please bow your head" I said. "Lord, I am here today with Mr. Randall Cameron. You know he doesn't have a strong faith, but he knows you exist.

Help him move to another level in you. If it is your will, allow me to be your vessel in this process. Give me the words to say. Open our hearts and minds to accept your will and your way. We invite you in now God. Come and sit among us as we converse. Let your presence be known and felt."

As I lifted my head I noticed an odd look on Randall's face. "You don't pray like church people" he said.

"What do you mean?" I asked.

"Well" he said, "when church people pray they say 'art thou' and 'thine' and words like that." He was looking at me now like he didn't believe I was a true Christian, or 'church person', as he called it.

I smiled and said "I just talk to God just like I'm talking to you and He hasn't failed me yet! He knows what you're going to say before you say it so you might as well just talk. If you're angry, he knows. If you're sad, he knows that too. You don't have to sugar coat things for God. He knows. But, you do have to say it. You can't just say, 'God knows my heart', like some people think you can. Sure, he does know your heart but sometimes you might wish he didn't. Our hearts are not always as good as we think they are. We might have good intentions, at times, but we might also have hidden agendas. Tell God what you really mean. Tell him what you want and need. Ask Him for help. You just have to accept Him and allow Him to work within you and then through you" I informed.

"Okay, you just went over my head with all that, but I am willing to learn more about God and how He can help me" Randall said. "My wife is a strong believer. For now, though, I need to focus on why I'm coming to see you. This is very difficult for me because it's something I've been carrying around for years. I feel like I just need to confess to someone other than a family member. So, I guess I'll just start…

"You see, my mother was an ungrateful woman and some of her ways rubbed off on my sisters and me. Amber, the sister you remind of, was the only one of us who was good and we ran her off." I was immediately alerted when he said his sister's name. Randall paused as he began to tear up and I knew for sure he and Arlene Cameron were related. Although she had only mentioned Amber's name, I was sure this was her son.

Talking about this had caught him off guard. I don't think he realized how emotional he was over what had happened to his family. I told him to take a moment and offered him some water. After he regained his composure he began again.

"My sister's father was just like our own. Even before she was born he was good to us. Riley was really good to us and for us. Before him, we struggled. We were actually afraid of my mother. But, when she met Riley things changed. She appeared to be happy before my baby sister came. I just don't understand what happened to her after that. It was like something came over her. Looking back, now I wonder if she suffered from some sort of postpartum depression" he said.

He stopped abruptly and gave me a horrified stare. "The things I say in here are kept confidential no matter what, right?"

Even though I had previously explained confidentiality to him, he needed to be reassured. "Absolutely! Everything will be kept between us."

He continued, stating "my mother would disown me if she found out about this. Not that I would really care, but she's what brought all of this back up for me again. I never really had a good relationship with her. But, a funny thing happened the other day. She called and told my wife that she was planning a family reunion and that she wanted to talk to me about it. I haven't really talked to my mother in years. I mean, sure I send her birthday and Christmas cards and may call for the holidays but nothing too meaningful. My sisters don't communicate with her very often either, from what I understand. It's strange that after all these years she wants to get us all together. She never cared before. Maybe she's dying or something. I don't know but I haven't returned her phone call. I wouldn't exactly call us a family. But, I tell you the one thing that would encourage me to go is if I knew that all my sisters would be there. I mean all three of them. The thing is, I don't think that's going to happen because my baby sister left and no one has any idea where she is. If I were her I wouldn't want to be found either. We were horrible" he admitted.

Had Ms. Cameron told him about me? Probably not,

because he said he saw my ad in the phone book. He also said he hadn't returned her phone call. Interesting!

"I need your help, Doc" Randall said. "I need to know what to do about my mother. I have so many feelings and emotions wrapped up in her that are unresolved. She did something to the man I considered my father that was so horrible that, to this day, I still haven't forgiven her. She lied and had him arrested and she waited until us kids figured it out and helped him. He lost his daughter over what she did and I lost my sister. I loved my sister but I was forced to mistreat her. I feared that if I didn't, my mother would take it out on me. You see, before my sister was born I was her most hated child. I was the dark skinned one. She would never let me go outside. She said I shouldn't be in the sun because I was already dark enough. What did she think I would look like after sleeping with a man who was two times blacker than tar? Whenever she would introduce us to people she would say 'these are my daughters, Sally Agnes and Molly Bea, and that's Randall'. I always felt like I didn't belong with them because that's the way she treated me. I honestly believe that if anyone had come by saying they wanted a little, black boy she would have given me away. I felt like the only ones who loved me were my grandmother and Riley."

"So, when my baby sister came along I was no longer the most hated child. She took my place. My mother was completely jealous of Amber because she was beautiful and she was Riley's pride. The problem with Amber was that my mother could not compete with her so she did everything she could to try to break her. She used the other kids to do her dirty work so no one could blame her. She lied to us to make us hate Amber and she made us do things to hurt her. I have to admit that I took part in it but I loved Amber. I don't think my mother or my sisters did. I think they really had it in for her but I can't say for sure. They could have just been pretending like I was.

One of my problems with my faith in God is because I prayed and nothing happened. I asked him every day to end the abuse for my sister, but he didn't. The other problem I had was that my mother claimed to be a Christian, yet she acted more like the devil himself! I prayed every night that one day she would come to her senses and realize what she was doing. That day never came and it destroyed my belief" he admitted.

Little did Randall know that his prayers had been answered. No, it hadn't come when he wanted it to and it hadn't looked like he wanted it to, but they had been answered. He never thought that his sister leaving may have been the best thing for her. He had overlooked the fact that her escape did end her abuse. His mother had also 'come to her senses' as he put it. My problem was that I couldn't tell him about his mother because of confidentiality. I knew I had to somehow get him to return his mother's phone call. That would be the only way he would find out. As we came to the end of the session, I prayed that God would give Randall the strength and courage that he would need to speak with his mother. I also suggested that he read and meditate on Mark 9:14-32 and ask God to help his unbelief. Before he left, he stopped by Gabrielle's desk to schedule his next appointment.

CHAPTER 7

Preparation

RANDALL CAME INTO his second session with his emotions all over the place. After our prayer I asked him to begin. "My wife talked to my mother," he said. "That woman is still as selfish as ever! Do you know what she did? She hired a private investigator to find my sister! Then, she called her. She didn't even take into consideration that she might not want to hear from her! I don't know how to feel. On one hand I'm so happy to know that my sister is alive and well but on the other I'm upset with my mother for doing it. And she's back to her old tricks again. Now she wants me to call Amber and ask her to come to this stupid reunion. How dare she do that to me!" he shouted.

He looked at me as though he was waiting for me to say something, so I did. "What part of this whole ordeal has you the most upset?" I asked. While he sat thinking about the answer to that question, I began to feel guilty. I had helped his mother with the private investigator who had found his sister. I didn't really think about how it might affect the rest of the family. If and when he finds out about my relationship with his mother he may not want to counsel with me anymore. I wished that I could tell him in order to get it over with but I couldn't. He would have to find out another way. Lord, help.

"I think I'm more upset with my mother because she has always been manipulative and controlling over us kids and she's still doing it" he said. "I thought I had escaped it by not talking to her or having much to do with her. Now I feel so torn because I really do want to talk to Amber but not because my mother wants me to. I want to talk to her because I want her to know how sorry I am about everything and that I love her and I always have. I don't think I should call her though. If you were in my situation, what would you do Doc? I mean, would you call her? What do you think she'll say? Do you even think she'll want to hear from me? I mean, she could have found me a long time ago if she wanted anything to do with me. Of course, I understand why she didn't but...I don't know." He was exasperated.

"What would you think about writing her a letter? That way you could tell her everything you want to say but you would be giving her the opportunity to respond only if she wanted to" I suggested.

His eyebrow raised, he got a slight grin on his face and tilted his head to the side. "Great idea Doc! Maybe I'll even get my sisters involved with this too! The only thing is...I really don't have a good relationship with them. What would you think about having them come to a session here with us?"

"I think that might be a good idea. Let's pray their hearts are receptive to your suggestion and for your strength and courage in asking them to come."

Randall went straight home to work on a strategy to get his sisters involved. First, he wanted to know if their mother had solicited the help of the girls like she did him. Then, he wanted to know if either or both of them were interested in this family reunion. He wanted to get their opinions before he put in the effort to try and contact their baby sister. He tried to figure out the best way to communicate with Molly Bea and Sally Agnes so he asked his wife. After all, she was a woman. Shouldn't she know how to communicate with other women?

"Brandy," Randall called to her from the bedroom. As soon as his wife entered the room he stated "I need your help with something important. You know that my mother wants me to contact Amber to try to persuade her to come to this reunion, right? Well, I think I should get Aggie and Bea involved. What do you think?" he asked.

"Well, sweetie," Brandy began "do you think your sisters would even be interested in coming to the reunion? I think that's the first thing you need to find out. If they don't even want to go then you'll have your answer. If they feel the same way you do, then you move on to the next phase. Why don't you call them both and tell them your feelings and ask them how they feel? You have to do it in a way that you make sure you give them an option. You said that you guys always felt manipulated by your mother so, you definitely don't want them to feel that way. Let them know that you have Amber's information and what you would like to do. Give them the opportunity to tell you what they want to do. Even allow them some time to think about it. Don't rush them. Tell them they can even call you back to talk about it later. You just don't want to make them feel obligated, manipulated or forced" she explained.

Randall completely understood where she was coming from. That was one of the reasons he loved his wife so much. She was nothing like his mother. She always gave him the opportunity to make up his own mind and never forced him to do anything. In a way, Randall could thank his mom for his wife. He had tried to find the total opposite of his mother and he had succeeded.

"You really want to have it set in your mind as to what you want to do regardless of what your sisters might want" Brandy added.

She knew her husband had always missed Amber and wondered what happened to her. For a while he had been too ashamed to try to find her. Then, it was simply that too much time had passed and he didn't think he should try anymore. He had given up on whether or not to search for her but he'd never stopped thinking about her.

After talking with his wife, he decided that he would call his sisters and invite them to dinner so he could talk with them together. Both sisters hesitantly agreed but were quite intrigued by his invitation. They decided they would have dinner on Wednesday night. That gave him three days to prepare.

CHAPTER 8

The Dinner

RANDALL BECAME MORE and more nervous as it neared the time for his sisters to arrive. He had spent three days preparing what he would say to them but he just didn't know how they would respond. He and his sisters weren't close. They had really lost touch after getting their stepfather out of prison. They knew each other's information but none of them used it very often. But, one thing they had agreed on was to never allow their mother to manipulate them again. This was one reason why Randall was so nervous. He felt like, in a way, their mother was weaseling back into their lives and using the love for their baby sister to do it.

There were three things that had given Randall confidence for this evening. First, he had prayed and asked God to be in the room. He wasn't quite sure that God heard him but he did feel a certain level of peace. Second, he had his wife there for support and she was a strong believer in God and in him. Last, but not least, he had prepared a great meal. Randall could throw down in the kitchen! His mom had never really liked to cook or do anything for them. So, one positive thing he took from his childhood was that he learned to do things for himself.

Randall's sisters arrived together. He greeted them both at the door. "Hi, Aggie...Bea. It's good to see you both. Come on in and have a seat" he invited as he accidentally bit his lip.

As the ladies entered the dining area, Brandy greeted them as well, with hugs. Randall was surprised at how they responded to his wife's welcome. They were not used to being hugged as far as his family went. They weren't a very loving bunch at all, but Brandy's family was. His sisters seemed to take kindly to Brandy and returned her affection as if they were old school chums.

"Rand has been cookin' up a storm for you guys," Brandy

announced proudly. "Are you ready to eat?" Both Aggie and Bea nodded their heads in agreement and moved to take a seat at the dinner table. After everyone was seated, Brandy blessed the table and asked God to be in the midst. Everyone opened their eyes and began to look at all the wonderful things on the table. Golden brown catfish fried hard, pot roast with new potatoes, chicken and dumplings, green bean casserole, fried corn, potato salad, baked beans, garden salad, hot water cornbread, crescent rolls and freshly brewed iced tea!

"And you won't believe this ladies but…your brother has even made a kitchen full of deserts! Please take some of this home with you!" Brandy begged jokingly, trying to lighten the air.

"Baby brother, you act like we at a family reunion! What you cook all this food for?" Aggie asked jokingly, following Brandy's lead. Randall cracked a smile and winked at Brandy.

"This is a reunion, Aggie. I haven't seen you guys in forever. I just wanted to make sure you enjoyed yourselves so that maybe you'd wanna come back." Randall was almost shocked at the irony in what his sister had said. He hadn't told either of them of his ulterior motive behind inviting them to dinner.

The rest of the dinner went well with everyone making small talk. Bea joined in with everyone else but seemed to be a little bit more reserved for some reason. Randall thought maybe she had some other things on her mind. Or maybe this whole get-together thing was just a little too much for her right now.

After dinner, Randall asked everyone to move into the living room so they could be a little more comfortable. He started to become nervous again because it was time to bring up the real reason he had invited his sisters to dinner. He asked everyone to sit in sort of a semi-circle so that each could be seen by the other, then he began.

"Ladies, I have asked you here for a reason. I need your help to make a decision that will affect us all. I want you to be involved because this is a little bit more than I want to handle by myself" he admitted.

Aggie and Bea were now looking at Randall, Brandy and

each other with quizzical expressions on their faces. Bea was beginning to get nervous because she knew this could only be about one person… their mother.

"Has our mother called either of you lately?" Randall questioned.

Both ladies, in unison, said "no, why?"

Randall continued by informing "well she called me about three weeks ago and I got a real shock when I finally called her back. Before you guys say anything, just let me get the whole story out and I promise I will give you both time to think and respond." The sisters agreed and Randall continued.

"She has concocted an idea to have a family reunion." He saw the rolling eyes and heard the sighs but kept going. "She called and asked me to help her and I haven't decided what to do. I don't really know if I care to see her or any of our other family members, for that matter. I invited you guys to dinner to help me make the decision because if you don't want to go there is no reason to proceed. But, there is one major part of this story that I have to add before you share your feelings."

He paused as a surge of all his emotions went through him. He didn't know how Aggie and Bea really felt about Amber and now he was almost afraid to say her name for fear of bringing up all those old memories. He was stalling and his sisters began to get anxious.

"Rand, are you alright?" Brandy asked.

"Yea babe, I'm sorry. I got lost in my thoughts for a moment" Randall confessed as he snapped back to the conversation. "Our mother has found Amber" he announced.

He was confused by the reactions he got from his sisters. Bea seemed to be thrilled. Her face lit up like the Six Flags man doing his little dance! Aggie, on the other hand, looked like she had just swallowed a persimmon. Randall didn't know what to do with either reaction so again he just pressed forward.

"She wants me to contact Amber and try to get her to come to this reunion. She had already spoken with Amber herself and although she didn't get the dial tone she didn't get a response either. She said that she simply listened to her talk and then hung up the phone at the end of the conversation without saying a word" Randall repeated what he'd been told. "I would love to talk to Amber but I don't want to make her feel uncomfortable. I would even be willing to do this family reunion bit if Amber would come" he admitted.

Randall's last comment sent Aggie over the edge. "How dare either of you bring that up after all these years! No one has seen or heard from that girl in I don't know how long. What is your mother up to Randall? Why would she only call you? Why would she not ask me to call Amber? I don't understand this at all!" Aggie ranted.

Randall, Bea and Brandy all sat staring at Aggie like she was the creature from the Blue Lagoon. They had no idea she would react this way and even less of a clue as to why. Everyone wanted to ask her to explain her feelings but no one moved. It was like they were trapped and sat like frogs perched on a log until she finished.

"I am not going to put up with anymore of your mother's crap!" Aggie yelled. "I don't want to have any part of bringing her back into our lives. And in case you're wondering which her I mean I'm talking about both of them. I don't want to see your sister or your mother!"

Aggie sat down with her arms folded across her chest. Tears began to roll down her cheeks as her chest heaved in and out. She had really gotten herself worked up. Even though they all thought she had a temporary moment of insanity no one said anything to her. To break the eerie silence Randall jumped in.

"Bea, how do you feel?" He asked.

"Well, I would love to see Amber," Bea responded. "I have missed her so much. Not a day goes by that I don't wonder why she left."

At that comment everyone turned and looked at Bea as if she had walked into a Phi Beta function wearing pink and green! Was she serious? Had she not grown up in the same house as the other siblings in this family?

"Bea, what on God's green Earth do you mean you 'wonder why she left'?" Aggie asked.

"You were the one that put her in the trash can" Randall reminded.

"What?" Bea questioned. "Put her in the trash can? I never put her in a trash can. Why would I have done that? That's cruel."

"Molly Bea, you cannot sit up here and tell me that you don't remember putting your sister in a bag and dumping her in the trash can!"

"Yes, I can because that never happened!"

Bea was becoming angry now. She looked as though she was frightened and ready to run. She didn't seem as though she were lying or in denial. She spoke with such conviction that Randall began to believe that she really didn't remember. He decided that for now, he would let this slide and move on to asking the ladies if they would attend a counseling session with him to talk more about this situation.

"Ladies, ladies!" Randall shouted over their bickering. "Can we just get back to the matter at hand for a moment? I would like to give you all the last bit of information for the night and then you can tell me how you feel about this and the plan of action we should take." He looked at each of the ladies one by one until he was sure he had the attention of everyone in the room. Then he stated "...I've been seeing a therapist."

He saw the rise in Aggie's chest so he put his hand up to stop her from interjecting. "I told her all about this situation and she has a suggestion. I would like for you all to attend my next session so that we might discuss this in detail and make a decision. My next session is Saturday morning so I would like you to think about it and let me know by Friday night whether or not you want to attend." The ladies agreed they would think it over and respond by Friday. The rest of the evening would be long and sullen for each of them.

Randall walked his sisters to their cars and came back inside. Brandy was standing in the doorway with a look of amusement on her face. She hadn't been around Randall's sisters much or any of his other family members for that matter. She didn't know what to expect but she certainly hadn't expected what she witnessed tonight. If it hadn't taken place in her living room she would have sworn she was watching Andre, Jamal and Hakeem Lyon go at each other! She gave

Randall a much needed hug as he walked back into the house. They both knew that nothing about this family situation was going to be easy or pleasant.

CHAPTER 9

Sally Agnes

ON HER WAY home, Aggie was absolutely furious. She couldn't believe her mother and brother were basically plotting to bring Amber back into the family. Aggie hadn't been able to have a relationship with her brother, sisters or her mother. She didn't want to relive her nightmare of a childhood, but it was beginning to look as if it might slap her in the face.

The conversation tonight was causing her to go back in time. Sally Agnes had been born the oldest of all four children. She was a tall brown skinned woman with piercing eyes and a big heart. She had a love for her children so big that she had actually enabled them. Although she tried not to show it, she was bitter inside. When she was born, her mother was young and hadn't really meant to get pregnant. Every chance she got, her mother would take Aggie to a neighbor or family member so she could go out and get her groove on. Aggie spent more time with family and friends than with her mother. She had grown accustomed to that until Bea came along.

Molly Bea was her mother's pride because she drew so much attention. Bea looked exactly like their mother and she was smart. Not that Aggie wasn't smart. It was just that she was never told. Their mom got a lot of attention from simply having an extraordinary child. Bea. She never took into account that her firstborn child was just as extraordinary. She just didn't resemble her. Bea looked like the first clone in history. She had her mother's deep brown skin and hour glass shape even as a young girl. Their mother was proud of that. She began taking Bea everywhere while leaving Aggie at home. That would make any child resentful but Ms. Arlene Cameron was either too clueless to understand that or she just hadn't cared. Whichever was the case, Aggie came to resent the both of them. She kept quiet and didn't say much but every time Bea got to go somewhere and she didn't, she just became more and more bitter. Aggie couldn't understand why she was being penalized for things she had no control over.

She felt as if the only reason her mother had kept her around was to be the maid. Everything her precious Bea wanted she got. Aggie began to hate them both. But, something happened to change Aggie's heart about Bea. Bea was too young to know what Aggie felt but she had a kind heart. She began to share everything she got with Aggie and as they grew, they became best friends. Aggie was still treated like the maid by her mother but having Bea as a sister and a friend made things much easier.

When Randall was born, Aggie got more relief. Arlene treated him worse than she had treated her. No one understood why either. Yes, he was dark skinned. So? Black is beautiful and her little brother was adorable, but her mother hadn't thought so. She treated him like crap. Aggie tried to protect him by keeping him out of their mother's way. She thought Randall was gorgeous and since her mother didn't want him she decided to make him her baby.

Shortly after Randall was born, Arlene found a poor, lovable, unsuspecting teddy- bear-of-a-man to marry her. Riley was wonderful! He made sure that all the children were treated well when he was around. He didn't have any children of his own so he treated Arlene's three as if they were his. Then, the Lord blessed him with the gift he had been praying over for years. God sent Amber to him. But, for some reason, the ultimate blessing for Riley was the ultimate torture for Arlene.

The birth of their baby sister signified the end of life as they knew it. With Riley, every day was great. No one was treated differently from anyone else because he wouldn't allow it. Riley told his wife that if she expected him to be the father of her children that he would need to have a say in how they were raised. Amber changed things. Their mother flipped her wig when she was born! Riley loved his only given daughter but he treated the other children no different. Their mother was another story. She not only reverted back to her old ways, but she became even worse.

When she began to torment Amber, Aggie had to join in for fear that if she didn't it would be turned on her. She figured Amber had her father to protect her. Aggie thought that as long as she went along with her mother she would be able to protect herself and Randall. Bea was never in any danger. Aggie had tried to live a double life. She tried to love Amber in private and hate her in the presence of the warden. This situation held Aggie hostage until the day she moved out. She had tried her best to put her entire childhood out of her mind but it was coming back to haunt her. She had never truly gotten over it all.

Aggie knew that everyone was wondering what had gotten into her at Randall's house. They didn't know how she felt growing up because she never shared it. She never told Bea even after they became adults. She wanted to forget it all and now she might have to face it all over again. The anger she had shown at dinner was because of her deep hurt, frustration and fear. Thinking about her mother and Amber made her feel like that lonely, unwanted, scared little girl again. That little girl who didn't just have low self-esteem but no self-esteem at all. She could never show anger as a child for fear of punishment. But, now that she was an adult she could act any way she wanted to and she was mad!

Aggie really didn't have anything against Amber. She just wanted her baby sister to be left out of this so she wouldn't have to relive the past either. She felt that if any of them spent too much time with their mother they might all pay a heavy price. Everyone except Bea, that is. And on the subject of Bea...what was up with that?

Aggie decided that she would call Bea to finish the argument they had gotten into at Randall's house. She just couldn't allow her to get away with not taking any of the blame for Amber running away. They had all participated and she was determined to make Bea remember.

"Hello" Bea answered after the third ring.

"Bea, we need to talk." Aggie persuaded in a tone that let Bea know she was still upset and not getting off the phone until she was satisfied.

"Yes, I know... You mad ain't you?"

"Heck yeah, I'm mad! How you expect me to feel after your denial tonight?"

"Well, Aggie I'm afraid you just gon' have to be mad 'cause I still don't know what you talking about. I didn't put nobody in no trash and I resent the fact that you keep trying to tell me I did!" Bea made this statement with such fury that it backed Aggie off a little.

Bea and Aggie only lived one block away from each other so Aggie decided to drive to her sister's place. She felt as if she would get a better picture if they were face-to-face. Nearly running a red light, she made it there in record time. Without hesitation Bea opened the door before her sister reached the porch.

"Okay Bea, let me see if I can jog your memory." Aggie said as she stepped into the corridor, deciding to give Bea the benefit of the doubt. Maybe she had just forgotten.

"I'm going to tell you what happened and after I finish the whole story you tell me if you remember." Bea agreed to listen. After all, she was frightened. Maybe hearing the story would help jog her memory. Aggie began the story with the intent to make her sister admit what she had done.

"It was the week before we got out of school for Christmas break," Aggie said. "We'd had a hard freeze the night before so we couldn't go to school that day. We were bored so we started playing in our room and Randall came in to bother us. Amber was in the room as well. She was playing on the floor by herself. Well, when Randall came in he took the toy you were playing with. So, you decided you would take the toy Amber was playing with. She was the only one who wasn't bigger than you."

Randall was younger but he was still bigger. He had grown so much that year. "When you took Amber's toy she started screaming as if someone was trying to cut her throat. Then she hit you so you started screaming at the top of your lungs in order to get her in trouble. But, for the first time in your little life the tables were turned on you. Everyone in the room said it was your fault. Your mother didn't take your side for the first time ever. All she said was 'you better all shut up!'

"You took it hard because she had always chosen you over everyone else but that day, for whatever reason, she lumped you in with the rest of us. You were ticked! You blamed all of us but the only one you could win against was Amber. You stood there staring at her for what seemed like forever, with this glare on your face that made you look even more like your mother than you already did. Then, you got a trash bag out the kitchen. You put it over Amber's head, pushed her backward so she would fall, grabbed the bag from the open end and pulled so that her little body was completely inside. You picked up the bag, with her laughing and squealing inside, 'cause she thought it was fun. She thought you was playing a game with her. You carried her right passed your mother and on into the kitchen. Not until you threw her into the 13 gallon can did Amber realize that you weren't playing with her. We don't think it hurt her when you threw her in but it scared her. She started crying."

"Your mother didn't even blink. I almost thought I saw her smirk. I went to the can to get the baby out but she grabbed and twisted my arm so hard I thought she would break it. She wouldn't let me get the baby out! Randall didn't even try. He just stood there with tears streaming down his face. After a few minutes, I guess you had a change of heart. You tried to get Amber out but your mother just gave you this look. You froze and didn't go near the can. She went back to the couch to watch television as we all stood near the can, petrified at what was happening. Amber was screaming. She was so scared. She was in a black garbage bag, inside the trash can, with the lid closed. I honestly believe your mother was gon' let her suffocate!

I know God sent Riley home that day. He walked into the house and no one even heard him come in. Amber was still kicking and screaming when he walked in. He ran and got her out. She looked like she had been in a sauna. Her skin was flushed, her hair was wet and she had been crying so hard for so long that she couldn't stop. I was so happy to see Riley save her that I just burst into tears. Your mother tried to explain the situation by saying that we was just playing with Amber and that she had just begun to cry when he walked in. But, Riley was nowhere near a stupid man. At the least, she had been neglectful. He wanted to leave her but she talked him out of it by using us. He stayed but things were never the same after that day."

Bea had begun crying from the moment in the story where Aggie said Amber began to cry. By the time Aggie finished the story Bea was crying uncontrollably. Aggie watched Bea begin to gasp for air and as she moved toward her. Before she could reach her, Bea passed out! Her body went limp. Aggie tried everything she could to revive her. She put cold compresses to her face, fanned her and even shook her. Bea was out! Aggie called Randall and then 911. Randall told her to elevate Bea's feet above her heart and that he was on his way.

Aggie wanted to freak out because she knew she had caused this reaction. She hadn't meant to hurt her. She simply wanted to make her remember and take responsibility for her part. She didn't want to be blamed for this. It was Bea's own fault. No one told her to hold her breath and try to cry at the same time!

Aggie began to talk to Bea in hopes that she could hear her. "Bea I'm sorry for this. Please wake up. You can't die on me. Then, I would have no one to talk to." Aggie noticed that Bea was breathing but it was shallow. Her brother and the ambulance were on the way. She was hoping to wake her sister up before anyone got there.

CHAPTER 10

Molly Bea

ONCE BEA CAME to, she realized what she thought was just a story… wasn't. It really happened. She had no memory of it, but she now knew it was true. Why would Aggie lie about something like this?

Just like Aggie had hoped, by the time the paramedics arrived on the scene, Bea was awake. Randall and Aggie were at her side. She was still dazed and the ambulance crew wanted to take her to the hospital but she refused to go. Bea had always been stubborn and when she got something into her head that she was or was not going to do… she stuck to it. The paramedics gave her another quick exam and told Aggie and Randall to keep an eye on her for the next few days and left.

After the paramedics drove away, Randall turned on Aggie and demanded to know what happened. The sisters both looked at each other as if to see which of them was going to start the story or if the truth would be told at all. After a long, pregnant pause Aggie stated "it was my fault. I just had to confront Bea about that trash can thing and it couldn't wait. Bea cried so hard she passed out."

"It wasn't your fault," Bea admitted. "It was just that the story you told was so horrible that I couldn't believe it actually happened to us. I feel like there are so many parts of my life that are missing. That was definitely one of them! I honestly did not remember that and I still don't. It scares me that I could have forgotten something like that. Maybe I blocked it out on purpose because I couldn't handle knowing what I did to my sister. I think I really do need to go to that therapy session with you Randall. Count me in. Maybe this lady can help me with why and how I could've put this incident out of my mind. I'm afraid but now, more than ever, I need to talk about the things that happened back then. I have a feeling that I've put some other things out of my mind like I did with this.”

“I’m going to spend the night with you okay Bea,” Aggie offered.

“No way” Bea said with authority. “You guys have your own lives and I’m fine. I just need to relax a while and prepare myself, mentally, for Saturday. I think this is gon’ be very difficult for me and maybe you guys too. Aggie, are you going?”

Aggie wasn’t quite sure about what to do. She wanted to be there to support her brother and sister but this thing might be a little bit more than she could take. But, she began to think about letting her baby sister down, again. What if they had the opportunity to get her back in their lives with or without their mother? What if Amber really wanted them in her life? Aggie had tried to make sacrifices for her siblings growing up and she never felt as if she had been successful. Maybe now that they were adults she could do something that would benefit them all.

“I’ll be there,” Aggie finally conceded. “I’m hesitant but I know we need to do this as a family if we gon’ do it at all.” Aggie and Randall sat and chatted with Bea a little while longer. They were stalling to make sure she was alright since she had refused to go to the hospital or to allow Aggie to stay with her. They stayed until neither of them could keep their eyes open much longer then they left.

Bea was completely worn out by the time her brother and sister left her house. She was ready to say her prayers and go to bed when the horror of what she had done to her sister crept back into her conscious. She didn’t understand how something so vivid and horrid could have been forgotten. Bea began to ruminate on the incident that her sister had described, so much so that she began to see the scene as if she were floating over it instead of being physically there. She saw herself, her brother, sister and her mother. The neglectful smirk on her mother’s face was a plain as day. Her brother’s tears and her sister’s panic were visible, but she couldn’t see her own face. She could even feel the emotions of everyone else in the scene except hers. She couldn’t hear the baby but she knew she was there. There was no sound. There were only emotions. Bea went numb.

She was now lying in her bed frozen. She figured the reason she couldn't feel anything in the picture was because she didn't actually remember being there. It was almost like she was seeing it for the first time. She couldn't move. How could she not have remembered such an incident? The scene she was picturing now must have been from what her sister had described.

Bea could not remember why she didn't have a good relationship with her mother. She had been her favorite child, so everyone else said. She simply knew she didn't want to be around this woman. Now she was beginning to understand. How could anyone want to be around someone who would do this to her children? What kind of a mother would allow a child to suffocate when she could have saved her? The truth was that her mother was that kind of mother. Bea was angry but not confrontational. She began to think about what she would do instead. How could she get back at her mother for being so cruel? Then she thought...maybe this was just an isolated incident. Maybe her mother had not been that cruel. Maybe she had just been playing along with a game for the kids and was really was going to save the baby before Riley beat her to it. Maybe…

CHAPTER 11

The Brainstorm

RANDALL CALLED EACH of his sisters early Saturday morning to remind them of the commitment they had made to join him in his counseling session. Both ladies were mentally preparing themselves because they had no idea what to expect.

"I'll be there to pick you up around noon" Randall informed Bea. "You live the closest to me so I'll stop and get you first."

"Okay Randall, I'll be ready. How should I dress? Is she nice? Is she going to know what I'm thinking even if I don't talk?" Bea had a million questions. Randall could tell she was nervous so he thought for a moment about how to put her mind at ease.

"Don't worry, Bea. Contrary to popular belief, therapists are not mind readers. She's not a psychic. Besides, the focus of this session is about Amber. I figure she'll pretty much just want to know your feelings about this whole family situation and how we should go about it. Go ahead and get yourself ready and stop stressing. I have to call Aggie and make sure she hasn't backed out on us. I'll be there at noon." Randall hung up the phone and Bea continued to worry.

"Aggie, I'll be there to pick you up at a quarter after. I'm gon' pick Bea up first and then head over to your place. Is that alright with you?"

"Well, I really had planned on driving my own car. I could follow you couldn't I?" Aggie asked with apprehension in her voice. Randall told her that her idea was fine but didn't understand why she just wouldn't ride with them.

Aggie had her own agenda. She didn't want to be stuck in the counseling session if things became too scary for her. She had planned her escape route in advance.

Randall, Brandy, Bea, and Aggie arrived at my office right on time. I welcomed the family in and prepared to begin our session. Bea reminded me a lot of my mother just by appearance. I guess I should have expected that since Randall had told me that I reminded him of his sister. But, I thought he was talking about Amber. Oh, well…

"I guess we should begin with some introductions." I could see the tension in some of their faces and knew I needed some sort of ice breaker. I requested "Please start from right to left and tell me your name and birth order."

Randall began. "I'm Randall and I'm the third born and the only male child." "I'm Aggie. I'm the first born and the forgotten child." "Hi...Bea. I'm the second born and my sister would consider me the favorite child."

"I'm Brandy and I'm Randall's wife. Just here for support."

I thought it was interesting that I only asked for name and birth order but they each felt the need to define themselves. I thanked them all for coming and gave my usual introduction of myself and my beliefs. I asked if anyone had any pressing issues they would like to add to the prayer before I began. Everyone appeared to be a little tight and anxious so I asked them all to stand and hold hands. They did as I asked and I began to call on the Lord. I knew, without a shadow of doubt, that this family needed Him whether they acknowledged it or not.

As I prayed I could feel the tension leaving the hands I was holding. I ended the prayer and encouraged everyone to sit. I had blocked out two hours for this session because I had a feeling that it was going to be challenging to get all three siblings to where they needed to be.

"Randall has told me about the family reunion and the circumstances surrounding your younger sister from his view point. I would like to hear from Bea and Aggie on what your view points are. I'll begin with Aggie, being the first born. How do you feel about the reunion, in general, and about Amber?" I asked.

At the sound of her name Aggie flinched. I didn't know if

it was shock or pain on her face. I didn't know Aggie but from what Randall had described, anything could come out of her mouth.

"To be honest with you Dr. Payce, I really don't want to go to this reunion" she admitted. "I mean, I don't care if they have it. I just don't care to be there. For me, it brings up too many negative feelings. My mother is not a good woman and since I left home I haven't really had many dealings with her. As for Amber, that poor child needs to just stay wherever she is. This family treated her so bad that I don't even want to face her."

She paused with her brow wrinkled and her eyes shifted up and to the left. Had she intended to come out with that? She had admitted that she didn't want to face her sister. Neither of her siblings seemed surprised by her statement but they did appear quizzical about her current discomfort. I couldn't tell whether she was embarrassed, guilty or ashamed. Maybe it was a little of each. But, I wondered if she had thought anything through. What if Amber wanted to see her family again? After all, it had been years. Maybe she had forgiven them. Just about then, Aggie decided to admit her thoughts out loud.

"I apologize…" she said. "I just realized how selfish my thoughts are. It is what I really feel, but it's selfish of me not to think of Amber's feelings."

"How do you guys think Amber feels?" I asked.

Bea spoke up. "I think now that we all grown up she might want to see us again. Maybe things wasn't as bad as they seemed at the time."

I'd heard Randall's version and I was getting a negative vibe from Aggie on how life was growing up. Why was Bea the only one that didn't seem to have negative feelings? She said her sister considered her the favorite child. Everyone seemed to think that but I don't get the sense that she was shielded from the violence. She witnessed it just as the others had. Why did she not even appear remotely traumatized?

"At Randall's last session I mentioned writing Amber a letter. I think that maybe you should all think about contacting her in this manner so that she will have the opportunity to hear what you have to say with the option to respond if she so chooses. Randall is in agreement. What do the rest of you think about that idea?"

Everyone in the room agreed that writing her a letter would be fine. I took out some paper and gave them each five sheets. I asked them to begin brainstorming to decide what they each wanted Amber to know. I told them that after they finished brainstorming they could discuss what they had written and begin to detail what they each wanted to contribute to the letter.

While they wrote, I observed them. Brandy helped Randall with his ideas. Bea was writing diligently but Aggie appeared to be struggling. I didn't want to break anyone's train of thought so I didn't move. I also wanted to have the chance to hear what they had planned to say before they sent the letters. I began to think about whether or not I should go over to assist Aggie. Instead, I began to try and put some of the pieces of this family puzzle together in my head.

I began with Randall because he was the one I was working most closely with. I knew he'd been scarred by the abuse from his mother and didn't want to have much to do with her. But, he also seemed to be all for the reunion if it meant that he would see his baby sister again.

Aggie was really struggling with this whole situation but she was transparent. She'd made it known that she was upset with her mother and didn't completely agree that Amber should be dragged back into this family.

Bea was the most difficult to understand. Her attitude and behavior were delightful but her point of view wasn't consistent with the rest of the family. I understand that each member of the same family can have different points of view but she seemed to be totally unaffected. This behavior lead me to believe that she was hiding or protecting something or someone, whether she was aware of it or not. Maybe she had suppressed or even repressed it. Whichever situation we were dealing with, I was very interested in finding out.

Lost in my own thoughts, I hadn't noticed that they were all staring at me. As I came back to reality I asked, "did you guys need my help?" They had all finished brainstorming and were ready to share. I decided to allow them to speak in the order in which they were sitting.

Randall began. "I would call her 'rabbit' just like I used to. Do you guys remember that little face that she would make where she wrinkled her nose several times in a row?" Randall asked his sisters with no response. "She was so cute" he continued. "I would tell her that I was sorry and that I had always loved her. I would ask her to allow me the opportunity to apologize in person or at least by phone. I would tell her that I have never stopped thinking of her and that when she's ready I want to try to have a relationship with her again. I would tell her about the reunion and invite her, of course. And I would definitely give her my information so she could contact me at any time" he finished.

I didn't make any comments about his brainstorming nor did I allow anyone else to do so. I simply moved on to the next person. "Aggie, would you please share with us what you've written" I prompted.

Aggie looked at me with hesitance in her posture. She was sunken into her seat as if she had no spine. Her head was down and I could have sworn her eyes were closed. But, I couldn't tell. I had seen her struggling with her writing but I had wandered off into la-la land myself and didn't know if she ever wrote anything on her paper.

She finally began to respond. "I do want to apologize for my part in her torment but I really don't think I had a choice. I would tell her that I don't want to have this reunion but that if she really wanted to come I wouldn't try to stop her and I would like to see her. That's about it in a nutshell for me" she concluded.

It was now Bea's turn. She jumped straight out of the gate without me having to ask for her thoughts. She read "I have missed you so much! I wish I could see you and I'm sorry that you had to go away and leave us. I hope you will come to this reunion because our mother really wants you here and so does everyone else. Please respond to this letter. We want you to be a part of our family again. We have been apart far too long." Bea finished her statements, looked up and smiled while all the other family members looked at her in astonishment.

"Go ahead and talk about what you feel about each others' ideas for the letter" I said. And as soon as that last word left my mouth Aggie lit into Bea!

"What the heck is wrong with you Molly Bea?"

"What are you talking about Sally Agnes?"

Ooh, I thought. Full names were being used. That was never a good sign during a conversation.

"You just sat there and acted like Amber left the family and abandoned us for no reason!"

"Well, that's what it feels like to me!"

"Bea, you don't know whether to wind your butt or scratch your watch!"

Both ladies just sat there staring at each other like they were about to smack down on WWE. Why were they on such different pages? I had been wondering that question since they first began to talk from their own perspectives. I thought I had better intervene before any blood was drawn.

"You seem to have very different views of your lives growing up" I observed. "Maybe we can deal with some of those differences later as our time is almost up for this session. I would like for you all to come back next week but I do need you to complete a homework assignment so you will be prepared for next time. I want each of you to begin writing a letter to your sister. When you bring them back next week we'll combine all three letters into one and send it off. Are there any questions before we dismiss?" I asked.

No one said a word. I then asked if anyone would like to offer our closing prayer and to my surprise Aggie offered! Her gesture both impressed and concerned me. She had just gotten into an argument with her sister and I didn't know what this prayer might sound like but I allowed her to take over. I silently prayed that she would take this seriously and not allow her emotions to interfere with this important conversation with God. We all bowed and she began.

"Dear Lord, help my anger. Help me to understand my family and help them to understand me. Thank you for bringing us all here today even though I really didn't want to come. Lord, help us through this week and make sure we all return next time so we can do what's best for our family. Thank you for listening Lord. Amen."

Wow! That wasn't what I expected at all but I thanked God that he heard the prayer I sent up before she sent hers. I dismissed the family and told them I would see them all the following week at the same time. As they left I heard Randall say "I really need you two to do something else with me before we leave each other today..."

CHAPTER 12

The Call

MS. CAMERON HAD been calling Randall daily to find out what was going on. She had left him message after message but he wasn't returning her calls. She had given him Amber's information and she wanted to know if he'd done what she'd asked him to do.

She began to rant to herself. "If I knew where he live I'd pay him a visit! I thank he did dat on purpose. I can't believe my own chil'en shut me out they life. I was only mean to Amber so I know why she don't want to talk to me but I don't understand the other three. They was just as mean to her as me. Why should they be let off the hook and not me? I know they was chil'en but they was still wrong! Can't they see I'm tryin' to git the family together? Why they punishing me? I paid for what I done to my daughter! Don't I deserve another chance?"

After asking that question she experienced something that would change her life forever. She heard and felt, at the same time, a voice say "No! But you will have one." She fell to the floor in terror and began to pray. "Lord, please help me. I'm hearing voices. I don't wanna be no schizophrenia! I need you God. I'm sorry. Please forgive me. Please stop the voices. I'll do anything if you stop the voices!" she pleaded.

She instantly felt calm and then the phone rang. For a woman who claimed to have known God for so many years, she clearly hadn't ever heard his voice.

"Hello" Arlene answered with hesitance.

"How are you?"

"Well, it's about time Randall! I been callin' you and callin' you. What took you so long to get back to me?"

"I had a lot to think about and that's why I have Aggie and Bea on the line with me now" Randall informed.

"Good afternoon, ladies." Arlene spoke to her daughters as

if they were acquaintances and they responded with the same coldness.

"Hello." They both stated in unison.

Randall continued. "We just wanted you to know that we've decided to write Amber a letter. That way she can take the time she needs to respond if she wants to."

Arlene began to boil on the other end of the phone. She didn't ask him to write a letter! She asked him to call. She also told him not to say anything to Aggie and Bea because she didn't want the girls to know yet. She didn't need of either one of them talking Randall out of what she wanted him to do. She said all these words in her head, but she knew better than to speak them out loud. She knew she had to remain calm when she spoke because she was on the spot. If she had any hope of getting what she wanted this moment was crucial. If she ever wanted to have a relationship with her children again she needed to step lightly. She also had to remember that she had rededicated her life to Christ. So, she took a few seconds and looked at her WWJD bracelet. What would Jesus do? She asked herself that vital question before she spoke again.

"That's fair" she said. "We'll just pray for God to touch her heart so she'll be able to respond."

The siblings were shocked into speechlessness! They had never heard their mother talk about God unless it was to benefit her. She used to say things like 'God told me I should take the money for your birthday presents and buy me a new outfit so I can look nice for your party.' She would never ask God to do anything for someone other than herself. Not even for her own children. This statement took them all by surprise. It both surprised them and put their guards up.

"Well, we all have assignments to do so we'll talk to you later" Randall reported. They really had plenty of time to do the assignments, but sintce the silence on the phone was loud enough to drown out a 747, everyone said goodbye and hung up the phones.

CHAPTER 13

Who's the Poet?

I'm not Molly Bea
there's something special about me
I sometimes close her eyes
'cause she couldn't take what she might see.
I hate the mother
she doesn't have a dad
I'd allow her to kill herself
but it would only make the mother mad.
No one understands me
I do not feel pain
I keep a smile on her face
to hide the guilt and shame.
Hide and seek
too much at stake
these are my words
she's not even awake.

BEA WAS RAMBLING through her office supplies trying to find paper when she ran across this strange but captivating poem. It was written in a child's hand so one of her siblings must have written it out of frustration. She read it over and over trying to figure out the riddle. Aggie must have written this, Bea assumed. She felt like she always had to protect me and I know she cannot stand our mother. I'll have to ask her about this later, she thought to herself.

Finally finding some clean paper, she could start brainstorming about what she would like to say to Amber in her part of the sibling's letter. As Bea began to try and write she realized she didn't have many memories of her baby sister, even though she had lived with her for seventeen years. Aggie had told her an awfully disturbing story last night that she was desperately trying to forget. Other than that, she could recall not one memory of Amber.

Bea was the second child her mother had given birth to and had gotten a great deal of attention simply because she resembled her. Bea never really liked that much because she didn't get to have her own identity. Everyone always said, 'look at little Arlie looking just like her mama'. No one had cared that her personality was nothing remotely close to her mother's. All they went on was looks. Bea often thought her looks were more of a curse than a gift. She began to feel really sad after thinking about how she'd felt as a child. She put her clean pad of paper on the desk and picked up the phone.

"Hey Aggie" Bea said before her sister could even say hello. "How are you coming with your part of the letter?" She was asking in hopes that her sister's paper was as clean as hers.

"Well, little Ms. Bea, if you really must know, I'm writing a tell-all. I'm telling our baby sister about how things really were and that she would be crazy to come back here. Don't get me wrong. I would love to see her. But, if she comes back to take any more abuse from that mother of yours, she belongs on the funny farm with the rest of us!"

"Why do you hate your own mother so much Aggie?"

"The question is...why don't you, Bea? Why do Randall and I take the things that happened to us so personally and you just gloss right over them. It's like you weren't even there or you just don't care."

Bea was too ashamed and frightened to admit that there were a lot of things she simply didn't remember so she just decided to change the subject.

"I don't know what you mean Aggs but I do have a question for you."

"Don't think I don't know you're changing the subject but go ahead and ask your question."

"Ok. Did you write poems when we were little?"

"Girl, I don't have a poetic bone in my body. You were the one writing all them weird poems and hiding them in crazy places. You was always talking about your mama so I figured you was hiding them from her. That's why I don't understand why you act like you don't remember things. You was always mad at her."

"Aggie, I have no idea what you're talking about. I don't write poetry. Did you ever see me writing it?"

Aggie thought about that for a moment. She had never actually seen Bea writing the poetry. She had just assumed it was her. "Naw, I didn't ever see you, but I found them in our room. I guess it could have been Amber or Randall writing them. Come to think of it, they had more reason to hate her than you did. Why you asking me about poems anyway?"

"I found one in my stuff when I was looking for paper."

"Oh, well I have one of those crazy things too."

"You do? Will you read it to me?" Bea asked. "The one I have is like a riddle and I want to see if they're all like that."

"Well, I'll have to find it. I'll call you back in few minutes."

To Bea, it seemed as if Aggie was off the phone for hours but it was literally only a few minutes later when Aggie dialed back. Since Bea had practically been sitting on the phone, she snatched it off the hook before the first ring could finish.

"I have it here." Aggie stated without saying hello. "Let me get my glasses and I'll read it to you." Bea heard Aggie shuffling around and then she began to read.

I don't exist
they can't see me
but they don't know her
who's Molly Bea?
Sleepwalking through the day
she doesn't know I'm here
through the torment and torture
I have no fear.
She'll survive
though the others, I'm not sure
they have no protection
while she remains pure
She's not effected

After the poem, Bea said good-night to her sister. She jotted down a few brainstorming ideas for her part of Amber's letter, put it away and attempted to go to bed. But, something about those eerie poems haunted her. Who was the author? What did the riddles mean? Why had they both included her name? Could she have written them? It was like trying to solve one of the Riddler's mysteries in the Batman movies. Bea decided she would bring the poem she had to the next session with the family and Dr. Payce. Someone needed to confess to writing those crazy things and to explain what they meant. Once Bea had made that decision she was able to drift off to sleep.

CHAPTER 14

Letters

AGGIE HAD FINISHED her letter to Amber and boy was she right about it being a tell-all! She started from the beginning of what she knew of their mother's life. She planned to let everyone know just what kind of person their mother really was. She was excited about disgracing the woman who had made her feel less than nothing all her life. She even thought about sending a copy to her mother in the mail. She secretly hoped that reading the letter would scar her mother as deeply as she had been scarred by her. That way she could be rid of her for good without having to go to jail behind it!

When Aggie was a child she used to plot on how she would get away from her mother or get her mother away from her. But something always deterred her plans. She recalled, vividly, the first time she attempted to take her mom out. She had tried, on several other occasions, simply to leave. She asked if she could go to live with her grandmother but was denied. Aggie had even become so desperate once that she asked if she could be adopted by some members at her grandmother's church! Of course, the church members thought it was cute and would have loved to have her but her mother hadn't shared their sentiment. Ms. Arlene Cameron would never give up Aggie. That would have stopped some of those checks from rolling in.

Aggie had been an intelligent child and was deemed so when not in the presence of her mother. Arlene had proclaimed that Aggie's father had a mental illness and it had a genetic impact on Aggie. She didn't know who her father was so she couldn't really protest what Arlene said. But, one thing Aggie did know was that there was nothing wrong with her brain or any other part of her anatomy. Her mother was the crazy one.

She should have applied for her own check! Then she wouldn't have had to hold Aggie hostage. Her mother's mentality about not letting her go was part of the reason the harmful thoughts began to take over.

Aggie had almost given up on escaping when one day, on their way to the bus stop, a horrible feeling began to arise in her. She was carrying Randall and Arlene was holding the hand of her precious Bea. Arlene had planned to go downtown to shop. Of course, Aggie and Randall were being dropped off at their grandmother's because their mother was only taking her golden child along. Aggie didn't mind that because she loved going to her grandmother's house. There was always food and her grandmother always told funny, little stories. She sang all the time too, which made everybody around her feel good.

Aggie got a thought in her head that was rather disturbing, but just might work. If her mother was out of the picture she would get to go and live with her grandmother whom she loved and who loved her back. The funny thing was that the entire time Aggie was gearing up to make an attempt on her mother's life she was feeling like something or someone else was in control. These didn't appear to be her own thoughts. It was more like the thoughts were being fed to her or piped in from somewhere. She didn't like those feelings but she figured if it would get rid of her mother she would just deal with it.

Anyway, while standing at the bus stop, an idea popped into her head. You should push your mother in front of the bus! She wondered why she had never thought of that before. They had been to that same bus stop several times. Nevertheless, it was a compelling thought and she began to try to plan how she could carry it out.

Before she had time to plan anything, another thought popped in, sort of like the ding on the iPhone text message indicator. Pretend like you're bending over to tie your shoe and bump into her. If the kid gets killed too that's all the more attention you'll get at Grandma's.

Aggie never wanted to hurt Bea, but again, if it would get rid of her mother she might just have to make that sacrifice. So, she got as close to her mother as she could stand, without touching her. As the bus approached, she began to make her move. She squatted down low so she would have more power, like the original Super Mario brothers! But, as she made her move something happened. She felt this strange warm wind across her body and the next thing she knew she was on the ground! Her mother hadn't moved from her place, yet Aggie had completely missed her target and had fallen to the concrete. What was even more weird was that it didn't hurt when she fell. It was almost like someone or something had pushed her and then someone or something else had braced her fall. Oh, well…she picked herself up off the ground and looked around to see how many people had witnessed her mishap. No one, not even her mother, appeared to have seen her fall! How strange. The funny, bad feeling she had before she fell had disappeared as well as the desire to hurt her mother.

After a few failed attempts, she stopped having the thoughts of harming her mother. She stopped trying to escape and put her efforts into taking care of Randall because he had become her mother's new target.

As Aggie sat remembering that incident she also began to recall something her grandmother had talked about. She was always saying this boy or that girl had 'the demon' in them. Aggie never understood what that meant. She just thought that was what old people said about little bad boys and fresh-tail girls. But, she was beginning to think it was more than that. As she sat thinking about other times the thoughts to harm her mother came up, she began to connect those times with the same funny, bad feelings. A thought would pop into her head and then she would try to carry it out but it would fail. Now it wasn't just the fact that it failed that was bothering Aggie, it was how it failed. Were there really demons that could take control over someone, even a child? And if there were demons, there must be a force just as strong or stronger on the other side. If evil had made her want to harm her mother, then good had certainly rescued her.

Aggie vaguely recalled a story that she'd heard at her grandmother's church. It was something about a demon-possessed boy. She ran to get her Bible, hoping to find the story.

Now, she hadn't cracked that thing open in years so, it was unlikely that she would find it without help. She was just getting ready to call her sister when she just opened to the page that was bookmarked. Mark 9:14-29 was talking about a boy whom a demon had a hold of and wouldn't let him go. It would throw him down and try to kill him, but it was no match for Jesus.

Maybe her mother *had* really believed in Jesus all those years! Or maybe Jesus believed in her! Maybe that's who was saving her mother from her little schemes that weren't really hers. Maybe Jesus liked her mother even though Aggie didn't. *Hmm. What kind of God is this who even rescues mean people?* Aggie had always thought that you had to be perfect in order for God to like you. Maybe He had seen some sort of potential in her mother that she hadn't seen.

After her little detour down nightmare lane, Aggie finished her letter to Amber and thought it was pretty good. But, after reading it, she didn't feel much like showing it to anyone. She remembered another saying her grandmother used to use... *vengeance is mine.* She remembered that one from a church service as well. She didn't know what it meant then, but she knew what it meant in this moment. It was like it had been fed or piped in again. Only, this time, it wasn't giving her a bad feeling and it hadn't come from her head. It had come from inside. It was warm and smooth. Kind of like the time she had fallen to the ground, without being hurt and with no witnesses. Aggie needed someone to talk to about this so she decided to call her brother...

Randall was struggling with what he should say in his letter to Amber as well. He understood that his would only be a small part but he felt like he needed to balance his sisters out. Aggie might be too aggressive and Bea would be as clueless as she had been acting. He had made a good start while brainstorming in session but now that he had more opportunity to think, he wanted to make it better.

His main objective was to be as honest as possible. He didn't want Amber to think for a moment that she was being manipulated or being brought back into an ugly situation under false pretenses. He really didn't care if she ever spoke to any other member of the family again. He only knew that he finally had a chance to reach out to his sister without fear. Sure, there was a risk that she would reject him but it was a chance he was willing to take.

He tried to remember what Amber was like as a child. He attempted to pull from his memory bank anything that might help him reach her heart. He recalled that by the time she left, her trust of anyone and anything had faded. He replayed offering her a slice of his orange one day. She looked at him and then to the orange and said 'no, thank you'. He hadn't really understood why she'd declined because he knew she loved oranges. Their mother had left the house for a few moments and he took an orange from the refrigerator without permission. He just figured she didn't want to get in trouble if they got caught.

As Randall pondered on that memory, he realized that not only had Amber been worried about getting caught, but she had been worried about him trying to hurt her. It suddenly became clear to him that at the time he'd made the offer, he hadn't taken a bite out of the orange himself. Amber had been afraid that he was trying to poison her. Wow!

Where did that come from? All these years, he had been thinking about that day and not once did it cross his mind that Amber was afraid of him! Randall now knew what he needed to do. He had to make sure she knew she didn't have to be afraid anymore. No one, but her father, had ever protected her before and Randall was determined to be her hero now. In order to do that he would need to regain her trust. But, how in the world could he do that through a letter? He thought he could do this on his own but now he needed some help.

"Brandy", Randall called as he walked up on his wife dancing in the kitchen as she washed the dishes. She was such a happy person. Anything she did she tried to have fun with it.

"Will you help me with my letter? I kinda know what I need to do. I just don't know how to do it."

"I'll do my best honey, but since I didn't know Amber

personally, it might be hard for me to help. But, I know something you haven't tried yet" Brandy stated with her eyebrows raised in excitement. That gesture made Randall curious, of course.

"What haven't I tried?" he asked, with just as much excitement.

"Prayer!" she said, already on her knees before she finished the word.

Randall rolled his eyes in disappointment. He thought she had a really good idea. "Brandy, what is praying gonna do? It takes too long for Him to answer anyway. I tried it as a kid and it never worked. I know it works for you but if He knows it's me asking, He's not gonna answer."

Randall stopped talking as Brandy just looked up at him with a sad, but hopeful expression. She couldn't believe she had been married to him all these years and had never known he felt this way about her God. She'd known he wasn't a strong believer but she had no idea he felt like God had a personal dislike for him.

"Randall," Brandy said, "I'll talk. You just kneel beside me so we can be in agreement."

Randall conceded because by the look on her face and the tone in her voice he knew his wife was not going to let this prayer thing go. Brandy prayed all the time but she had never insisted that he pray with her. This time was different and as soon as his knees touched the floor he felt different. He felt woozy. Not the nauseas sort of woozy, but more like a happy daze. Almost like one might feel from drinking just one too many hard sodas if one drank hard sodas…

He decided not to share that thought, of course. He also began to feel warm and light like he was floating. Before he opened his mouth to tell his wife how strange he felt, she began to speak.

"Our God, my husband and I are coming to you tonight to give thanks, honor, glory and praise. You are the only one who is worthy and we acknowledge that. You already know that I have been praying for his family and tonight he joins me in prayer. He is attempting to make contact with his sister, Amber.

Lord, help him find the words to say and help her heart to find his words meaningful. Strengthen our faith as a couple and individually. Reveal yourself to Randall, Lord. He needs to see you. He needs to understand how much you care about him. Touch his heart. Bless him with your light that he may speak only the truth. We ask for courage to get through this test and we ask for your power to break through the barriers. Let forgiveness reign through this situation in your most holy name. Amen."

"Now get to writin'! You have no excuses. God is with you. He always has been but now you know for sure." With that, Brandy went back to her dishes and dancing.

That made one of them who knew for sure, Randall thought. He didn't know anything for sure about this God of hers. But, he did know that she believed. So, maybe he should try it. After all, it had seemed to work the night his sisters came over.

He went back to sit at his desk and just stared at the paper. It was still blank. "Faith of a mustard seed, Rand!" Brandy shouted from the kitchen. She had said that to him and explained it so many times but not until right then did he really get it.

"If I just have a little bit of faith instead of doubting all the time, God will meet my faith and pick up from there" he said to himself out loud. What would it hurt? Doubting sure wasn't getting him anywhere. "Lord, I don't want any of these words to be from me. You talk to Amber. You're probably the only one she would listen to."

Randall leaned back in his desk chair to think but as he did he dropped his pen. That woozy feeling was back. He picked up the pen and by the time Brandy came in to check on him he had written two pages.

"Prayer works, doesn't it honey?" Brandy asked with a smile. She had always believed it did. She just wanted so badly for her husband to know and knew he didn't write two pages on his own.

"Tell me more about this God of yours and how prayer works." At the sound of that request Brandy's soul lit up and her eyes filled with tears. Nothing was going to get in the way of this conversation! Most certainly not the telephone.

The answering machine clicked on at Randall and Brandy's home as Aggie tried to decide whether or not she would leave a message. She really wanted to talk to someone so she decided to hang up and try her sister…

Bea was plowing along with her letter to Amber but something was bothering her. She couldn't get those poems off her mind. She now knew it had been either Amber or Randall who wrote them. What she was struggling with was, which one and why? Why was she the only one that didn't have all the negativity against their mother? And, since she didn't feel the negativity, why had she not really had a relationship with her either? Why did she have all these gaps in her memory?

She knew that her siblings weren't lying about things that happened, but why was she the only one who didn't or couldn't remember? Maybe she had put it out of her mind a long time ago, on purpose. What do the shrinks call that? Suppression? Maybe she had suppressed all those awful memories. Speaking of shrinks, maybe she should talk to Dr. Payce about some of this. But, she didn't want anyone else to know what she was going through just yet. The poems were one thing. She didn't write those, but the memory and time loss were a different matter.

I'll just look her up in the phone book, Bea thought. I think that was how Randall found her. I hope so because I'm not getting on that webernet thing! Maybe she would consider meeting with me before or after our family session. I just really don't need my brother and sister to know about this right now. I need to sort some things out before I talk to them about it, but I'm tired of looking like an idiot every time we have to discuss our family life. It's time I do something about it.

She couldn't find Dr. Payce in the phonebook so she had to get on that webernet thing. It was easy to find with *Google*! You noticed her picture before you saw her name. *Boy, this picture sure looks a lot like someone I know. Duh, I just saw her last week. What's wrong with you woman? She is someone you know.*

Bea dialed Dr. Payce's office and got Gabrielle, her receptionist. "Good morning, Gabrielle" Bea acknowledged. "This is Molly Bea Cameron. I'm not a current, individual client with Dr. Payce, but I do see her along with my brother, Randall Cameron. I have a question. Do you think Dr. Payce would be willing to see me on an individual basis?"

Gabrielle placed Bea on hold. "Dr. Payce, I have Molly Bea Cameron on the line and she wants to know if you will take her on as an individual client even though she has been attending family sessions with her brother Randall" Gabrielle spilled all in one breath.

That's interesting, I thought. "Put her through, please."

"Sure, Dr. Payce. Here she comes."

"Good morning Bea, how are you?"

"Well I could be better, Dr. Payce. That's why I'm calling" Bea stated with hope.

"Gabrielle tells me that you would like to begin individual sessions. Is that right?"

"Yes. I have some things I want to discuss that I'm not ready for my family to know about yet. There are things that even I don't understand so I know they wouldn't.

"Ok. I can understand that. Would you like to come in before your family session on Saturday?"

"Yes, that would be great" Bea stated. She was somewhat excited and relieved at the same time.

"Ok, Bea. I'm going to send you back out to Gabrielle to confirm your appointment time and I'll see you soon."

I had been wanting to get a hold of Bea because I knew something was going on with her. I just didn't know what. Here was my chance to get started. Hopefully having a session with Bea wouldn't ruin what might happen in the session with the family. Oh, well. I might just have to take that chance. Getting to the bottom of Bea's problem would be important to the family as a whole.

CHAPTER 15

What's Wrong

BEA SHOWED UP for her first session ready to talk. It was Thursday and her next session with her family was in three days. She had decided that she couldn't wait until Saturday. She wanted to have more insight about herself before she had to face them again. She needed to understand why her view of the way they had grown up was so different from her brother and sister. As she sat in the lobby, waiting for Dr. Payce to call her in, she rehearsed what she would say. She had started making mental notes of things her siblings had mentioned. Things she should know but didn't. She knew Dr. Payce wasn't a miracle worker or a mind reader, but she was a Christian. That had to count for something!

I finished my prayer and saw that I had about five minutes before Bea's appointment was to begin. I decided that I'd better make a trip to the bathroom and get a glass of water because once we got started I didn't want anything to distract me.

I had no idea of what to expect from the upcoming session. I knew there was something to be discovered but I just didn't know what. On the way back to my office, I noticed Bea getting herself ready.

"Come on in" I invited. "Have a seat and we will begin with prayer. Is there anything you would like to add?"

"No, not this time." Bea was ready to jump right in. That was a good thing. God was already working!

After the prayer had come to a close, Bea thought she'd just shoot straight from the hip. "I know there's something wrong with me" she stated with conviction.

I decided that since she felt there was something wrong with her, I would give her an opportunity to tell me what she thought that something was.

"What makes you say that, Bea?"

"Well really, there's something wrong with my whole family, but I'll start with me."

She took a moment after making that statement. I wasn't real sure of what was going on with her but I was praying that God was dealing with her. After a long pause she began to share her thoughts and feelings.

"There are so many things I can't remember. My sister and brother have told me things that I should know but I just don't. I have no idea where those memories are. For one thing, there's one particular birthday that I don't remember. It was my sixteenth. That's like, a major milestone for a teenager. My mother had planned for a special day with just me and her. My brother and sisters were at my grandmother's house. They were going to spend the night. My step dad had gone out of town on business but he had already given me money for my birthday before he left. My mother didn't know about that. He'd made me promise not to tell her."

"When I woke up I could smell something good coming from the kitchen. She had told me to go to bed early, the night before, so we could get up early and start our day. She stayed up watching television all night. I could hear her laughing from my room and I could hear a male voice from the movie that was playing. My bedroom door was closed so I had no idea what she was watching but she sure was enjoying herself. I figured that was the real reason she wanted me to go to bed early. She just wanted some time alone. Everyone was gone from the house except me and she knew I wouldn't bother her.

"Anyway, I finally fell asleep and by the time I woke up it was morning. The smell of something sweet was filling my room. I jumped up, threw on my robe and ran into the kitchen. That's where my memory ends. I have no idea what happened to the rest of my sixteenth birthday." Bea began to tear up. The pain of not being able to remember something that important had to be tormenting her.

I began to wonder where she had put that pain for so long. She really couldn't remember. Had anyone ever asked her about her birthday? Had she ever asked anyone about it? Had she been too fearful or had it even crossed her mind until recently? Well, now was as good a time as any to ask. So, I dove right in.

"Bea, when was the first time you realized the memory of your birthday wasn't there?" She sat and thought for a moment. "Well, I guess the first time would have been when my brother and sisters got back home that night. They asked me how everything went and before I could answer, my mother jumped in."

She said 'Oh! We had the best time! We ate and shopped all day long!' "I didn't say a word because I didn't remember if we'd had a good time or not. As a matter of fact, I couldn't remember anything from the entire day. I thought maybe I had worn myself out and just forgot. No one ever asked me about it again after my mother told this elaborate story about what we had done. I was too embarrassed to admit that I had no recollection of any of it. I assumed that it happened the way she said and I just let it go."

I took some time to think about what Bea had just said. Her memory stopped in the kitchen that morning. What had she seen when she walked in there? Was she traumatized by something? I wasn't sure where to go with getting her to remember anything about this particular day because I didn't really have much to go on. I decided to go with the incident about her putting Amber in the trash can. That was something I knew a little bit more about since it had come out in a previous session with the family.

"Bea, let's go back in time, a little bit, to Amber and the trash can" I suggested. Bea's posture tensed. I wanted to know if she was able to remember anything at all from this incident. "From the story that your siblings have told you, do you remember anything about that day?" I asked, hoping to get a response.

"Well, actually" Bea started "I do remember playing in our room together. Randall came in and took something of mine. So, instead of fighting with him, I took what Amber was playing with. Amber started to scream, of course, and my mother came in. I'm sure you remember all of that from the story my siblings told. But, the story changes for me after my mother came in and yelled at us. I recall that part, but after that…nothing. I don't remember putting Amber in the trash can. I don't remember our dad coming home early and saving her either. The next thing I remember from that day was dinner. My guess is that it was too traumatic for me and I blocked it out. But, until my sibs confronted me with it, I didn't remember it at all. It's still insignificant to me until you add the part that I can't remember. What do you think Dr. Payce?"

Honestly, I wasn't quite sure yet. It's possible that her brain shut down for her due to not being able to handle what was going on. But…there were other ideas flying through my mind.

"It's quite possible that you blocked these events out" I said. "We know the incident with Amber and the trash can was traumatic. We don't know what happened on your birthday but my guess is there was trauma there as well. We definitely have some work to do, Bea. Our session time is almost up, but I would like to see you again on an individual basis if you'd like."

Bea agreed to continue her individual counseling and I gave her a homework assignment to have done before our next session. I wanted her to write down as many incidents of "blacking out" as she could remember. I wanted to know just how many times this had taken place and from what age it had started and ended. She had a piece of a memory and then it just ended abruptly. I explained everything to Bea in detail about the homework assignment and got ready to walk her out when she dropped a doorknob bomb.

She pulled a piece of paper out of her purse with a child's handwriting scribbled on it. "I didn't write it. I confronted my sister Aggie about it, but she said she didn't write it either! So, Randall or Amber must have wrote it. I think I want to talk about this in our next family session."

As soon as I read it I knew who wrote it. I asked her if I could make a copy of the poem for myself and she agreed. I said good-bye to Bea and reminded her that I would see her on Saturday with the rest of the family.

The Cameron family ordeal was turning out to be more

than I ever bargained for. I was definitely beginning to doubt my skills. But, really that's not relevant. I depend too much on God to think that I really matter in this. He had sent these people to me for a reason and I knew that eventually we would find out why.

I needed a break so I decided not to go in to work on Friday. I didn't have any clients scheduled because it was a paperwork day and my brain was too tired. On my way out of the office I told Gabrielle I wouldn't be in tomorrow and that she could take half the day off as well. Gabby was a great assistant and if I wasn't going to be there why should she have to be?

As soon as I got settled in the car I hit #1 on speed dial.

"Hey mom, how's it goin'?" I was trying to sound as cheerful as I could, but I was feeling down and wanted to hear her voice. She had this way of always being able to make me feel better. But, when she answered the phone I could tell she needed me more than I needed her. The problem was that she wasn't going to tell me what was wrong.

"It's going alright with me" she said. "How's it going with you, Ms. Counselor? Are you still seeing the woman you were telling me about that had treated her children so terribly?" she asked.

I really didn't want to talk about me or the Cameron's, but maybe this would be the only way I might work her into talking about herself. "No, I'm not seeing her anymore but there's an interesting twist" I began. "Now I'm seeing all of her children! Well, all except for one. It's amazing how God works, huh? The woman's son called me up. He saw my picture and thought I looked like his sister and…" I stopped in mid-sentence because I heard my mom gasp as if she couldn't breathe. "Mom…are you there?" She didn't answer me. "MOM!"

"I'm here" she finally said, sounding as if she'd just had the wind knocked out of her.

"What happened? Did you choke or something?"

"Yeah, yeah. I was drinking some root beer and it went down the wrong way. I'm okay now. Goodness, that sure is some interesting stuff you're dealing with." "Yeah, it is. Are you sure you're okay? I thought you had passed out on me for a minute."

"Nope, I'm fine. You don't sound like you're doing all that well though."

How did she do that? She always knew when something was wrong. I'm the therapist here and she's beating me at my own game! At this rate, I'll never get her to confide in me.

"I'm okay. I just thought I'd call to hear your voice. I'm really tired but you sound just about like I do. How's life treating you?" I asked, then started to pray.

My mother proceeded to try to convince me that everything was just fine. So, I let her get away with it. I knew she didn't want to burden me. What she just didn't understand was that her burden was a part of mine whether she knew or not. We ended our conversation on a good note. I had made it home and decided to go for a swim. I floated and prayed.

Lord, I'm having some issues! You already know about it but I have to confess that I've been worrying. I know that worrying does me no good but I can't stop. There's something wrong with my mom and she won't tell me. I'm not asking you to tell me what it is because I probably couldn't do anything about it anyway. I'm not even asking you to remove the burden because it could be something she needs to go through. What I'm asking is that you show her the way. I know she talks to you and I know she listens to you and I know she needs your help. I know you'll come through and because of that I know she will too. I'll be going to bed soon so we'll just let this serve as my bedtime prayer too! Lord, I ask for your protection as I sleep through the night. And by the way, if my husband knocks on the door to wake me up in the morning that would be great! Just saying...In Jesus name, Amen.

CHAPTER 16

Tyson

TYSON HAD BEEN feeling horribly since he'd said what he said to Andrea. He never thought she would go back and repeat it word for word to Sasha! If he'd known that he would have come up with another lie that was less painful! Especially since none of what he'd said was true. Since the day Sasha left town he had been ridden with guilt. He just didn't know what, if anything, he could or should do about it. He didn't really know, for sure, why she left. He could only assume that what he said about her hadn't helped the situation. The story around the office was just that she was offered an opportunity she couldn't refuse. Andrea had been sworn to secrecy so her lips were sealed. Now she decides not to talk? It was probably just as well that she wasn't talking because she would see pigs fly before he told her anything else!

He couldn't believe he had even told that lie about Sasha not being his type. Honestly, he thought she was gorgeous! He just couldn't bring himself to go there with her. In actuality, he couldn't understand why someone like her would be interested in him. He felt like he was just plain while Sasha was amazing. She was smart, pretty, sweet and in a powerful position in the company. He'd thought maybe she'd been infatuated with him for some reason and that she didn't sincerely liked him. He never really talked to her. He had been thinking about her for a while but he would never have approached her. So, when Andrea caught him off guard he did the easiest thing that came to mind. He lied! Of course, he regretted it now but in no way did he think he wouldn't have an opportunity to make it right.

True, he wasn't ready for a relationship but if he were he would be honored to be with Sasha. Before she left, he only thought about her occasionally. That was mostly when he saw her around the office. She was actually pretty sexy but he had to keep his thoughts under wraps. He most certainly didn't need any rumors going around. Now that she was gone he thought of her constantly. He wondered if she was okay…what she was doing…whether or not she hated him. Just the typical questions that would torture even the most sane person if they believed they might be the cause of someone else's unhappiness! He hoped, with all his heart, that she wasn't unhappy. He didn't know how but he knew that one day he would make this right. He needed to get himself together but he had every intention of finding her and telling her the truth, even if it meant him being rejected. But for now, it would have to be business as usual.

Tyson knew what a good relationship should look like because his parents were still together and they were happy. He knew he wanted to have a wife one day and make her just as happy. He often wondered what it would be like to be married to Sasha but he didn't figure he would ever get to find out after what he'd done. Regardless of what he thought, he was going to man up and apologize to her even if it led nowhere. The only problem was that he had no idea where she was and even if he did, he had no idea of how to approach her after what happened. He would figure it out for himself eventually because he wasn't asking Andrea nothing!

CHAPTER 17

In Crisis

AHH...FRIDAY. I REALLY wanted to take this day for some much needed rest, but I had so much to do. I barely had any groceries in the refrigerator and my bedroom looked like I had asked a two-year to clean up. I needed a plan if I was going to get everything done and have some time to relax too. So, I decided I would make a list.

First, I would get my house in order. No pun intended. Then, I would go make groceries, as my friends on the coast would say. You know, I never understood that expression. To me, if you gon' "make" groceries it means you gon' cook! Anyway...then, I would grab some lunch and come home and chill.

As I got ready to leave, with my hand on the garage door opener the phone rang. I was tempted not to answer but something told me I needed to take the call. I ran back into the kitchen and grabbed the phone off the hook as I noticed the screen reading Aubrey Payce.

"Mom. Are you alright? Why are you calling me from home?" I bombarded her with questions. She was calling from her home number when she was supposed to be at work.

"Well, I knew you were off today and there have been so many things on my mind and my past is about to catch up to me and I don't want you to be hurt and..." She was talking about as fast as a fifteen-year-old girl texting her BFF! It was almost like listening to Charlie Brown's school teacher, sped up and in reverse. I couldn't keep up.

"Mom...breathe. I don't know what you're talking about. What about your past? How would I be hurt?" I kept asking questions and she kept rambling, until... she burst into tears!

"I had hoped I would never have to tell you any of this," she cried. "I wanted to protect you from the pain I'd experienced and until now I'd been successful." She began to cry so hard I didn't know what to do. She finally stopped talking because she just couldn't get the words out.

"Mom, just take your time. You don't have to get it all out right now. I'm listening when you're ready." I tried to wait as patiently as I could but I was having my own meltdown on the inside. My brain was moving as fast as she'd been talking but I had no clue of what to think. I needed to break the silence. "Mom, are you still there?" I asked.

"I'm here sweetie" she answered. "I'm sorry about all that. I just needed to get that out. I'm sorry I used you to vent." I gasped for air… in shock. Here I was thinking she was finally going to talk to me and now…nothing. What had she gotten out? I didn't hear anything I could understand! I was trying my hardest not be angry.

"Mom, I'm sorry but I didn't understand a word you were saying. I mean, I heard you but I can't make sense of any of it. Aren't you going to start over? Don't you want me to understand what it is you're going through?" I was almost in panic mode. I might not ever get this chance again!

"No baby. I'm fine now. I just had to get that off my chest. I never meant to bother you with any of this stuff but I couldn't hold it in. It was weighing on me but I do apologize."

I felt like my mom had just been on the witness stand, told her life story and then recanted the whole thing. I was done! "Well, mom I was on my way out when you called. If everything is alright I have some errands to run" I said trying to hold in my frustration. "Okay. Call me later, if you get chance."

"Sure Mom, I'll talk to you soon." I had to get off the phone before I exploded. We said our usual I love you's and hung up. I was so frustrated that I just sat down instead of heading out the door. Shopping and cleaning would have to wait.

Before I get could get moving again I had to pray, meditate and listen for about an hour. I was trying to piece together the story that she had been rambling on about. The only thing I really understood was that she was about to have to face something from her past and evidently it might affect me. I didn't know why it would, but I guess anything that affects her is bound to have some effect on me.

After I had worn myself out, racking my brain with my mom's rant, I was finally ready to go. I hated any type of shopping and after that conversation I was not in a good mood. I really just wanted to get a few items and get back home. But, pulling up to the store I knew that wasn't going to happen. There were people everywhere!

It took me forever to check out. The lady in front of me had about three hundred dollars worth of groceries. She had two shopping carts, four kids and three animals! I prayed the whole time I was in line because that was ridiculous. I know people love their pets but ma'am… was it really necessary to bring them all to the store? I really wanted to ask that question but my better judgement prevailed. With the mood I was in, I might have just ended up on a viral video for acting all the way out of character. And Lord knows I do not need to lose my credentials over a grocery outing.

Once I finally got back home it was time to relax. I turned the lights off and the television on. I was trying to watch Stomp the Yard but all I saw was the back of my eyelids.

I woke up to a ringing phone, movie credits and my clock reading 7:20pm. I had been asleep for hours. I needed to wake up so I could get ready for bed! Who's calling me?

"Hey Andrea. What's going on girl?" I answered.

Now, Andrea had been talking to herself all day. She'd sat at her desk watching Jamie follow Tyson around the office and thinking, Sasha would just die if she could see this. Was this really the type of relationship he wanted? Why would he be letting this go on if it wasn't? Andrea was beginning to lose respect for him. She didn't think he was a bad person for not thinking that Sasha was his type but she didn't know what to think about Jamie being his type. He knows everyone is watching his every move. He's management for goodness sake! She desperately wanted to call Sasha and once she was home and settled, that's exactly what she did. Now she was trying to figure out how to talk to her about this without upsetting her. Tyson was someone Sasha had feelings for. And he was the reason she'd left town. Andrea wanted to get Sasha's input but she knew she needed to keep some of the intimate details under her hat. She would have to think about her wording very carefully before. Too bad she didn't figure all of this out before she dialed her number!

"Drama girl. Whassup witcha?" Andrea commented in her usual slang.

"I'm doing well. I'm dealing with this family in counseling who are going through and they're taking me through with them! I know I'm supposed to leave that stuff at the office and give it to God and I'm usually good at doing that. But, this case is different for some reason." I didn't even realize I felt that way until just then.

"Well, I guess I won't bother you with the mess going on down here then."

"Why? What's wrong?"

"Nothing with me. It's your boy, Tyson."

Uh oh. Here we go. I had actually gone almost a full day without thinking about him. Now here she comes with something to send me back. I was going to have to decide whether or not I wanted to entertain it. And, I really didn't. I'd had a peaceful evening and was not ready to let go of that.

"Andrea, I love you and everything, but I really can't handle any Tyson news tonight. I just woke up from a long nap and I really need to get ready for my day tomorrow. Can I call you on Sunday after church?"

"Sure" Andrea said. "Have a good night and I'll talk to you on Sunday."

I figured I'd better get busy fast before I started thinking about Tyson on my own. I hadn't eaten dinner or ironed my clothes. I decided to turn my ringer off because I really didn't want to talk to anyone else tonight except God and I didn't need the phone to talk to Him.

CHAPTER 18

A Letter to God

I WAS IN the office bright and early Saturday morning. I needed to catch up on some of my paperwork since I had taken my usual administrative day off. I was expecting the Cameron's at eleven o'clock so, I had about four hours to get my work done.

As I sat, typing my case notes, I started thinking about the offer Mrs. Warren had made. It had been weeks and I hadn't given her an answer yet. She hadn't asked me again or anything. I was just wondering if maybe she had forgotten. Maybe she was waiting for me to make the next move. She put the offer on the table and it was my choice as to whether I would accept or not. I mean, what would it hurt? I could definitely use some guidance spiritually and otherwise. I guess my hold up was that I was trying to make sure she wasn't taking the place of my mother. Of course, my mother would always be my mother but a mentor might be nice. Being a therapist is a hard job. Most therapists need therapy! We carry other people's issues around with us sometimes and if we aren't careful, their issues will become ours. I could use someone to bounce ideas off of. I'm in this city all by myself with no friends or family. This might be the opportunity I need to help further the vision I have in my heart. I don't profess to know or understand everything in the spiritual realm because sometimes God has to hit me over the head with what he's trying to tell me. And even then, sometimes I still don't get it!

I decided that tomorrow, after church, I would have a serious talk with Mrs. Warren. That is, if I could get to her. Everyone always rushed up to talk to the Pastor and his wife after service. Maybe I would just call her on the phone this evening. I was sure I'd need to talk to someone after meeting with the Cameron's.

Eleven o'clock had come sooner than I expected. I heard the buzzer at the front door. If Gabrielle isn't in I keep the door locked so clients have to be let in instead of just walking in on me. They were a little early but I wouldn't dare leave them outside. I let the Cameron family in and asked them to have a seat in the lobby. I needed a few more moments to gather my thoughts. I could hear them chatting out there while they waited for me. Everything sounded fine. There was no bickering. Hopefully they'd all completed their assignments and were ready to get the letter to Amber completed and mailed.

"Come on in" I called to them from my office doorway. "It's good to see you all here again. Have a seat wherever you'd like today and we'll begin with prayer. Is there anyone who wants to offer the prayer today or anyone that has something they would like to add to it?"

I was surprised when Randall said, "I'd like to offer the prayer today if no one else would mind."

While I only felt emotion on the inside without allowing it to show on my face, everyone else in the room showed outwardly what I was feeling. They were surprised, but pleasantly. Everyone gave Randall some sign of their approval although not verbally. His wife squeezed his hand, Aggie nodded toward him and Bea simply tilted her head to the left and smiled.

"Begin when you're ready Randall" I prompted.

"Before I start the prayer I would just like to tell you all why I have asked to do this. I had an experience over this past week that I still don't quite understand but I know it was supernatural. I couldn't get anything written on our homework assignment and I went to Brandy. She made me pray with her. I never said a word though. She just prayed for me. I went back to my desk and still didn't have anything but the moment I prayed for myself and picked up my pen it was like someone else's hand was attached to my body!"

Randall started getting excited and in my mind I was saying "Go God, Go!" Randall went straight into his prayer.

"Lord, I just want to say thank you. I know I don't have much of a relationship with you but I think I'm ready to start working on that. I'm here with part of my family and I want to be here with my entire family one day soon. I'm not sure what has come over me but I just realized that I feel this way. Lord, help us reach out to our little sister. We allowed her to leave our lives and that wasn't right. Help us to learn to love each other and recover from everything we've gone through as individuals and as a family. Thank you again. Amen."

"I'd like to hear from everyone" I said. "What are you all thinking and feeling right now?"

"That was a wonderful prayer, honey" Brandy said. The joy of hearing her husband pray was all over her face and in her voice. She was trying to hold back tears.

"Where did that come from little brother?" Aggie asked. "I didn't know you prayed."

"Well… I don't" Randall said. "I mean, I didn't. But, after the experience I had this week I need some answers. I know I didn't write this letter on my own and I want to know who did. I know it was a blessing and I just need to know more about it. What else can I do but pray?"

"Wow…it feels so good in here" Bea observed. "I came in not knowing what was gon' happen. I was gon' hold some things back from you guys and now I feel like I just need to be honest about everything!" Bea looked at me, smiled and winked, as if we had a secret between us. "May I share what happened in our session, Dr. Payce?"

"Sure. You guys can talk about anything you want in here" I reassured.

"Well" Bea began, "I just wanted you all to know that I'm aware that something is wrong with me. After hearing some of the stories you told, I realized that parts of my memory are missing. I used to have "blackouts" that I never told anyone about. I was always too embarrassed to say I didn't remember. I blew 'em off for a long time because I didn't know what to do. I knew people would think I was crazy if I said anything to anyone."

The family was looking at Bea like she was an alien. They had no clue of what she was talking about. I could tell that they were trying to figure out whether or not they had ever seen her 'black out'.

"After trying to work on our assignment I knew I had to do something about the gaps in my memory because I didn't want any more surprise stories from you guys. The one about the trash can was enough to last me a life time but I have come up with another one." Bea stopped and looked at me as if she were asking my permission to continue.

"Dr. Payce, I know today wasn't meant to be a Bea session but I just feel like I want to talk about this. I need their help." Bea waited for me to respond.

"Bea, this is your family's time. You guys can use it any way you like. It's more important that you have your family's permission than mine." I wanted this family to begin the healing process as soon as possible. Now was as good a time as any. Bea turned to her family and asked them if they would be willing to use this time to work out some things. They agreed and she began.

"I need you guys to help me with something. This may actually be something only our mother can answer but I'm just not ready to talk to her yet." They all nodded their heads as if they understood what she meant by not wanting to talk to her. Bea continued "Do you remember my sixteenth birthday?"

"Not really…"

"Just what your mother told us…

Bea's siblings really didn't remember anything significant about her birthday or any of the other events she brought up. It was beginning to look like there were only two beings that would be able to help her sort out the gaps in her memory. One was God, whom she probably wouldn't mind talking to. The other was her mother and that was going to be a challenge. Since Bea was at an impasse, the family agreed to move on and begin writing the letter to their sister. They had all done their homework assignments and were ready to combine the letters. It was decided that they would hand write the letter so it would be more personal. They would each write their own parts so Amber would see that each of them had contributed. They wanted to be sure she knew that each one of them had been active and willing participants. This was going to take a while.

So, while they were writing their letter I decided to write one of my own. I was going to write a letter to God.

The family was in a huddle like they were strategizing for first and goal! They seemed to have their plan together and didn't appear to need my help so I decided to move to my desk. I pulled out my stationery and prepared to write my letter.

Lord, I have to admit that I don't treat you like I should. I don't spend enough time with you and you know I don't deserve the blessings you send to me. Yet, you send them anyway. I want to love you like that. I want to love others like that. I want to give you what you deserve from me. Sometimes I worry that you won't bless me with the desires of my heart. There is no reason why you should but your word says you will.

But, the truth is that most of the time I don't know what I want. It's a good thing you know what I need. I am so happy I know you. I think about people who don't know you and feel sorry for them. I don't know how to get through life without you and I don't want to find out!

Yet, sometimes it seems as though people who don't know you have all the success. Why is that? Your word says the first will be last and if we want to be great we have to be small. Well, it goes something like that. I don't know where those exact scriptures are but you know what I mean. But, above anything else, I want to do what you say. I know...I don't always listen to you. I miss what you're trying to tell me a lot! Help me to train my eyes and ears to know you. I want you to make my desires line up with the desires you have for me. I need your help with that because my wants and desires are strong and sometimes they can get a little out of control. Sometimes I think they'll overpower me!

Just as I finished the last sentence I looked up to find that the Cameron's were just about finished. I'd have to finish my letter at home. I folded it up, stuck it in my purse and went back over to where the family was sitting. They looked to be finishing up and I assumed, for the moment, that they were pleased with what they had done. Before I could make any comments they asked if they could read the letter to me. Of course, I gave my approval and Randall began to read. They each read their own parts of the letter. Surprisingly, it flowed very well. They appeared pleased with their accomplishment and in turn, so was I. The session was coming to a close so we discussed the details about who would put it in the mail. Each family member had put their addresses and phone numbers in the body of the letter. The only thing left to do was stamp, mail and wait for a response. I suggested the family return in two weeks whether they had gotten a response or not. I wanted to make sure everyone was okay with what does or doesn't happen with Amber.

I walked most of the family to the outer office doors but asked Bea to remain behind for a few moments. I suggested that she seriously consider inviting her mother into her next session. She made no guarantees but did promise to give it considerable thought. Bea was to return for an individual session the following week, with or without her mother.

I locked up the office and headed for home. I wanted to call Mrs. Warren once I got there but my letter to God was just burning to get out of my purse! I went to my desk, turned my light on and began to read over what I had already written. It was alright, but I didn't feel like I was getting across what I really wanted Him to know. Maybe I'd give Mrs. Warren a call after all. I hoped that might give me some time to think about what I really wanted to say to my Savior.

"Good afternoon Mrs. Warren. This is Sasha Payce."

"Hello, Sasha. I've been wondering if you were going to call."

"Yes ma'am. I must admit that I've been dragging my feet, but I'm ready now. I would love for you to be my mentor. I do feel that I could learn a great deal from you in the therapeutic world as well as the spiritual."

"And I would be delighted to be that for you with God's help, of course."

"Of course!"

Mrs. Warren hadn't had any lunch yet and Pastor was at the church preparing for tomorrow's sermon. We decided to meet for an early dinner to discuss where we wanted to begin with our new relationship. She was paying and I was always up for a free meal!

CHAPTER 19

Service

SUNDAY MORNING SERVICE was life changing! Pastor gave his personal testimony, which I had never heard before. He talked about the way he was in his youth and if what he said is true, I know the Lord forgives.

"…My brother and I were forces to be reckoned with" Pastor stated. "We thought we had no one to answer to. We were grown and we could do whatever we wanted. Sure, initially we just wanted to be foot loose and fancy free but eventually our carelessness turned into something we couldn't control. Satan had established a serious hold on us that neither of us could get out of. We got into the drug game. We was making money and couldn't nobody tell us nothin'. We was living the good life. We had cars, a house, women, you name it! It was all going perfectly until my brother decided to have a taste of the stuff we was selling. At that point we was like Adam and Eve. We both knew not to get into that but it got us anyway."

I don't think Pastor realized he was gonna be so emotional about this. It looked like he was caught off guard by what he was saying.

"Amen!"

"Hallelujah!"

"Preach Pastor!"

The congregation cheered him on. I'm not sure if they were giving him support or edging him on because they wanted to hear the rest of the story. You never know about us church folks. But, Pastor continued on anyway.

"One day I left the house to make a quick run to the store" he said. "We were due to have some company over to the house that night and we needed a few supplies. I couldn't have been gone but twenty minutes and when I got back my brother had started the party without me. He had the music blasting and he and the drink in his hand was making out! I didn't know what had happened at first. I was shocked!"

"You see, neither one of us smoked or drank before that day. Sure, we had tried a couple of things here and there but neither of us had ever been drunk or high. At that moment my brother was both! I didn't understand it. I didn't know what had gotten into him but he was having such a good time I decided to join him!

The entire time I was getting high I knew I shouldn't have been. But, I did it anyway. After that first high there was no turning back. We couldn't stop and from that day forward our empire slowly buried us. We lost everything because instead of selling and making the money we were smoking it all ourselves. After we ran out of money we started selling our cars. We knew we had hit rock bottom when were on the streets just like our customers! Our house was foreclosed on for not making the payments and we were broke and homeless all within two months of that first hit!"

Pastor paused but seemed to gain some momentum. "That's not even the whole story but I only said that to say this…God is good!"

"All the time…"

"Yes He is…"

"Won't He do it!" The congregation went wild again.

"I know He's good because I was out there. I was at a point where I didn't know whether I was coming or going but by the grace of God I am here! He was looking out for me when I didn't know I needed looking out for. When I was too stupid to know there was an unconditional lover called Jesus! I want all of you out there to know that Jesus is real! If He could save me from the state I was in He can save anyone! If you don't hear another word I have to say hear this…Jesus loves! Jesus saves! Jesus heals! Jesus delivers! Jesus provides! Jesus is everything you need and when you're smart enough to realize it, He'll be everything you want!"

Pastor did this little spin around thing that made his robe fly and the church erupted! It sounded like a Friday night football game in Texas, but this praise was for the Lord. I dropped my Bible because it was sitting on my lap when I jumped up. It landed flat on the floor and was still open. Good, I thought. I won't have to try to find where the scripture reading was. But, when I picked it up I discovered that it hadn't fallen to floor on the same page I'd been reading from. The page had flipped to Psalms and the first passage that caught my eyes was chapter 100 verse 1. It read… *Make a joyful noise to the Lord, all the earth.* I dropped the Bible again and jumped out of my seat to give the Lord a shout of praise because the Word told me to! I was enjoying myself in the spirit that was filling our beautiful sanctuary.

On my way home I remembered I needed to call Andrea back. I was in such good spirits that I felt like I could handle whatever it was she was going to tell me. I decided to stop off and get something to eat because I didn't feel like making anything for lunch. I was already going to have to cook for dinner and I didn't see the point in cooking twice in one day.

I arrived at home and no sooner than I put my lunch on the counter the phone started ringing. It was Andrea. *This girl was relentless!* She must really have something important to say. The truth is that I know it's just gossip. She's going to put it in the form of an inquiry but it's just gossip. I'll call her back when I finish eating. There is no way I'm gon' let her ruin my lunch!

I let the voicemail pick up. I'm glad I have call notes so I can't actually hear what she's saying. Sometimes I wished I could hear it so I could more effectively screen my calls, but today… for Andrea, I didn't want to hear it. I had actually planned to call her but her relentlessness to talk made me change my mind about wanting to hear from her. I finished my meal and decided to call her back before she called me again. I had read every scripture I could find on gossip and none of it was good. I was going to be polite but I wasn't going to participate in it.

"Hey, Andrea I noticed you called me. Whassup?" I asked.

"Well, I had called you yesterday to talk to you about this issue I'm having. I know you're a therapist and you're not supposed to counsel with acquaintances but…" Andrea was rambling.

I really wanted her to get to the point. She was never a person to beat around the bush so, I was really getting curious as to what was going on. Maybe she hadn't called to talk about Tyson. Maybe it was about something else.

"Andrea, what are you trying to say?" I couldn't take it anymore. "You're rambling and I haven't made sense out of anything you've said." She sounded like my mother had that night she called me to vent. Maybe the problem is not with them. Maybe it's with me because lately, I've been having some problems with conversations that I'm supposed to be following.

"Well, I have something on my mind that's seriously irking me" Andrea said. "I just wanted to know what you think about um…" Andrea trailed off and stopped talking.

"Andrea?"

"Um…I'm getting another call. Can I call you back?"

"Sure. I'll talk to you later."

We both hung up the phone and I went to praising the Lord! I was so glad she got another call. *Wait a minute*, I thought. *She doesn't even have call waiting. But, I heard the click.* You know, the sound the call waiting makes when someone else is beeping in on the other person's line? *Oh well, maybe she got it put back on her phone.* I just jumped and danced anyway. I didn't care why she had gotten off the phone. I was just so glad she did!

I finally had time to sit down and finish my letter. I was really getting into it now. I was also trying to figure out exactly what to do with it. It was a letter I couldn't mail! But, I wanted Him to have it. *I know*, I thought. *I'll finish writing the letter and take it to the altar. I'll tell Him in prayer.* That simple little plan made me feel so good. Writing was rewarding in and of itself. But, having the chance to deliver it to the one it's intended for makes the process all the better!

CHAPTER 20

Favors

BEA SPENT THE rest of her Sunday, after church, contemplating whether or not she was going to call her mother. She tried everything she could to get it off her mind and decided to call her sister and ask her opinion.

"Nyellow" Aggie answered.

"Hey" Bea said, assuming her sister knew who was calling. "I need to ask your opinion about something and I need an honest answer."

"I'm all ears" Aggie replied. Aggie lived for this kind of stuff because she was a busy body and it sounded like this was going to be juicy. "You remember yesterday when I was telling you about what Dr. Payce said?" "Yeah. What about it?"

"I've been thinking about whether or not I should ask our mother to come to counseling with me. And well, I want to know what you think. I mean, if you were me, what would you do?"

"Well, Bea I guess it would depend on what I needed from her." That statement was Aggie's way of trying to get more information out of Bea than she was probably ready to give. "What is it that you need from her that you think only she can provide?"

Bea knew what Aggie was trying to do but she didn't have time for games. "Aggie, I already told you I need to figure out why I have these gaps in my memory and why you guys remember things I don't. That's all this is about. There's no gossip and no secrets."

"And you think she's the only one who can help you?"

"It seems that way."

"Do you think she would use anything from the session against you?"

Bea had to take a moment to think about that one. She

never really thought about that. Now that she was an adult there was really no one her mother could tell that would have any effect on her. She was fine with her brother and sister knowing. She didn't really associate with any of her mother's family or friends... if she had any. So, if she told any of them she really wouldn't care.

"Well, what could she possibly do with the information, Aggie?"

"Humph. You don't know her like I do." Aggie made that statement under her breath.

"What'd you say?"

"Aw nothin'. I was thinking out loud about a stupid commercial I just saw."

"Oh. Well, what do you think? Should I bring her to the session or not?"

"Honestly Bea, you have to make the decision as to whether or not you want to ask her. If she's the only one who can help you then I don't guess you have any other choice but to ask. Just be prepared for her to disappoint you." Aggie didn't want her sister to be hurt.

"You think she gon' disappoint me?" Bea asked with concern.

"Think about it, Bea. I mean, really take a minute and look back on the memories you do have. Was your mother ever there for us? Like, really there for us?"

Bea didn't have an answer. As she thought about it, the only person they had ever really been able to depend on was their grandmother. She never really thought about that before. It was possible that her mother may not even agree to come to the session with her. If that happened she might never get her questions answered.

"Let me think about this some more, Aggie. I'll call you later."

Bea hung up the phone and just sat on the edge of her bed. If her mother couldn't or wouldn't help her, who could? Although her grandmother had a great memory she was never around when any of the blackouts occurred. She needed her mother for this one and she didn't see why there would be any problem getting her to commit to the session. Bea only had to figure out the best way to ask. She remembered the way Randall talked about his recent experience with prayer. Maybe that was something she needed to try.

"God?"

Oh wait, Bea thought. *I don't know how to do this. I haven't prayed in so long. I have no idea what to say. What would Grandma say? She prayed all the time.* Bea thought about that and started over.

"Lord, I need you. I've been in trouble for a long time and I'm just now deciding to do something about it, but I have a problem. I think I need my mother's help and we don't have a good relationship. I need to figure out how to ask for her help. I know my grandma used to talk to you and you would answer her. Now my brother is talking to you too. Pretty soon I guess you'll be hearing from my entire family. I don't mean to bother you. But, I need you. I don't think I have any other options. I know you don't really know me but…anyway, Amen."

Bea got off her knees not really knowing if her prayer had gone beyond her ceiling. She'd tried as best she could remember from listening to her grandmother, but she just wasn't sure if it worked. After all, she never really talked to Him before. Why should he answer now? Oh, well. She knew she couldn't wait too long on God so she came up with a plan B. If God wouldn't help her then she might just have to guilt her mother into it. They had contacted Amber like she asked so she needed to do this counseling thing for her.

Arlene had really enjoyed the morning service especially since the pastor allowed her to lead two songs this week. He was wrapped around her finger. She was an usher, the secretary and a deaconess for the church. She sang in the choir and welcomed the visitors. One would think she was the first lady! She would love to have that title and even allowed visitors to believe she did. Whenever they would mistakenly call her the first lady she would not dare correct them. She simply smiled and hugged them. That way, when and if she was confronted she could say truthfully, that she never told them she was the pastor's wife.

She was trying to walk Holy but her flesh wasn't going down without a fight! She knew she was wrong and that was a start. At least she thought about it. Before she started trying to live a righteous life she wouldn't have cared whether it was wrong or not. This was going to be a long, slow process. But, it was something she would have to do if she was ever going to get her children back. She really wanted to understand why she lost them in the first place. She needed to be honest with herself and with God. Of course, He already knew who she was but she would to have to face herself.

Arlene really wanted this family reunion to happen. She was trying to be as patient as possible with her son but it felt, to her, like he was dragging his feet with this Amber situation. But, she knew she was not in control of this. This was up to her children. For the first time since they were born, she would have to let them dictate how something turned out. She was so used to telling them what to do and not giving them an option. She had to admit that she liked it better that way. But again, she was going to have to change some of those old ways. Actually, she was going to have to change most of her old ways.

As Arlene headed for the kitchen she was thinking about what she might make for dinner. She felt like some fried chicken, greens, candied yams and corn. But she was at home by herself. Why would she cook all that food?

As she passed the telephone, on the way to kitchen, it rang. She jumped so high and hard that she bumped into the wall. She hit it so hard the pins in her wig moved! She hadn't taken it off after church and it nearly hopped off her head. She straightened it before she answered the phone as if someone could see her.

"Hello?" Arlene said, upset with whoever was calling because they had startled her.

"Hi. This is Molly Bea. How are you?" Bea was so nervous. She hadn't called her own mother in so long she didn't know how to talk to her.

"Well, hello Bea. I'm surprised to hear from you. Have you all heard from Amber?"

Arlene assumed that must be the reason her daughter was

calling. She also assumed Randall and Aggie were on the phone as well.

Bea couldn't believe her mother just jumped straight into talking about Amber. She hadn't even asked her how she was doing. She was just about to change her mind and make up some reason to get off the phone when…

"I'm sorry, Bea. I didn't even ask you how you were doing. Forgive me." Arlene said that with such sincerity that she didn't recognize it as her own voice. Bea was shocked and wondered if she had made those comments out loud.

"Thank you. I would be doing much better but there's something I need your help with." Bea hadn't meant to go there so quickly but it just felt right.

"Well, I don't know how I could help but I'll try."

"I guess I need to tell you a little bit about what's going on and what I need from you before you commit to it."

"Okay. I'm listening."

Bea was so amazed and stunned that it took her a moment to speak. The conversation seemed to have started off on the wrong note and all of a sudden it had begun to go even better than she'd hoped.

"Well, I've been seeing a therapist…" Bea waited after making that statement to see what kind of response she'd get. The other end of the phone was silent so she continued. "…And, through my first sessions I've discovered that I have some areas in my life that I don't have a good memory of. To be honest, there are some things I've recently found out about that I don't remember at all. I've tried to ask my brother and sister but they don't have the answers either. I really think you may be the only one who can help me. What I need is for you to come to counseling with me. I need you to see if you can help me work through some of these gaps in my memory. I know it's asking a lot but would you think about it? My next session is this coming Thursday and I would like for you to come with me. If you would just think about it and let me know by Wednesday I would really appreciate it." Bea ended her plea and waited.

She didn't wait long for a response but it was definitely not the one she'd expected. "Bea, I will go with you to your session on Thursday if you do me a favor first. Why don't you come over for dinner? I was thanking of a big meal I got a taste fo' but I just couldn't thank of no reason to cook that much food. And well, you just give me a reason. You could come over for dinner and then take some home withcha. Whatchu say?"

Arlene was shocked at what she had just asked. She hadn't invited her children over for dinner since they'd moved out. She didn't know where this was coming from. And the thought wasn't even a selfish one. She was truly reaching out.

Bea was even more shocked than Arlene was and had no idea how to respond. "Uh…sure? I'll come over." Bea only agreed because she didn't know what else to say. She figured it was the least she could do. She wanted something from her mother so it was only natural that she should return the favor. Even though she really felt that her mother owed her.

"Dinner will be at 7. I'll be 'spectin' you."

"Alright. I'll be on time."

Bea hung up the phone and felt like she was in the Twilight Zone. She felt like she had just been in the strangest conversation. The call had started out in such a way that she thought she would hang up without asking for what she needed. Then, it took on a totally different feel. It was like her mother had read her mind. And then, on top of that, she agreed to help her and invited her to dinner. Freaky, Bea thought. But, it might just turn out to be the start of something good. After all, she had started praying about it.

"Aggie!" Bea couldn't wait to call her sister to tell her who she was having dinner with tonight and to get her opinion on it.

"Hi, Bea. Have you decided what you gon' do about asking your mother to go to counseling with you?"

"Yep."

"Well…?"

"Get this…Not only did she say she would go with me but she invited me over for dinner! Tonight! What do you think about that?"

Aggie didn't respond. She was waiting for her sister to say April fools even though it was January. She couldn't imagine her mother doing this unless…

"Bea, are you telling me the truth?" Aggie asked that question with such seriousness behind it that it worried Bea.

"Yes. I just got off the phone with her. She invited me over because she wanted to cook this big meal but didn't really have a reason to. She said she would do me a favor if I did her one" Bea explained.

Aggie went silent again. She really didn't want to but she was thinking the worst of her mother. She was thinking that this had been too easy and that her mother had to have some ulterior motive for inviting Bea to her house. Aggie wasn't sure what Arlene was up to but she sure wasn't about to let Bea walk into it alone.

"Bea, call her back and tell her I'm coming with you and see what she says" Aggie insisted.

"No way. I'm going by myself."

"Fine Bea. Then I'm not gon' be responsible for what happens."

"Fine. Do you want me to call you when I get home?"

"Do whatever you want."

Both sisters disconnected the call upset with one another. Bea couldn't understand why Aggie just wouldn't believe someone could change. Everyone was changing. Randall was praying for goodness sake! If that wasn't a change she didn't know what would be.

Why would Aggie ask to go to the dinner with her? She acted as if she didn't even like their mother and now she wanted to go to dinner with her. Was she jealous? She did seem kind of worried. She said something about not being responsible for me and what might happen. What did she mean by that? What could possibly happen?

Bea began to worry herself into a tizzy. She began to have second thoughts as to whether or not she should even show up for this dinner but that thought disappeared quickly. Just as fast as she had gotten all worked up she calmed down. She knew she needed to do this for her own sake and the sake of the rest of her family. If this reunion stuff was going to work it had to start somewhere.

CHAPTER 21

Do Tell

RANDALL HAD PUT his precious package in the mail on Saturday. He was now sitting at work where he was supposed to be doing some financial planning, but he couldn't keep his fingers out of his mouth long enough to pick up a pencil. He needed to talk to someone so, he picked up his phone to call his wife, but was met by his sister Aggie on the other end.

"Hey little brother…"

"Hey Aggie…whatcha up to?"

"Trying to not call Bea…"

"Why you tryin' not to call her? Why don't you just talk to her?"

"Because she should be calling me. She had dinner with your mother last night and I was expecting to hear from her. She was mad at me so I guess she's being stubborn. I guess if I wasn't being so stubborn myself I would have told her to call me back. But, I didn't…"

"Why was she mad at you? What did you do?"

"What do you mean…what did I do? I was just trying to make her understand that she needed to be careful and watch her step around her mother. That's all…I was trying to protect her and she acted like I was being jealous!"

"Well Sis, you're the oldest. You know how this is gon' work out. You might as well go ahead and make that call. Don't let pride keep you from checking on her."

"I know…but I feel like I'm always taking one for the team. But, enough about me…what's going on with you today?"

"I put the letter in the mail to Amber on Saturday, but they probably won't pick it up until today. I'm so nervous. Do you think she'll respond? Will she even read it?"

"She'll probably at least read it. Now the response…that's a different matter."

"I'm having a hard time controlling my anxiety. I actually have her phone number so I could just call and put myself out of my misery. But, then I'd feel like a hypocrite because I'd be doing the same thing your mother did. I want to give her the space to respond only if she wants to. Whadoyou think?"

"Well, I wouldn't advise you to do anything your mother would do. So, give her some space. That girl has been gone for over thirty years. Give her the choice whether she wants to stay away or come back. Well, little brother, I'm gonna let you get back to work. If you hear from Bea tell her to call me."

Bea wasn't quite sure how to feel after dinner with her mother last night. She didn't know what to think either. She was beginning to think that maybe Aggie had been right about not going over there alone. She wasn't quite sure now of how the Thursday session was going to go either. She even began to wonder again about whether or not she should take her mother with her. Would it do more harm than good? Would her mother be honest with her? She knew she needed her mother's help but why was it so difficult?

Bea really wanted to talk to Aggie but she was ashamed to call. She didn't want to tell her about the doubts and she definitely didn't want to hear I told you so. Aggie would probably never say that but Bea didn't even want to give her a reason to think it. She was being stubborn and she knew it but Aggie hadn't called her either. But, now she needed her sister's help because she had gotten what she wanted. Sort of... Her mother had agreed to the counseling session. The only problem with that was that none of her children quite trusted Ms. Arlene Cameron.

Arlene woke up feeling great about dinner with her daughter the night before. She felt that it had gone well and she was actually excited about going to the counseling session with her. She had already been to counseling before and felt that it had opened her eyes to some things. She knew she was nowhere near where she needed to be but at least she was seeing some things differently. What harm would it do to get a free visit? She really hoped that going to counseling with Bea would trickle down to the rest of the family. If she does this good thing, maybe the rest of the family would come around. Arlene desperately wanted them to know she was trying and that she was serious about the reunion. If she could get all her children who were in arm's reach to agree, it would only be a matter of time before she got her baby girl back. She had already gotten the chance to hear Amber's voice. Now, she needed to make sure she could see her face.

Aubrey experienced a trying church service yesterday. Her pastor had really stressed the connection of family. He had tried to get his congregation to understand that although they may not have been born into the family they would have chosen, there was a reason why God had placed everyone where they were. Aubrey had never understood what happened to her and why. She had thought about it over and over and could never come up with a good reason. She just couldn't understand why God would allow anyone to go through what she did. Of course, she knew there were people who had experienced worse but she didn't understand that either!

It was now in her spirit that she needed to find out what had happened in and with her family. She didn't know if she really cared to see her mother but her father had never left her mind. Maybe she should at least find him. After all, he loved her. He just couldn't protect her anymore. His going to jail was what had given her the strength to leave the family. Without him, she didn't have a chance of surviving in that house. And while on the subject of her mother, what about that out-of-the-blue phone call? Was she really serious about this family reunion and did she really expect her to come? What a mess! Maybe if she ignored it, it would just go away. Her mother had said she wouldn't bother her again, but she was certainly not inclined to believe that. When had her mother ever done anything she said she would do? What would she tell Sasha? Did she owe it to her only child to allow her to get to know her biological family? Even though she got the point of what her pastor was trying to say, he didn't know her people.

Aubrey had always felt she knew what was best for Sasha

but now that her daughter was an adult she really didn't have the right to dictate her life. She really didn't have the right to withhold things from her even if she thought she was doing the right thing. Sasha was smart. Aubrey knew that Sasha wouldn't allow herself to remain in the dark forever. She would figure it out sooner or later. She had to figure out what to do before her past punched her and her daughter both in the gut.

CHAPTER 22

The Response

AUBREY HAD BEEN wrestling with the memories of her past life for several days now. She needed to make a decision about whether or not she was going to speak with her mother again, but she did wonder about her siblings. Did they know their mother had found her? What was their relationship with her like? They weren't exactly treated well but they weren't treated like she was either.

These questions went around and around in her head for days without answers. She needed some help but she didn't exactly have anyone to turn to. She had friends but they had no idea about her past and she had no intentions of letting them in on it. At least, not yet. She hadn't even revealed any of it to her own daughter. How could she allow perfect strangers into her most intimate life when she hadn't even allowed the only being that had come from her body access to it?

Wednesday evening had rolled around and Aubrey was still no closer to an answer for her questions than she had been in weeks. But, while thumbing through the day's mail she discovered an envelope that would surely light a fire under her. The letter was addressed to Amber Price and the return address was from the Cameron Family. What an interesting word... Family. That term was used so loosely. What did it really mean anyway? What are the qualifications needed to be considered family? Whether she agreed with it or not was another matter. Aubrey was faced with a letter from a family with a last name she didn't want to associate with.

They still think of me as Amber, she thought. She hadn't been that girl in years. She'd gotten rid of her when she got rid of them. Amber was a part of their family. Maybe that's the way she could keep her distance. She could be Amber while reading the letter. That way they couldn't hurt Aubrey. That sounded like something Sasha would advise her to do. Or at least something she might tell one of her clients.

Aubrey sat down and just stared at the letter. She hadn't been in touch with any of them in so long that she thought of the Cameron's as past acquaintances.

She wasn't obligated to respond but the least she could do was read the letter since they had taken the time to send it.

She just couldn't bring herself to open it so, she got up to turn the coffee pot on. She loved the hazelnut and any other flavored creamer she could find! Aubrey could drink coffee in any season or anytime of the day or night. She thought maybe if she could relax she would be able to open the letter and read it. One more thing might be needed as well so, she pulled out her journal book and began to talk to God with urgency.

As she finished her prayer and closed her journal, her coffee pot reminded her that her favorite indulgence was ready. She got up and got her "Queen of the Castle" coffee mug, came back to sit in her favorite chair and picked up the letter. She took a sip of coffee and then held the letter over the steam to open it. Upon opening the letter, she immediately noticed one of her sisters' hand writing. Without reading anything she scanned the page. In all, there were three different handwritten patterns. This was a natural thing for Aubrey to do. She's an analyst by trade so she's trained to look for things out of the ordinary. She's almost like an investigator except she doesn't use her skills to catch people. She uses them to catch glitches and malfunctions.

She knew she would have to read the letter to figure out who the other two individuals were, but she knew the first portion of the letter had been written by Bea. The legibility had improved with maturity but it was definitely Bea's handwriting. Aubrey took another sip of her coffee, placed it back on her end table and began to read.

Hi little sister. I hope this letter finds you well, Bea wrote. I'm writing to you because I miss you. I want to see you. It's been way too long. Our family is not whole without you and I want to change that. I know things didn't go too good for you when you was here with us. There are some things I'm having trouble with in remembering our childhood but I'm working on it. I feel like you are a big part of me learning more. I want to hear from you Amber. Aubrey cringed at reading her given name. *I only hope you want to hear from me too. I know, now, that things weren't always great but we are still family.* There was that word again. *Please contact me. You will find my address and phone number at the end of this letter. Please write or call. I love you, little sister and I send hugs and kisses from Molly Bea.*

Well that was sweet of Bea. Aubrey always remembered her being sweet, for the most part. Of course, Bea did have her moments... She wondered what she was talking about as far as remembering things in our childhood. What was it that she was trying to recall? She would probably be better off forgetting about all of it, Aubrey thought. She figured she'd better continue reading the letter to see what the others had to say. Her brother Randall was left handed so she figured the second writer was him since the direction of the script had changed.

Hey baby girl. How's my little rabbit? Aubrey actually smiled at that greeting. Randall had always called her rabbit because of that crazy little thing she did with her nose. She only did it for him because he got such a kick out of it. She hadn't originally been doing it to be comical. She had allergy problems and her nose itched all the time. The only way she could get it to stop itching was to wiggle it like that.

Well, I know that your mother called you and I know what she wants. She wants you to come to a family reunion. To be honest, I don't know how to feel about it but I know I would like to see you. I know we have a lot of hurt in our past but maybe this is how we start to get over it. Please call me. I don't want to pressure you but I do want to hear from you whether you decide to come to the reunion or not.

After reading her only brother's portion of the letter Aubrey's heart began to soften. She was still confused but she felt like her brother sincerely wanted to get to know her. Maybe it was guilt. Maybe it was regret. She really didn't know but she was beginning to think that maybe she would at least talk to him. She could only assume the rest of the letter had been written by her oldest sister, Sally Agnes.

Hi Amber, this is Aggie. I guess I'm the only one of us who thinks you should stay away. Don't get me wrong. I would love to hear from you and even see you. I just don't know if it's worth it. I don't know if I would go to the reunion even if you did come but what I feel shouldn't stop you. You should do what you think is best. I have put my contact information in the letter as well. Please call one or all of us. We really do love you.

Aubrey was actually impressed with the fact that her siblings had written to her, but in a way, she was somewhat upset. They had eluded to the fact that our childhood's sucked but it seemed as though Randall and Bea were sugar coating it. If she went to this, so-called reunion, she wanted an apology. She hadn't forgotten the things each of them had taken part in. Yes, she knew they were children at the time, but it was still painful. She hadn't forgotten any of it. She not only wanted an apology from her siblings but she wanted an explanation from her mother. She decided, in that moment, that apologies and explanations would be the only way she would come anywhere near her "family" again. Aubrey picked up the phone to call her brother.

CHAPTER 23

Facing Reality

BEA WOKE UP on the morning of her joint session with her mother not feeling well. She was a little nauseous but she knew she wasn't sick. It was just her nerves. She was glad she'd decided to take the day off work. Feeling beforehand that it was going to be a difficult day for her, she told her supervisor she'd be back to work on Monday. Today was Thursday but she thought she might need an extra day plus the weekend to recuperate.

Bea had been journaling since her first session with Dr. Payce. She wanted to try and remember as many "black outs" as she could. Writing the experiences down brought up quite a few instances. As she read over them they almost seemed like dreams she woke up from but simply didn't remember the endings. Maybe the journal could help Dr. Payce jog her memory during the session. Her mother should be able to shed some light on what happened during those times because in each instance her mother appeared to have been involved. Whether directly or indirectly Arlene was a crucial part of what she could remember. Bea definitely knew today needed to be a prayerful one and she might even offer the prayer before session, as she knew Dr. Payce would ask if anyone cared to. It was now just a waiting game because her session wasn't until this evening. Bea knew she needed to keep herself busy so that fear and doubt wouldn't set in. But, she couldn't help but think about her mother and whether or not inviting her was really going to work out in her favor.

Arlene woke up early singing! She was excited about going to counseling this evening with her daughter. Bea had been the most docile child and Arlene knew she didn't have to worry about any of her old ways being discussed during this session. After all, this was to help Bea with her problems. Not to discuss Arlene's past life. She had already gone to counseling and spilled her guts about all of that. Well, not all of it. She had ended her sessions before too much was discovered. Dr. Payce knew a lot more about the way things really were than she had ever shared with anyone. But, sharing it all wasn't necessary! Counseling gave her a good start but she figured she could do the rest of the work on her own. She did have to admit that she hadn't done much changing but she was a work in progress. At least she was thinking about things a lot more. Reaching out to her children was big! Bea was the easiest to start with. If there was one of the children that would be on her side it was Bea. The only reason she didn't go to Bea for help with the Amber situation was because she felt Bea was on the weak side. She wouldn't be convincing enough. Randall was the male child and she knew Amber had been the closest to him. If anyone could get her to come around it would be him.

Arlene had planned to spend her day just like any other day… window shopping. Maybe buy herself a new wig. She wanted to look nice for this counseling session. Bea hadn't said much about her counselor. Not even her name. Arlene thought she was being a little mysterious about the counselor and her previous sessions because she was embarrassed. She hadn't told Bea about her own counseling sessions for that very reason. Seeking help was her own business. Not because she felt like she was crazy. It was really because she might have to admit she was wrong.

Counseling really wasn't that big of a deal. Arlene had to admit she had never once felt like she was being treated in any other way than just a person struggling with life. She figured maybe after going with Bea she would tell her she had been herself. It didn't mean she was weak. *Although that's what she thought about her daughter.* It only meant she'd needed help, like most people do at one time or another in their lives. Dr. Payce had taught her that.

Even though I had plenty of clients on my schedule today I felt like I needed to be most prepared for my last session of the day. I was to see Arlene and Bea Cameron. There were some serious issues going on in this family and it was definitely going to take more than a couple of counseling sessions to work through all the pain they had been through. They were going to have to be honest with one another. I didn't know if they were ready for it, but ready or not the time had come.

Since the first day I met Arlene, I just knew something was coming. I still felt it. I was certain it was for the family, but for some reason I felt like it was happening to me. So much loss, yet something was still on its way. Moving away from my mother and my friends had a huge impact on me. Losing the hope of ever having a chance with Tyson had affected me most of all. Maybe I needed a new hope. Something else to look forward to... It's possible I had just gotten so involved with this family that God was allowing me to feel what was coming in their lives. I definitely sensed some difficult confrontations ahead yet it still felt like a victory.

I was scheduled for altar time tonight after the Cameron session and I was excited about it. Not only would I be presenting my love letter to God but I would also be in prayer for this particular family. Maybe He would reveal something to me that might give me a glimpse into what I was feeling.

As I was sitting at my desk, thinking about my day, my phone rang. Gabrielle was buzzing me to tell me a call was holding for me. I knew who it was. "Hi Ma," I answered. "You called at exactly the right time. One of my clients is fifteen minutes late so it probably means she isn't coming. And, even if she does she's going to have to wait for me now. How are you?"

"Well, I'm calling to get your advice" my mom admitted. Wow! I couldn't believe it. She had never asked for my advice before.

"Sure mom, I hope I can help. What is it?"

"Um," she said "I have a co-worker who's going through this family crisis. She wants to have a meeting with her family but needs to know how to do it most effectively. The family has been separated for a long time and have a lot of hurts and they just want to know how to start the healing process. What would you recommend if you were their counselor?"

"Well, I would probably set a meeting date for as many of

the members who could attend. You definitely want to extend the invitation to everyone involved and try to set the meeting at a time with the least schedule conflicts. Sometimes that's hard, but you have to at least try" I insisted.

"How would you facilitate the meeting? Would you have only family there or would you do it with a neutral party?" Mom was asking some great questions! I was beginning to think maybe she should be a part of it.

"Well, I definitely think you do need a facilitator but it could be a family member. It should be someone that everyone respects and someone they would consider a fair person. It might be a good idea to have rules as well. Like, the person who has the floor has to be called on so you don't have everyone talking over one another. Or maybe having an object where only the person with the object in their hand can speak. You know, some kind of way to keep order. Be careful with objects, though. Make sure it's something that can't be used as a weapon!" I had seen way too many family meetings get out of hand.

"The rules should be given before the meeting begins and everyone should have a copy of the rules in front of them. Make sure everyone who wants to speak gets a chance and make sure to try and resolve anything that can be resolved before the meeting is over. Remember that emotions will fly. Allow people to speak directly to each other. Confrontation can be a good thing but make sure the facilitator or facilitators can always regain control of the meeting. We don't want any physical altercations."

I knew all too well how physical altercations went. I experienced that on a number of occasions. Not with my own family, of course, because I didn't really have any. I was just always with my friends and their families. I'd attended several family reunions where it got ugly. I mean really ugly. Really… what's the point in two brothers waiting until they get in front of the entire family to start fighting? They live together for goodness sakes! Why couldn't they just fight at home and then come to the reunion?

"I know what you mean" mom said. "Those are some good

ideas. Thanks sugar lump." My mom was always calling me these funny little names she made up. It was cute. "I think I have a pretty good idea of what to tell my co-worker. Well, I think I'd better get back to work. I was just taking a break and thought I'd try to catch you and pick that brain of yours for a few minutes. Call me later and let me know how your day went."

"I've got a pretty long day today Mom and I'm going to church when I get off. How about I call you tomorrow?"

"Ok. I'll talk to you tomorrow. I love you."

"Love you too, Ma. Bye."

I hung up the phone feeling great. My mom had actually called me for advice. Of course, it wasn't for her own life but if what I told her works for her co-worker, maybe she'll seek my advice with her situation. I was now certain the rest of my day would go well!

That certainty only lasted until my last client of the day. "Dr. Payce, Bea Cameron is here" Gabrielle buzzed. "I'm leaving for the day so I will lock you guys in. Have a good evening and I will see you in the morning."

"Thank you, Gabby. Be safe on your way home." I got up from my desk and got to the door just in time to see Gabby on the outside of the entrance door pulling it to make sure it was locked. "Come on in Bea, Ms. Cameron" I welcomed.

"Well, hello Dr. Payce" Ms. Cameron said. "It sure is nice to see you again." Bea didn't say a word but she looked from her mother to me as if she had been betrayed. I knew this was not going to be a pleasant beginning to this session. "So, you two know each other?" Bea asked once we were behind closed doors. I looked at Arlene as she knew I wouldn't answer the question being posed.

"Yes, we do" Arlene answered. "I used to see Dr. Payce for counseling."

"Dr. Payce, is this why you wanted my mother to come here with me today? Because you already know something about me that you guys are keeping a secret? Aggie warned me not to trust my mother but no way did I think that I couldn't trust you!" Bea was angry now so I had to get the situation under control quickly.

"Arlene, may I disclose part of the reason why you came to see me?"

"Yes" Arlene agreed.

"Bea, your mother came to see me for very much the same reason you did. She wants to have the family reunion and she wants Amber to be there. She came to work through some things and to try and figure out what she needed to do to move forward successfully. I asked you to invite your mother into your session because there are things you're struggling with that I feel she could give us insight into. My intent was never to betray you or trick you in any way. I apologize if you feel that way. But, understand that I was bound to the same confidentiality with your mother as I'm bound to with and for you."

Bea didn't say anything for a moment. I was hoping and praying that we could just move forward from where we were because there was no way I wanted to lose Bea as a client. She had some serious work to do and I feared that if we ended on bad terms she wouldn't seek help elsewhere. We all sat there in silence until Bea asked "…May I offer the opening prayer?" Of course, I didn't mind at all.

"Arlene, would you mind if Bea offered the prayer?"

"Nope. You go right on 'head, Molly Bea."

We bowed our heads and Bea began her prayer. As I listened I could tell it was heart-felt. She was sincere in what she was asking. I was just thanking God that she didn't walk out of my office when she found out I knew her mother. She finished her prayer and we all took our seats.

"Tell me, have you spoken to one another about why I suggested you both come to session?" I posed the question to both of them but Arlene spoke up first.

"Not much. She just said she had some thangs she couldn't remember and thought I might could help" she answered.

"Well, that's pretty much it in a nutshell" I said. "Bea, I asked you to come up with some information the last time you were here. Do you have any of that prepared for today?" I asked that question prayerfully because if Bea wasn't prepared this session was going to be harder than it had to be.

"Yes" Bea said. "I started a journal after I left here the first time and I've come up with quite a few instances of..." Bea stopped talking and just looked at me and then at her mother. "Should we explain what we're talking about?"

"Sure, Bea" I said. "Why don't you go ahead and tell your mother a little bit about what you're really dealing with. Right now, I want you to talk to her as if I'm not in the room. I'll be here to help if you need me, but you really need to talk to her."

Bea looked at me for a moment with her eyebrows turned down and inward toward her nose. She was trying to be sure that I really expected her to have a conversation with her mother while pretending I wasn't in the room. I simply nodded my head in the direction of her mother and didn't say a word. After a few seconds of silence Bea began to look at her journal. She told her mother about the "blackouts" and started reading off the incidents one by one.

Arlene became more and more anxious with each incident she read. Bea had no idea what her mother's reactions were because she wasn't looking at her. She had her head down and never looked up. While Bea read, I watched Arlene. She was nervous. She shifted continuously in her seat. I was surprised that Bea couldn't hear the chair creaking. Arlene crossed and uncrossed her legs about ten times. For a moment there I thought about interrupting Bea and asking Arlene if she needed to be excused to the ladies room! She was definitely aware of those incidents but she didn't speak. She just continued to allow Bea to read.

Bea finally finished her list and looked up. "Do you remember any of those incidents?" She asked her mother.

"Well...um..." Arlene started to lie but before she could, I jumped in.

"Bea, why don't you go back to the very first incident you read. Let's take each 'black out' one by one. We don't want to overwhelm anyone. You don't have to get through all of them today. Read the first one again please" I instructed.

Bea read the first incident from her journal. It was the horrid scene with the children putting Amber in the trash can and Arlene not allowing them to get her out. "Now Arlene, keep in mind that this session is not about you. It's about Bea and her loss of memories. Please be as honest as possible. Do you remember this?"

"Well, uh…yes. You see, the chil'en was playin' with Amber and it went a little too far and…"

"Where was Bea during the incident?" I asked cutting Arlene off before she stuck her foot in her mouth.

"Well, she was right there with the other two. If I'm clear, she was the one started the whole thang" Arlene recalled.

"See, that's the thing. This isn't coming from her memory. This is coming from the account that her brother and sister gave. Bea doesn't remember anything after you yelled at them. Do you remember anything strange about Bea's behavior that day?"

"Well, no 'cept that. See, Bea wasn't a mean child. I couldn't believe it was her that started it. I figure one of the other kids put her up to it 'cause Bea wasn't a strong child neither. She didn't just thank of things like that. Now Aggie was. But, Bea? I never woulda 'spected nothin' like that outta her. I just figure she got real mad and flipped her lid that day. After her daddy come home and got the baby, Bea went back to being her old self. She went to her room and laid down 'til dinner that night."

Bea didn't appear to be shaken by her mother's response and she decided to move on to the next incident. As I watched Arlene, she looked relieved for Bea to move on. I'm sure she was ecstatic that we didn't go into the reason why she'd sat idly by and let that take place. With the next incident she wouldn't be so lucky. Bea brought up her sixteenth birthday.

"…I woke to something good cooking in the kitchen…" Bea was telling the story from her memory. "…I got out of bed, put on my robe and ran toward the kitchen and that's where my memory ends. What happened that day? We were supposed to go out and spend the whole day together but I'm sorry to say I don't remember anything we did."

Bea looked at her mother for answers. Arlene looked as if she had just swallowed a canary. She wasn't going to be able to get out of this one. Bea and I both sat there and stared at her.

"It's very important to Bea's healing that you tell her the truth, Arlene. When she came into that kitchen, what did she see that was so traumatic that she had a 'blackout'?" I needed Arlene to tell the truth. Bea needed Arlene to tell the truth.

"You tellin' me you really don't remember what happened that day, Bea?"

"I don't remember anything until Aggie and Randall came home from Grandma's" she answered.

I thought Arlene's eyes were going to jump out of her head. She and Bea just sat there in a staring standoff. I watched both of them, wondering what Arlene was hiding that she was assuming Bea already knew.

"Arlene, did you think for all these years that you and Bea had a secret you were keeping?"

"Well, Bea was always a sweet child and I figure she would always be in my corner. I can't lie. I did some thangs I shouldn'ta done and I thought she was just helpin' me keep 'em tucked away."

Bea looked at her mother straight on and asked "what happened that day?" She wasn't asking in a pleasant tone either. She was gritting her teeth and the veins in her neck were pulsating. I wasn't sure whether or not I should be frightened. All I could do was pray. I hoped Arlene was praying too because both of these women outweighed me and I was not about to get in the middle of a brawl! I positioned myself between them and the door so if they set it off, I could save myself first. Then, I was just gon' stand back and call 911. *Lord, sprinkle your calming spirit in this room.*

Arlene took a moment. Took a deep breath and began. "Bea, I can't understand how come you don't remember. You came outta yo' room and stopped dead in yo' tracks. Then you ran full steam ahead and throwed everythang off the table to the flo'. You threatened my company with a butcher knife and scared that man half to death! Scared him so bad he lef'. Then you went to yo' room and slammed the door. You took the knife witcha so I didn't go near you for the rest of the day. I ain't never seen you like that befo'. I didn't know what had got into you!"

At that point Arlene and Bea had the same confused expressions on their faces. Neither one of them had understood Bea's behavior. Bea couldn't remember it and Arlene didn't know what could have made her so violently angry.

"I have never been a violent person! Why would you say such a thing about me? I would have never threatened anyone like that!" Bea began to cry. "Who did you have over so early in the morning anyway?"

Uh-oh! That was the question I was waiting on! The question Arlene definitely did not want to be asked. But, in the answer to that question was the answer to why Bea had reacted the way she did. Arlene wasn't going to be able to weasel out of this one because I wasn't going to let her. She owed her daughter an answer. It was time she own up to some of the dirt she had done to her children to someone other than me and God. God had forgiven her but her children hadn't. She hadn't given them a chance to. She'd hurt them and she needed to try and make things right.

"Arlene, I'm afraid that you owe your daughter an answer. She needs to know what happened. That's why you're here" I prompted.

"I had a man friend over. I was lonely when yo' daddy went outta town and I invited him for breakfast" Arlene lied.

"Arlene, have you asked for forgiveness about this incident?" I asked.

"Yes" she stated.

"Do you believe you've been forgiven?"

"Yes."

"Then tell your daughter the truth."

She looked at me, as if she wanted to rip my head off! But, she started over and actually told the truth this time. She admitted that she cheated on Riley, the only father Bea knew. Arlene confirmed that the man had come over the night before and was still there when Bea woke up and this wasn't the first time it happened. The session continued with a great deal of emotion but there was some good work being done. By the end of it I was drained. I needed to run to the altar! I scheduled another session with the both of them but wasn't sure if they would come back together. That was rough! I was ready to go to the sanctuary where I felt safe. I seriously considered stopping by my house and getting my pillow and blanket so I could sleep right there on the altar!

Bea was beginning to figure out why her sister was so suspicious of their mother. After the joint session with Arlene, she didn't know if she ever wanted to do that again. She wanted answers but with each answer came more questions. Was her mother really that cruel? Why had she allowed her to put Amber in the trash can? Why had she invited another man to their home while her stepfather was out of town? Well, she really knew the answer to that question. Especially after Arlene admitted that it hadn't been a male voice from the television the night before. But, to cheat on Riley? Her mother was starting to sound like a real shady character. But, if Arlene was shady and cruel, so was she. Bea was realizing that she had actually hurt people too! Maybe that's why she had blocked out so many of her memories. Maybe she had just not wanted to remember. Everything she and her mother both had done was so vicious.

Bea could have just pawned the trash can thing off on being a jealous sibling but the butcher's knife thing really disturbed her. She began to feel like she was just plain crazy! She still didn't remember any of it. It was just being told to her in such brilliant description that she had to believe it. What reason did any of them have to lie to her? She wasn't certain of much but she did know that she was sorry for committing these acts against her family. How would she make any of this right? She would do her best, but she couldn't help but wonder why her mother never tried to help her before now.

Arlene had been cordial during the ride home in the car with Bea but as soon as she hit her front door she called off some words that would have shamed the devil! She started ranting to herself… "I can't believe what just happened in dat office! Dat session was supposed to be 'bout Molly Bea and Molly Bea only! How I get wrapped up in it? I ain't got no problem helpin' Bea but I ain't goin' back there again! I ain't 'bout to let no mo' stuff like dat come out. I knows I wasn't the best mama but they just made me look like a monster!"

Sometimes it hurts when we walk by a mirror. Arlene stopped in the middle of her rant after hearing those words! Where had that thought come from? What did it mean? What did a mirror have to do with what had happened this evening? It never hurt her to walk in front of a mirror. She was gorgeous, so she thought. *Stand in front of your mirror right now and be honest about what you see.* The voice was back and Arlene was about to get scared.

Instead of letting the fear take over, she obeyed. She walked toward her bedroom where she had a full length mirror. The closer she got to the bedroom the slower her pace became. She finally eased in front of the mirror and moved closer so that her reflection could be clearly seen. She breathed a sigh of relief as she saw what she always saw. A good-looking woman, finely dressed, nicely made-up and just as she had looked when she left the house. Arlene began to enjoy what she was seeing so much that she started to smile and blow kisses at her reflection. Everything was just where it should be. She could still turn heads. She had regained the self-confidence she lost for just a few moments after that session and after the voices. Now, she could go on with the rest of her evening.

She turned to walk away from the mirror but just as she did she had to turn back quickly to take another look. Just as she had taken her eyes from her reflection she noticed a change. She stared at her changing face in the mirror. The reflection was morphing into someone she didn't recognize. The more she stared the more changes she noticed until she could no longer see her face, as she knew it. She was now glaring at a face that most certainly could not belong to her. It was that of someone with no compassion or love for anyone. As she continued to gawk she began to see through the reflection straight through to the soul of this woman. It was dark and cold. This was a selfish woman who cared for no one. This soul and the woman with whom it dwelled were going to hell! As Arlene got closer to the image to get a better look, it changed back to her own reflection. She was so horrified she screamed out in terror! She had been given a glimpse of her own soul and a glimpse into where she was headed if she didn't change. Now!

Arlene had been allowed to see her true self. She had hidden this truth from herself for years and believed she had been hiding it from others. She fell to the floor in tears. She had to call out to God for help. "Lord, help me! I'm not dat woman. Am I? I can't be… I don't wanna be. I'm tryin'. I know I gotta do better. Help me to git my life right. I need you Lord. You the onliest one I got. My kids don't love me 'cause I didn't love them. Oh God! I really didn't love 'em! What kinda mama don't love her chil'en?" Arlene couldn't speak another word. She lay on the floor sobbing uncontrollably.

Arlene cried until she had not one tear left. She just lay in that same spot on the floor silently. All she could think about was the fact that she had not loved her children. Out of all the cruel and mean things she did to them, the worst of them of all was not loving them. She realized that if she had loved them she would never have done the cruel and mean things. She was paralyzed until she heard…*You're not dead and neither are they. Get up! It's time to heal.*

Those words had come from deep inside of her. She had to seek healing for herself and her children. She needed to start over with all of them. It was time to truly have a relationship with them. It's one thing to give birth to someone but it's another to be a parent. They didn't need someone to raise them anymore but they could still have a mother. She still had the chance to be a mother to her children. God had granted her that option because he could have taken her life for some of the things she had done. But, he didn't. He had given her the opportunity to repent.

CHAPTER 24

Deciding Factor

RANDALL WASN'T ABLE to sleep at all last night. He had heard from Amber. She got the letter and called him. He couldn't believe it! She sounded just like he remembered. Although it was wonderful to hear from her she asked him for something he was afraid he may not be able to deliver. He knew he would have to present what she wanted to the rest of the family in a way that they would easily receive. If he didn't, it might mean never seeing his little sister again. He'd asked his wife, Brandy, to pray with him last night. Now it was time to put a plan into action. He would use the upcoming family session to try and get Amber's wishes across but he desperately needed help. He knew, for a fact, that he wouldn't be able to pull it off on his own. He only knew it had to be done.

He had two days to come up with a way to get his mother to come to the family session on Saturday. The whole family needed to be there. Amber wanted a special meeting with the family or she wasn't coming to the reunion. Randall wanted to pitch this idea to his family all at one time and they all needed to agree. He prayed and planned. Now he needed his mother to agree to come to the session and his sisters to know that she would be there and to not back out because of it.

He picked up the phone and dialed the number, praying with each ring. "Hello?" Arlene finally grabbed the phone, after the fourth ring, right before the answering machine picked up. She had been unable to move after the humbling experience she'd had hours ago.

"Uh, hi" Randall said. "How are you?"

Arlene hadn't been real concerned about who was calling but she was pleasantly surprised when she heard her only son's voice. "Hello Randall" she answered back. "I'm doing a little better now."

"Well," he began, "I'll get right to the point of this call. Amber called me last night." Arlene gasped on the other end but couldn't speak. "She has some terms she's requested of the family before she'll commit to the reunion. If you want her here you really don't have a choice but to do what I'm going to ask. The four of us need to be at Dr. Payce's office on Saturday to discuss this. By the four of us I mean you, me, Aggie and Bea. I'll pick you up at 12:30pm. We have a one o'clock appointment. Will you be ready?"

Randall hadn't really given her an option and neither had Amber. If that's what they wanted then that's what she would have to do. She had been given another chance to have all of her children back together and she knew that if she didn't take this opportunity there may never be another one.

"I'll be ready Randall. I'll see you at 12:30pm on Saturday" Arlene agreed.

He hung up the phone with half his battle down. Now he would try and tackle both his sisters at once. He picked up the phone again to dial Bea. She was the more patient of the two. Aggie was calming down and mellowing out a little but she still might challenge him on this. He didn't want to take the chance of her hanging up before he got Bea on the line.

Bea picked up after the first ring. She must have been sitting by the phone. "Hey Randall" Bea answered. That caller id was great!

"Hi, Bea. I want to get Aggie on the line with us before I tell you what this call is about."

"Oh" Bea said "well, you're in luck. Aggie's sitting right here at the table with me. Hey Aggie, go get the other phone from the bedroom. This is Randall and he wants to talk to us both" Bea ordered. Aggie being at Bea's house was better than he could have hoped for.

She came back with the phone attached to her ear. "Hey little brother, what's going on?"

"Well, I've got some good news and some questionable news" Randall admitted.

"Well, come on. Don't keep us in suspense" Aggie barked.

"Ok, ok. Amber called me last night!"

"What did she say?" Bea asked barely able to contain herself.

"She basically said she would consider coming to the reunion, but only if we agreed to have a family meeting. She said our letter was nice but that's all it was. You both know Amber didn't leave because everything was just so wonderful. There were some more than serious problems in our family and she wants to talk about it." Randall finished and everyone remained silent.

"Alright, since you guys are obviously speechless at the moment, that was the good news. The questionable news I'm considering questionable because I don't know how you guys are going to feel about it. But, I have invited our mother to our session with Dr. Payce on Saturday. I had to if we're serious about getting Amber here."

Randall stopped talking again. He really needed to know what his sisters were thinking and whether or not they were on board with this.

"Well, baby brother, it sounds like we don't have a choice. I'll be there" Aggie committed.

"Me too. Whatever it takes" Bea said. "Do you have any idea of how we should pull this meeting together?"

"Not really. I've been praying about it and I'm hoping Dr. Payce can help us out with this. I just wanted to make sure you guys were going to be okay with having our mother at the session."

Randall and his sisters finished their conversation agreeing that they would all ride together to the meeting this time. Randall would pick everyone up, including Arlene. If they were going to pull this family thing off, they would have to start acting like a family. This could not be an act. This had to be real or it wasn't going to work.

CHAPTER 25

The Family Session

THE CAMERON FAMILY informed me that they would all be in attendance for the session and they were coming prepared to work. I was excited for them! I had no idea what they were ready to work on, but I could sense that it was something important.

Ever since Thursday night, after I got up from the altar, I had been feeling even more than usual that something was coming. I was feeling more and more like it was for me but still couldn't put my finger on it. I had no clue of what was about to happen but I did know I needed to be prepared for whatever it was. I learned from Pastor that sometimes it wasn't just that we were waiting on God but that sometimes He was waiting for us. Our blessings were waiting for us to get to where we needed to be to receive them so that once we had them we wouldn't lose them on account of not being prepared.

I had a lot of irons in the fire, so to speak. Things seemed like they were coming together. It was as if my desires and dreams were all in a beautiful, puffy white cloud over my head. It was coming but I was just waiting for my cloud to burst so it could rain down on me. In the meantime, I was just going to have to keep moving forward. I knew my job was important and for now, I was just going to be God's vessel.

It was Saturday morning and I was getting ready to have what might be my last session with the Cameron family, as a whole. Of course, sometimes we do get attached to the clients. Some of them just have that effect on us. But, it's important to only do what is right and good for them. We have to leave our own emotional needs and desires out of the session.

I had been having a difficult time keeping this family out of my personal thoughts though. There was something very special about them. Sure, I had worked with many families but none that had affected my life like this one. Many people give up on the counseling process right before their breakthrough. This was one bunch I hoped would see theirs all the way to the end. I wanted them to be as invested in themselves as I was in them. This particular family session was key.

Randall ran out the door because he was running late. He was flustered because Brandy wasn't coming to the session with him. He had to pick everyone up and still make it to the office on time. His family would definitely not like the way he would have to drive in order to make that happen but he couldn't stand being late.

He made it to Arlene's at 12:37pm and had called ahead from his cell phone to ask his sisters to go to one house so he would only have to make one more stop. They decided to meet at Aggie's and Randall made it there at 12:43pm. The family made it to their appointment at exactly 1:00pm. Randall had a smile on his face while the ladies looked horrified. Sure, they had made it on time but they had questioned whether they would get there in one piece!

I was ready for the Cameron's to get started as soon as they arrived and they were right on time! Everyone was present except Brandy. This was going to be interesting, to say the least. As far as I knew, the Cameron siblings had not all been with their mother like this since Amber left. After that, I believe they all left home.

I offered the prayer and we began right away. Randall took over the session. "Dr. Payce, you're the only one who doesn't know this yet, but I spoke with Amber this week. She wants something special from the family and that's why I've asked our mother to be here with us today" he informed.

"That's great Randall. I'm glad she responded to your letter. So, what is it that she wants?" I asked.

"She wants the family to have a meeting where we talk about the way things were and what happened to us" he said. "I believe the family is in agreement, but we need you to help us come up with the best way to have the meeting."

"Is the meeting supposed to take place before the reunion or are you guys just agreeing to have it once she gets here?" I asked.

"Those are the details we want you to help us with" Bea suggested.

"I guess we need to come up with a couple of options and then you can allow Amber to choose what she would prefer" I said. "We should come up with a scenario that affords her the opportunity to come before the reunion even occurs and one that allows the meeting to take place just before or after the reunion. We want to come up with a face-to-face plan as well as one that allows you guys to have a phone conference. The key is that Amber needs to feel like you all really want her here and that you'll do whatever it takes" I suggested.

The family definitely agreed they needed options and the final decision would be Amber's. We worked on those plans for an hour. After the session Randall decided he would call Amber back to give her the options and that the family would adapt to whatever she wanted.

CHAPTER 26

The Planning

"HI SASHA, THIS is your mom, give me a call when you get home." My mom had left a brief message on my machine. She sounded like she was excited and worried all at the same time. I figured I'd better do as she asked and call her back.

"Hey, Ma. Whatcha doin'?"

"Not much. Just making a salad for dinner" she said.

I was surprised she didn't say she was making chicken. My mother could do wonders with a chicken! I lovingly thought of her as the "Bubba Gump" of chicken. She could make baked chicken, fried chicken, chicken salad, chicken spaghetti, chicken a-la-king, lemon chicken, chicken soup, chicken tetrazzini, chicken tacos… and the list could go on. You name it. If it could be made with a chicken she could make it!

"I'm just returning your phone call. What's up?"

"I got a surprise for you!"

"What did you buy me?" I asked excitedly.

"Actually, I bought me something" she said.

I didn't get how buying something for herself could be a surprise for me. "What did you buy?" I asked.

"A plane ticket to see you!"

"Woo-hoo!" I squealed with delight. I hadn't seen my mom since I left town. I got so busy with my private practice that I hadn't had time to go back to visit her or my old friends.

"That's great, Ma! When are you coming?"

"I'm going to come the first week in July."

That was good. It was a couple of months away. That way I could be prepared to take a few days off so I could spend some quality time with her.

"Cool. I'll be ready for you. Is there anything in particular you'd like to do when you get here?"

"Nah. You can just show me around to the things you like to do. Of course, I want to visit this awesome church you're always telling me so much about. I want to meet your mentor and the pastor for sure."

"No problem. It's done! If you think of anything else just let me know."

"Alright baby. Well, I'm gonna get myself ready for work and let you get some rest too. Call me later this week. Don't get too busy for your mama."

"Yes ma'am. I will definitely call you later this week.

I love you Ma and I can't wait to see you." "I love you too. I'll talk to you soon. Good-night. Don't let the bedbugs bite!"

"Good-night, Ma." I laughed. My mom still said those crazy little things she said to me when I was a kid. I didn't mind, though. It let me know I was still her baby even though I felt older than dirt.

Aubrey hung up the phone with her daughter in conflict. She was excited to be going to see her only child, but she didn't know how she would to tell her about the true reason she was going to Collinsberg. She was to reunite with the family that supposedly, she didn't have. She could only pray the relationship she and her daughter shared would stand up to this secret.

Aubrey had agreed to the reunion. The family would have a short meeting the night before, just to get reacquainted. The actual "throw-down", as Aubrey was thinking it would be, was to take place the day after the reunion. If there were going to be any hurt feelings no one wanted it to show in front of the rest of the family members. Aubrey had every intention of staying in town after the reunion and talking with Sasha. She would allow her daughter to meet her family after the reunion. She needed to keep this little secret of hers from her daughter until after this reunion was over.

What a great day! It looked like the Cameron's had a good chance of getting Amber back in their lives and my mother was coming to see me! As I was helping the Cameron's plan their family meeting I couldn't help but think about what my mom had recently asked me about. It seemed as though she had a co-worker in this same situation. I offered to be the mediator for the Cameron's and I wondered if she would be interested in being the mediator for her friend's family.

I had a lot of work to do but I just wanted to end the night on a great note. But, before I turned in for the night I decided to pick up my Bible. *But he was pierced for our transgressions, he was crushed for our iniquities; the punishment that brought us peace was upon him, and by his wounds we are healed.* As I meditated on that scripture from Isaiah 53:5, I really tried to figure out what it meant to me. It occurred to me that part of the passage was past tense and part of it present tense. He was pierced, he was crushed, the punishment was upon him, but we are healed. That means it was already done. Even though we may be going through something in the present, we have to remember that He has already endured it so we have victory right now. The Cameron's could be healed from the past. They would still have to go through the process but it was already done! I could rest easy tonight having been reminded of that.

PART II

Reunited

CHAPTER 27

Reunion Interrupted

THE REUNION WAS finally here and sure, I was invited but that didn't mean I should go. I could get into a lot of trouble for things like this yet I still had the urge to go. So, I decided to take the risk. I couldn't stay long though because I needed to meet my mother at three o'clock. I couldn't wait to see her! I grabbed the address to the park and ran out the door.

Trying to find a place to park was a nightmare. There were people everywhere! I had only been to other people's family reunions. I didn't have family so it was hard for me to believe all these people were related. I was sure some were second and third cousins but there were still so many of them. They were all different shades and hues. Some light skinned some dark some medium brown. It was kind of exciting and scary all at the same time!

As I opened my car door and was about to put my left foot on the ground, a man approached me. I didn't know who he was from Adam but I'm sure he thought I was related to him. He was wearing plaid shorts, a white wife beater and tri-colored striped socks. The left sock was raised to his knee and the right one hovered at mid-calf. The black house shoes on his feet completed his outfit. I was sure they called him 'Uncle Somebody'. But, before he could say anything to me Randall ran up to save me.

"Doc, you made it! Good to see you. What made you change your mind about coming?" he asked.

"To tell you the truth Randall, I really don't know" I said.

"Well, come on up and meet Amber."

"Okay, but I can't stay long. I just wanted to drop by."

As we approached the family I recognized Arlene, Aggie and Bea but there was someone else there with them. It had to be Amber. As we neared the huddle she turned her back toward us and started to walk off, but Randall called to her before she could move away.

"Amber…I want you to meet Dr. Sasha Payce" he announced.

My mother's face was the last thing I saw…

"Sasha!" Aubrey reached out to catch her daughter before she fell but her brother beat her to it.

"Randall, take her over there and lay her on the bench" Brandy ordered! "If she doesn't come to in a couple of minutes we're going to call 911!" Randall carried the young woman he knew as Dr. Payce to the shaded area and laid her gently on the park bench.

"Somebody grab that towel and dip it in the cooler to make a cold compress" Aubrey demanded. She had never witnessed her child faint before. She agreed with Brandy to call the ambulance if Sasha wasn't revived in a few moments.

When I opened my eyes I was looking into the faces of my entire family. The family I had known only as the Cameron's. My uncle Randall had caught me before I hit the ground, so I found out. The shock of finding out that my mother was the Amber that I'd been helping them with over the past few months, had been too much! Too many thoughts were going through my mind at once! The fact that I had been sharing the secrets of this family with my mother, not knowing this was a part of my own family secret. The issue of having been counseling with my own relatives for months. The revelation I'd been given from asking God to show me what was coming in my life. The fact that I was now going to have to stop counseling with them and that I definitely wouldn't be the mediator for their family meeting. Understanding that I was now a part of that meeting, as a family member! It was just too much!

I was trying to focus my eyes while praying for the feeling to come back to my legs. I just lay there and stared blankly at each of them unable to speak. Even if I was able to speak I didn't have anything to say. I didn't know what I was feeling. I could hear them murmuring but I had no idea what they were saying. I didn't know whether I should be happy or mad. Happy in the sense that I now had a family like I'd always wanted but mad because my mother had hidden this from me all my life! Then came the questions. Had the Cameron family came to me because they knew who I was? Had I been used to get to my mother? How was I supposed to treat them now? How would they now treat me? The lights went out again. I could hear my mother fussing and then the sirens and then nothing…

When I woke up, the second time, I had no idea where I was. The only thing I saw was a white ceiling. I could hear faint beeping noises but couldn't make out where they were coming from. It was only when I tried to get up that I noticed the nurse. Oh my goodness! I was in a hospital room. That was definitely somewhere I didn't want to be. I didn't want anyone to be poking and prodding on me. I started to get upset and panicky until I heard the calming voice of my mentor, Mrs. Warren. How did she know I was in the hospital? The racing thoughts were starting again but this time I figured I'd better stop them before I went out again.

"Dr. Payce is your daughter?" Aggie asked.

"Was she talking to you about us this entire time? Did you know about us before we knew about you? Did Dr. Payce… Sasha… whoever she is… know who we were all this time?" Randall asked beginning to get upset.

The Cameron family was in shock. They heard Amber call their counselor by her first name after she was briefly introduced to her as Dr. Payce. They had let that go for a moment because of the fainting and the ambulance and the hospital situation. But, now that they knew she would be alright they wanted to know what was going on. The family was now out in the waiting area while Mrs. Warren visited with Dr. Payce.

"Yes. Your Dr. Payce is my daughter, Sasha. She had been telling me about this interesting family she'd been working with. She never told me any names but it didn't take me long to figure it out. I just didn't say anything to her. Finding out that I'm Amber was just as much of a shock for her as finding out that she's your niece is to you" Aubrey stated honestly to Randall.

"I don't believe she would have fainted over something she already knew about Randy" Aubrey commented. *She was the only person, besides his wife, that could ever get away with calling him anything other than Randall.* "I have to admit that I didn't care much about how any of this would affect you guys but I never wanted to hurt my daughter. She's everything to me! That's a major part of the reason why I stayed away from here. Of course, I needed to get away, but once I was grown I could have come back. But, I had Sasha and I wanted to protect her from this. Never could I have imagined that she would find out about you all like this. I had hoped she nor I would ever have to see you again" Aubrey admitted.

The family shouldn't have been surprised to hear this from Amber but they all gawked at her as if they were. Maybe the shock of the whole situation had everyone off kilter. No one really knew what to do or how to respond to one another. They all needed time to take this in.

"How are you?" Mrs. Warren asked.

"I don't know" I said. "My head isn't clear yet. Just give me a few moments."

"Well, your mom got my number from your cell phone and called. I hope that was okay."

"Oh. Of course. You're about the only one I really want to see right now."

Mrs. Warren sat on the edge of my bed and touched my hand. She closed her eyes and began to pray. I closed my eyes as well. I knew I needed all the prayer I could get and if someone was willing to sit and pray with me I had no objections. I felt lost. I needed to talk to the one who had never betrayed me and never would.

Mrs. Warren finished praying and was probably looking at me, but I couldn't open my eyes. It wasn't that they were stuck or that I had passed out again. It was because I didn't want to come back to the world just yet. I wanted to stay there with Him in that moment. That was the only place I felt safe. I wished so much that my "Ty" had been there to comfort me.

Why my thoughts always went back to him I didn't know.

I seemed to always think of him when I felt alone. I would always imagine his arms around me. I had even had a dream once where no one could comfort me but him. It was the strangest dream. It was gruesome. I had been anxious during the dream and my body was literally tense but in the end I ran to him. I was so afraid and nervous and all he said was…'it's okay. Just sit down.' Just those few words offered me all the comfort I'd needed. What was so amazing was that I was able to interpret that dream. Usually I couldn't interpret my own dreams but this one I could. I really think it was more of a revelation for me. I ran to his house and he was the only one who could calm me. In the dream, it wasn't the fact that I loved him that had been so comforting. It was his spirit. I truly felt I had been sent to his house. I secretly wished I was at his house right now because I most certainly didn't want to be here.

"What are you thinking about?" Mrs. Warren asked.

"Nothing" I lied.

She wouldn't have understood even if I had told the truth. No one knew about Tyson. I was always too embarrassed to talk about it. Thinking of him did comfort me but it also made me feel like a fool as well. I was in love with someone that could have cared less about me. So, I just kept it to myself.

"I need your help, Mrs. Warren. I cannot handle this by myself" I said.

"I'm here" she said. "Whatever you need. But, right now just get some rest. We'll talk more when you get out of here."

I agreed with her and closed my eyes again. The only problem with that was it's where Tyson was. There was no way I could rest my mind with him there. He had kept me awake many nights and this one wasn't going to be any different.

I stayed in the hospital for two days just for observation. They ran tests, tests and more tests but found nothing significant. I could have told them they wouldn't find anything. There was nothing wrong with me except that I had just found out I was a part of a very dysfunctional family! I mean, who isn't? I know every family has its problems, but my issue was that I was just confronted with something I didn't even know existed. Most people grow up knowing their family is dysfunctional so there are no surprises. I grew up with just my mom and until now I thought she could do no wrong. Well, I was wrong. Now, I was going to have to deal with her and them. Just thinking about all that was reason enough for me to pass out again. Isn't it something how I can handle other people's issues with such ease, but when it comes to my own problems I can be such a wimp? Passing out.... I can't believe it! I wanted to get out of the hospital so I knew I had to go toward the light. Somebody had a lot of explaining to do. I wanted to know the truth and I wanted to know the whole truth. Now! I wasn't waiting for any family meeting either. My mom was going to have to spill!

CHAPTER 28

Show Before the Showdown

IT WAS TIME for me and my mom to talk. Now I knew what she had been hiding from for the past several months. She was hiding from herself. More importantly she was hiding herself from me. I was tired of it and it was time I let her know!

"Mom. I understand why you would leave your family. You were being abused. I even understand why you would hide those secrets from others. But, what I don't understand is why you would hide it from me!" I stared at her waiting for her to come forward with some answers.

"I'm sorry" she said. "I thought it was best. There was no way I would have allowed anything to happen to you and I didn't even want you to know that those things happened to me." My mom dropped her head. She had tried to protect me for all the right reasons but it just wasn't coming out the way she wanted it to.

"Ma, I can understand that, to a certain extinct. I understand that, as a child, you should have shielded me but I've been an adult for a long time. Were you ever planning to tell me?" I was beginning to get emotional. I had been holding back years of frustration about her treating me like a child. I didn't want it to sound like anger but it was.

"Honey, I had hoped, foolishly of course, that I would never have to tell you. I changed my name, praying they would never find me."

"Right, Amber" I said sarcastically.

"Look Sasha, I know you're upset with me and you have every right to be but you will not disrespect me! I don't care what my birth certificate says but I know what yours says. I'm your mother and nothing will change that! And if you use that tone with me again I will slap you into the middle of next week come Monday! Are we clear?"

Dang. My mama wasn't playing. I had never seen that look in her eye before. She was serious as a heart attack about slapping me! I was mad but I wasn't crazy!

"Yes ma'am" I quickly replied.

"This family meeting still has to happen" she stated. "Everyone needs to be there and now you're included. I want you to know how things were and why I did what I did and why things are the way they are. Do you think you could get Mrs. Warren to be our facilitator?"

It clicked with me then that she had been asking for my help. She asked me how to facilitate a family meeting. Of course, she had said it was for a friend but she asked me and not someone else. "Sure" I said. "I'll ask her."

"Well, I want to continue this conversation then. You've heard parts of their side of the story. I don't want to just give you another account. I want us all to get this out in the open so the real story comes out. Everyone sees things from their own perspective. I want you to hear the truth."

"Okay, Ma. I'll call Mrs. Warren and try to set things up."

My mom and I decided to call it an evening. I would call Mrs. Warren in the morning. Right now I needed to think some things through. I was still trying to wrap my head around the idea that I actually had a family and it was the Cameron's. A family that had shared some of their deepest secrets with me in confidence. Horrible secrets. Finding out that I'm a major part of the reunion in more ways than one was exhausting. I had some guilty feelings mixed in with everything else. My mother is the one they hurt and I helped them find her.

Lord, I need you again. Of course, you know I need you always. But, I'm experiencing so many different emotions that I don't even know where to begin. I'm upset with my mother, on one hand, because she kept some very important information from me my entire life. I do understand her reasoning for doing it, but I guess, I just don't agree with it. I now have an entire family that I don't know much about and what I do know isn't good.

As their therapist I know Bea has some VERY serious issues. But as a family member I want to call her Aunt Sybil! I mean, I don't know how many personalities she might have in there and which one might come out or when. And, Arlene...or should I say Grandmommy Dearest...what kind of mama is this?

Lord, I know you were at work in all of this because it wouldn't have happened this way if you weren't. I mean really, what were the odds that I would move to this town and that my own family would choose me as their therapist out of all the therapists here? I know I asked you to reveal some things to me but never did I think it would be anything like this!

Like, this woman messed up ALL her kids. I haven't even met the grandkids yet but I'm one of 'em! As much as I'm upset with my mom for keeping them from me...I love her for it. I might have been just as messed up as everyone else!

Lord, now that you've shown it to me, I need you to tell me what to do about it. I don't want to make anything worse. I've been a part of the solution from the beginning and I want to continue to be that. I just don't know how to do that now. As a counselor, I can keep my distance from the situation and the emotion. As a part of the family I can't do that. How do I approach this healing process now that I'm one who's been hurt? I've been betrayed, at least by my mother, if not by the whole family. I don't know how much they knew about me or whether they knew about me at all. I don't really know what I know right now. I'm so lost. I need to get a handle on my emotions. I need to be prepared for this meeting because I have a lot of questions that I want answered. Lord, I just need you to be there. My life has been good this far and I thank you for that. You have shielded me from a great deal of hardships and pain but now I have to face some things. Be with me. Be with us all. Speak through me and for me. Help me to continue to be a part of the solution and never contributing to the problems.

I want to throw a quick prayer in for Tyson as well. I have no idea what he's going through but I want him to know that I'm always here for him. The only thing is, I can't tell him that. Would you let him know for me? No matter what he thinks of me, my feelings haven't changed for him. I will always think of him as my Ty. Take care of him. For all things I give you glory. Amen.

Sasha had been on Tyson's mind more than usual. Some nights he couldn't rest for thinking about her. It was guilt. It was the fact that he actually cared about her. He had to admit that he wasn't handling things properly. He wasn't praying like he should. The truth was, he didn't really know how or what to pray in this situation.

He had been feeling a spirit of confusion for a while but couldn't put his finger on where it was coming from. He realized he needed to get rid of that before he could do anything about Sasha. He would have to get to the bottom of where the confusion was coming from before it cost him his joy.

"Lord, it's me Tyson. I know I haven't come to you formally in a while but it's about time I did. My life isn't horrible but it's not all it should be. There is something missing. I don't quite know what it is but I know I have to get to it. You have something for me. I know you do. But, as long as I live in the comfortable state I'm in I won't have it. I know there may be some things and/or people I need to add and/or remove from my life. But, I need you to show me which ones and how. I feel stuck. I feel like I'm not going anywhere and I know I won't until I get things right with you. Well, that's what I'm trying to do right now. Help me to get things right with you."

Tyson finished his prayer and just lay in his bed quietly. He was listening to see if God would speak. Thoughts, hopes, and dreams filled his mind but he wondered if they were from God or just things he wanted. He needed discernment. He knew his life would never be what it was supposed to be if he didn't align his will with His will. It was just that it was such a difficult thing to do. He knew he would be granted the desires of his heart but only if his desires were what God really wanted for his life.

Tyson realized he had to get closer to God. He knew he

had to spend more time with Him. He had stopped doing that and now he knew he needed to get back to that place. That would be the only way he would get his life on track. He didn't know if that included Sasha or not. He really didn't know what to think about that. He only knew he wanted what was right. He would have to make a decision now. Who was he going to serve? It would either have to be himself or God. Serving himself wasn't working. He was confused whenever he was inside the church. He knew the right things to say and do because he had grown up in the church. But, he also felt like the same confusion and darkness that followed him every day usually went right on into the church with him. He couldn't understand that. How could sadness and anything dark be in the church?

As soon as that thought passed through his mind, he was reminded of the last sermon he heard about the fact that Satan was once in Heaven. The pastor said "spirits are entities we cannot see. But, they often dwell within individuals and are able to deceive us. We look at the person and we like them because of one reason or another. Maybe they have a great personality, connections we need or we feel safe around them. It's not anyone we could ever be interested in as more than just an acquaintance so we just occupy our time with them. Well, this would be the very person Satan uses to attack you. The spirit might be very sweet and inviting on the outside. It might tell you things you want and need to hear while slowly poisoning your spirit. Confusion, depression and deceit are lurking. They wait within this acquaintance until the perfect opportunity to strike. Truth gets mixed with lies. They make you think they could be a better friend to you than anyone else. You begin to alienate the people you should really be getting close to. Now confusion and deceit are following you around trying to get in the way of the grace and mercy that should be following you. They make things as clear as mud for you. They become the only ones you talk to because they're the only ones who understand you… supposedly. They care about you. At least, that's what they lead you to believe while, all the time, evil's plan is working."

Tyson suddenly knew what and who had been causing him such confusion. He didn't know if he could get rid of the spirit but he could definitely get rid of the person with whom it dwelled. Jamie went to church but had no relationship with God. Tyson would have to figure out a way to remove Jamie from his life. He truly believed that God had revealed that to him and if he was going to align himself with the will of God he couldn't have anyone in his life that would hinder that. He needed to make room for the right things and the right people and he needed to be open to whatever and whoever that might be. He didn't know if Sasha would be a part of his life in any way, ever again. But, what he did know was that eventually he would have to make amends for any pain he may have caused her.

I woke up feeling a little better than I did the day before, but I needed some help with my new-found knowledge and fast! "Good morning, Mrs. Warren. This is Sasha."

"How you feeling sweetie?" Mrs. Warren asked in that lovely voice she had.

"I'm doing a lot better, thank you. But, I have a favor to ask of you. Do you have a moment to talk?"

"Of course. Let me clear my other caller. Hold one moment please." I could hear her fumbling around and then I heard a beep and click. "Hello. Are you there Sasha?"

"Yes ma'am. I'm here."

"Alrighty. Let's talk. What's on your mind?"

"Well, as you know, I just found out the family I'd been counseling with is my own. My head is still spinning about that but my problem is this... They were supposed to have a family meeting, for which I was supposed to be the facilitator. Well, that idea went out the window when I became a part of the family. So, my favor from you would be for you to facilitate the meeting for us. And, before you answer, please don't feel obligated. This may get real ugly. I'm not even sure I'll be able to handle it. But, if you would consider it, I would be grateful. Another thought that came to mind was that if you knew any other counselors you might be able to recommend. One for the family and one to continue sessions with them on an individual basis. They're still going to need help. A lot of help. I just can't be the one to do it anymore." I'm sure she thought I would never stop talking, but I just had to get all of that out before I forgot anything.

"Sasha, I believe I can help you with all of that. I will facilitate the family meeting and I'll give you some referrals for continuation of care for the family after the meeting."

I knew I had gone to the right person. Mrs. Warren and my pastor were really the people they claimed to be. If they said you could count on them, then you could count on them. Mrs. Warren and I discussed the arrangements for the meeting. I told her I would check with my mother and the rest of the family to find out when they wanted the meeting to begin. I took Mrs. Warren's suggestion on how the meeting should go, but I told her I would give her total control. We prayed before we hung up because that's just who she is but I surely appreciated it. I didn't need anyone trying to help me that wasn't getting direction from the Helper.

CHAPTER 29

Showdown

MOM AND I walked into the church right on time to start the family meeting. Mrs. Warren greeted us at the door to her office. Arlene and Bea were already present. *I guess I should call them Grandma and Aunt Bea, but I'm not even sure they would like that.* Randall must have been pulling in right behind us because he was walking through the door as we took our seats.

It was now five after six and Aggie wasn't there. I don't know what everyone else was thinking but I know what I was thinking. She's not coming. She was always the resistant one in session and not showing up to the family meeting would be the ultimate act of defiance.

Everyone sat in silence until Mrs. Warren decided to begin. "Well, I know we're still waiting on one more. Sasha, would you get her number and attempt to call to see if she's coming?" Mrs. Warren asked. Why she chose me to make the call I don't know. Maybe because I would probably be the only one Aggie wouldn't be rude to. Nevertheless, I got up to get the phone number from Bea and on my way to the door she walked in.

"Excuse me for being late. I ran into an accident on the highway" Aggie stated. She took her seat and Mrs. Warren began.

"Now that everyone is here we'll begin. I would like to start with the session rules. We're all adults here and I know we'll all show respect for one another whether you like or agree with what is said or not. I know that emotions may run high throughout the session and that's to be expected. I understand anger but we will not yell or curse at anyone. That kind of behavior will not get us the results we want." Mrs. Warren was talking to us as if we were in kindergarten but she was saying what definitely needed to be said. "I want you all to think about something" she continued.

"I want you to realize what God has done and is doing for all of you right now. He needs you to know that this is a time to heal. He's the healer and that's why you've all arrived at this point. Do you think any of this was a coincidence? If you do, you're wrong. If you can't see the hand of God moving in this family I suggest you open your eyes and look a little harder. It wasn't a coincidence that Arlene went to Sasha for help and it was definitely not a coincidence that Randall found the same counselor. There are hundreds of therapists in this area and most of them advertise in the phone book and the internet. He was drawn to her picture. She looked like his sister. Of course, we've all discovered why that is." Everyone either chuckled or smiled at me. It felt good to belong to a family even though this one was like a powder keg with a match about to be set to it!

"Sasha came to this town not knowing she even had a family and look at what she stumbled upon. If that's what you think happened, you're wrong about that as well. She was lead here. She may not have known she was being lead but she was. God had been orchestrating this reunion before He placed it on Arlene's heart. Now that you know this, you all have to do something about it. He's not going to just continue to drop things in your lap. From this point on you're going to have to work for it. He hasn't brought you this far to leave you but you can all turn your back on this blessing if you so choose. I don't want to see that happen. So, let's get some things established here…"

Mrs. Warren pulled out pieces of paper and handed each family member a sheet. They were handouts of the session rules. I thought that was cool. It meant we'd have some order to go with the madness. It was exactly what I'd suggested to my mom when she asked. Mrs. Warren began to read from her sheet.

"Rule #1: Only the family member with the gavel will be able to speak. The only person who may speak without the gavel is the facilitator. The facilitator will be the distributor of the gavel. The family member who is speaking must also stand and face the family. If that family member is requesting a response from another family he/she may give the gavel directly to another family member after speaking or asking their question."

Of course, I was thinking this gavel business might be a little dangerous. I don't know about giving angry people blunt objects! I've seen way too many *Lifetime* movies for that! I'd been to the hospital once already this week and really didn't feel like making another trip. But, I was confident that Mrs. Warren could maintain control of the session.

"Rule #2: There will be no cursing or yelling at anyone.

Rule #3: All family members have the opportunity to speak if they chose to.

Rule # 4: A family member who has been asked a direct question must answer the question as honestly as possible. If you do not know how to respond to the question you will be allowed time to think about it but will be asked the question again before the end of the session.

Rule #5: Family must attempt to resolve issues during sessions that can be resolved."

As Mrs. Warren finished going over the rules she asked if there were any questions. Since no one had any she offered a prayer, which was much needed. She also had us play a funny game to break the ice before the real session began. She said she did that for two reasons. One was because the family hadn't been together like this ever as adults and needed to get to know one another. The other was so that we didn't just begin the session by tearing into each other. After the ice breaker was over Mrs. Warren opened the floor but gave the gavel to my mother to kick things off.

"I feel it's only right that Aubrey begin the session since she's the one who requested it" Mrs. Warren stated. My mom walked up to receive the gavel and turned to face her family.

"Well," she began, "I would just like to start off by asking everyone to respect my name change. I am no longer Amber. I'm Aubrey. Amber was a little girl who came from a family of hatred and I want to leave her in the past for now." Everyone nodded showing respect for her wishes. Not necessarily did they agree with it but they did respect it. That was a good start.

"I know you've been counseling with Sasha and that's great. That's the reason why I didn't tell her I knew who you were when she started telling me about you guys. I knew that if she'd discovered her relation to you she would've had to stop seeing you. I was afraid if that happened, you might not have continued your therapy and I didn't want to risk that. I wanted you guys to get the help you had come looking for. I admit that what I did may not have been the right thing to do, but believe it or not, my heart was in the right place. But, I would like to take this time to apologize to all of you for that. I need to give a special apology to my daughter."

My mom looked me directly in my eyes and said, "...I'm sorry sweetheart. I never meant for any of this to hurt you. I thought I could protect you and then I thought you would be able to help them. Mrs. Warren was right, though. I believe that all of this was orchestrated by God and this was the way it was supposed to happen. Regardless, I ask each of you to accept my sincere apology."

Everyone gave their own signs of acceptance. After my mom felt confident with what she'd just done, her demeanor changed. Her brow and jaw line hardened as she began again. "Now to get to the point of why we're all really here... You guys started counseling and have begun to work through some of your issues. I hear that you each shared your thoughts and remembrances from life growing up. You even shared thoughts of how I might feel. But, I want to tell you all how it really was for me growing up in that house..."

She paused. I don't know whether it was to get control of her emotions, to gather her nerves or what. All I know is that the next time she opened her mouth she sounded like someone I'd never met before. Her voice softened and moved up the soprano scale a couple of octaves. She sounded more like a girl than a woman.

"I didn't know I was being mistreated at first" she said. "All I knew was that I liked it much better at Grandma's house unless my dad was home. I knew, for a fact, he loved me. But, I didn't know about any of you until I got a little older. I drew courage from somewhere. Well, I only knew it as somewhere back then. Now I know what it was. I started asking my friends at school about how their families treated them. I quickly found out that my family was wrong. That is, except for my dad. I'm sure he never knew the real reason I would have such a fit when he would leave the house. He probably just assumed it was because I loved him so much and couldn't stand to be away from him. If that's what he thought he would have been partially right. The other part was about survival. I knew I needed to be alone with you guys like I needed a hole in my head! And the more I was alone with you the more I wondered when the day would come that I would have that hole in my head.

"I remember a lot of things about my life back then and most of it was bad. I was always afraid so, I just tried to stay out everyone's way. I know I was my dad's favorite. That was only natural. I was his only child but that didn't give any of you the right to treat me the way you did. And, as I look back on it, I know some of the things you did were out of spite and anger and jealousy. But, I really want to understand why you would allow things to be done to me that could've killed me."

Mom paused and stared at Arlene. Then she began to walk toward her. I got a little nervous. She walked right up to her mother, without saying a word and stopped in front of her chair. She reached her arm out toward her. Now mind you, this is the same arm that controlled the hand that held a wooden gavel. My mom held the gavel out toward Arlene asking only with her eyes and her posture for her to take it. Arlene answered the question by receiving the gavel and standing up. My mom took Arlene's seat as Arlene headed to the front of the small office to face her family. As she turned to face us she looked petrified.

"Well" she began "like Amber, I'm sorry, Aubrey… I owe all you an apology. I wasn't a good mama and I know dat now. I just wanna say I didn't learn dat by myself. Mrs. Warren was shole right 'bout God's hand bein' in it. Goin' to counseling with Dr. Payce and prayin' helped me to see what kinda person I was. I got a good ugly dose of the real me. I'm shame and I don't know if I can never make it right.

"Aubrey, I'm gon' try and answer what you asked as best I can. Believe me when I say I know it ain't nothin' I can say or do to take back what I done. I let some of them thangs happen to you 'cause I was jealous. Jealous of Riley's love fo' ya. He loved you so much and before you was born I was the one he was givin' that love to. Now, I ain't saying' once you come he stopped loving' me. I'm just sayin' I felt like you was takin' too much of him from me. I let what I felt build up 'til I was angry. I knew I couldn't say none of dat to him. And since we bein' honest, I thought if the chil'en hurt you they wouldn'ta blamed them. They'da said it was just a accident. They was kids. Everybody took thangs easy on kids. If I'da been the one to get rid of you, that woulda made me a bad person. That's just the way I was thankin'. Now I know if anything woulda happened to you, by my hand or theirs, I woulda been to blame. Honestly, there ain't not one good reason why I hurt you. Not one reason why I let the other chil'en hurt you. But, I am sorry it happened."

Arlene dropped her head and handed the gavel back to Mrs. Warren. She took the seat next to me because Mom had taken her seat when she handed her the gavel. I didn't know how I felt sitting next to this woman either. I'd heard the stories before, but those things had been done to Amber. I was now looking from the view point of these things having been done to my mama! Since the room had gone quiet I figured I'd say what I needed and wanted to say. I walked slowly toward Mrs. Warren to obtain the gavel.

As I turned to face my family I realized how much we all actually favored one another. I looked at each of them, including my mom, in the face before I began to speak. "I want to commend all of you on just being here" I said. "I know how difficult it was for most of you to participate in any of this. I know I'm the youngest member of the family represented here but I hope you'll accept my words just the same."

"Go 'head on and speak baby" Arlene interjected. I was sure she just wanted the attention off her but I continued anyway.

"As you all know, I was not aware of my relation to any of

you until a couple days ago. I'm still trying to take all this in but I heard some things during my counseling with all of you that seriously frightens me. As your therapist I could remain impartial. Now, as a member of the family, I am deeply disturbed. I know these feelings are partly due to the fact that the brunt of the evildoing was aimed at my mother. I'm probably as protective of her as she is of me and I have to be honest with all of you. I really don't know how I feel about any of you personally. My feelings and opinions have changed about you to some extent. This is the main reason why therapists don't counsel with their family or friends. This is also why we don't get involved with clients once we're in treatment or once treatment has ended. It distorts and changes the dynamics of the client/ therapist relationship.

"When I was able to keep you all at arms-length you seemed like individuals who were truly sorry for what happened in your family and I was able to see that. Now, I just can't seem to get passed the fact that you hurt one another and now that hurt has trickled down to the next generation. I don't know any of my cousins so I can only speak for myself, being a part of your next generation. I'm hurt. My life has been affected whether any of you realize it or not. I grew up without a family because of things done before I was even born. I resent that! I don't resent any of you but I do resent the situation. As a therapist, I understand that sometimes you do the best you can. It may not have the best outcome but at least you tried. I feel like this family spent more time trying to hurt one another than trying to help. That is, until now.

"I didn't grow up around you and that may have been for the best. I don't know. I could be completely wrong about the things I've just said but it's the way I feel right now. I would like to get to know each of you but I want to come into a family who is interested in making things right with one another and with God. I don't want to come into a family of lies and secrets. So, I'm asking you all to open up and put it all out there. Let's put everything on the table so no one goes away feeling like they weren't heard. Lies and secrets rip families apart so, I'll only be a part of a family that has no secrets."

I handed the gavel back to Mrs. Warren hoping I hadn't overstepped. Technically, I was a part of the family but I was the most recent addition so I didn't know if what I said weighed much, but I had to put it out there.

Everyone kind of sat there for a moment. No one even looked around the room. Mrs. Warren didn't seem to mind the silence at all. She looked everyone in the face asking, with only her eyes, if anyone wanted to take control of the gavel and speak. Finally, Aggie got up and walked toward Mrs. Warren. My first thought was uh-oh. She's about to light the flame to the powder keg.

Aggie seemed sullen as she walked. She moved slowly, with a slight shuffle and her shoulders were slumped forward. After receiving the gavel from Mrs. Warren she stood with her back toward the family. I don't know if she was praying or what. But, when she finally turned around I saw tears in her eyes. She locked her eyes onto Arlene's face and didn't let go. I could tell that Arlene wanted to break the gaze but she couldn't. Aggie attempted to speak but nothing came out. She closed her eyes, dropped her head toward the floor and I saw one tear drop. When she raised her head again she was ready.

"You hurt me deeply" she said as she hardened her stare at Arlene again. "You never loved me. You treated me like I was some child you were being paid to keep. No, I take that back. You treated me like the child someone had pawned off on you without paying you to keep. You used me, but you didn't love me. I felt like more of a mother to my sisters and brother than you were.

"I didn't ask to be brought into this world. You had no right to treat me the way you did. You had no right to treat any of us the way you did and I want to know why. Why, after having the first child that you never wanted, did you keep having children? I know you knew how babies were made. There's only one way to keep yourself from getting pregnant! We won't go there but you know what I'm getting at.

"If you didn't want me, why did you not just let me go to live with Grandma like I wanted to? Why did you try to convince me that I was crazy? Never mind. I know why you did that. You owe the government a whole lot of money!"

Aggie couldn't help but laugh at her last comment. I laughed too because I knew exactly what she was talking about. Those crazy checks Arlene had lived off for all those year! She lied. There was never anything wrong with Aggie or any of her children, for that matter. She had taken the government for a ride!

"I really don't have much else to say, but I would like to apologize to my baby sister for the way things went down before you left home. None of the things that happened were your fault. I'm sorry I didn't do more to help you" Aggie admitted as she looked at my mom. "But, I would like an explanation from you" she turned back toward Arlene. "I need to know what you were thinking all those years and why."

Aggie set the gavel back down on the podium where Mrs. Warren had come back to stand. Mrs. Warren extended her arm to Arlene for her to again receive the gavel. Arlene was hesitant but there was no way she was getting out of this. She stood and walked toward the gavel slowly, almost like she was walking *The Green Mile.*

"Sally Agnes" Arlene began, "I got to be honest with you and tell you it ain't no good reason why I done any of them thangs I did back then. You right in sayin' I never wanted no chil'en. Sho', I wanted 'em 'cause everybody else had 'em but I didn't want to take care of 'em. But, I want you in my life. I want all of you. I'm tryin' to show it now. That's how come I'm here and that's how come I asked you to the reunion. I want us to be a family and start over."

Arlene turned to put the gavel down and before you could hear wood meet wood Aggie was out of her seat. She moved toward that podium like something was chasing her! When she grabbed it I leaned forward because I thought there was getting ready to be a knock-down-drag-out. I thought Mrs. Warren and I might have to take her down! I had work on a locked psych unit for a couple of years so I knew how to do it!

Aggie turned to face Arlene with the gavel in her hand and Mrs. Warren didn't budge. I thought, *how could she be so calm?* I was thinking we might have to call the ambulance again. At least this time it wouldn't be for me. Aggie broke my thoughts when, in a raised voice she said, "wait just a minute!"

"Do you think you gon' get off the hook that easy? You ain't said nothing! Yea, I know what you tryin' to do now. You gettin' old without your family around you. You alone and lonely now. Now, you want to treat us like family and you want people to look at how successful your children are and you want to take credit for it. Well, have I got news for you. It's not gon' happen like that! If it happens at all, you gon' have to come up with something a whole lot better than what you just gave us!"

Aggie was only about a foot away from Arlene's face and she still had that gavel in her hand! Mrs. Warren still didn't move. I was beginning to develop a whole new respect for her because I was freaking out…inside. I had my therapist face pasted on the outside.

Aggie shoved the gavel back toward Arlene. Arlene reluctantly took it and looked around at the rest of the family looking for help, I guess. I'm sure she wouldn't have minded if anyone jumped in but we all wanted to know those answers too.

"Aggie" Arlene started again, "I knows I hurt you. I really wasn't thankin' much 'bout yo' feelin's or nobody else's back then. You didn't really matter. You was kids. Kids didn't have no say in nothin'. It was all 'bout me.

Is that what you want to hear?" "Is it the truth?" Aggie asked.

"Pretty much" Arlene admitted.

"Then that's what I needed to hear. All I was ever interested in was the truth."

Arlene gave the gavel back to Mrs. Warren and she and Aggie both took their seats again. Mrs. Warren stood up once more but this time she did speak. "Well," she said "I think you guys have had enough for today. This is some pretty emotionally draining stuff we're dealing with and I don't want the tension to get too high. We haven't heard from Bea or Randall at all so, I want you two to be prepared to speak tomorrow. That's not to take away from what anyone has said today or what anyone might say in future sessions. We'll resume this meeting tomorrow night at the same time. Does anyone have any questions before we dismiss?"

No one said anything so we dismissed with prayer. Man, right when it was getting' good! Not that I wanted to see anyone throw down but it was getting interesting! It's hard to be objective when you're dealing with family. Like I said before, I didn't know that experience until now.

I returned home with my mother riding shotgun. I wasn't exactly sure of how she felt about the family session, but I was indifferent about it at the moment. I got some things off my chest, but I wasn't sure if anyone was getting the answers they wanted. Sure, Arlene admitted she never wanted children and had apologized for treating them cruelly, but now what? Was it going to be finished after everyone had their turn or their individual explanations and apologies? I kind of wanted to know what my mother was thinking, but on the other hand, I didn't. I knew this meeting had been much harder for the rest of the family than it was for me. They lived it. I'd only heard about it.

If she wanted to talk about it she would have to bring it up. She never really liked sharing her burdens with me so I didn't want to push her to it if she wasn't ready. I had the feeling that one day she would open up to me more and let me in. Until then, I decided to continue to be patient.

We were scheduled for another family session tomorrow. I wondered what it was going to be like. For a moment there, I thought Aggie was gon' strangle Arlene tonight but she'd restrained herself. Tomorrow it would be Randall and Bea's turn to speak. They were much more laid back so I wasn't worried about needing security with them.

CHAPTER 30

Advise Me

TYSON WAS ON the internet trying to find Sasha's number. He had tried to *Google* her already and only her old address was coming up. The only person they had in common was Andrea and he really didn't want to talk to her about it. She was part of the reason he was in this predicament in the first place.

He knew he shouldn't blame anyone but himself and he was going to work on that but for now, he had to get that information. He'd been praying about what he needed to do and he thought he'd been given an answer. He needed to contact Sasha. He needed to honestly explain his comments and let her know how he really felt. He would leave it to her to pick up the ball from there.

He had talked to his mother about what she thought he should do but she was really no help. So, he decided to ask his dad. He didn't really talk to his dad much about women so he had no idea what kind of response to expect. But, he called him up anyway hoping he wasn't too busy.

"Hey Dad" Tyson greeted.

"Hey mijo, que paso?" Mr. Juarez replied.

"Not much Dad, but you're not going to speak to me in Spanish all night are you?"

"Naw, son. What's going on?"

"Honestly Dad, I got woman troubles."

"No way. Not my boy."

"Yeah Dad, ya boy got issues."

Tyson could hear his father laughing at him under his breath, but at this point, he didn't care. His parents had been together forever and he needed some advice. Sure, they'd had problems in the past but they'd overcome them and he needed to know how.

"Dad, could you stop laughing long enough to help me?" Tyson wasn't angry with his father for laughing. He had a slight smile on his face himself.

"I wasn't laughing at you, son. Of course, I want to help you. Tell me what you think the problem is."

"Ok. Well, there was this woman at work, Sasha that liked me. Or at least I think she did. I found this out through a friend of hers. I always thought Sasha was attractive but I never really thought about dating her or anything. At least, not until I found out how she felt about me. Or, how I thought she felt about me. But, I did something stupid. I lied. I basically told her I wasn't interested and I didn't do it in such a nice way. I said something to her friend who blabbed. And the truth is, I didn't really mean what I said at all. It was just that I was caught off guard. Now, Sasha's gone and I don't know how to find her except by asking this same friend and I really don't want to do that. I need to talk to Sasha but I don't know how."

Tyson finished his story and his father just sat there in silence. So, Tyson just sat there as well. Until he heard his mother in the background he wasn't even sure if his dad was still on the phone.

"Sorry son. Your mom was within earshot and I didn't want to talk with her so close in case you didn't want her to know what was going on."

"Whatever Dad, I know you're just going to tell her when we get off the phone" Tyson said with a chuckle.

"No, honestly. If you don't want her to know I won't tell her. I realize this is serious for you, son. Sure, I tell your mom a lot of stuff but if you want this to be just between us then that's what it'll be." Tyson knew his dad was being honest with him at that moment.

"Well, Dad for now I would like it to be between us if you don't mind."

"You got it, mijo. Now, let's see what we can figure out." It sounded to Tyson like his father was ruffling paper. "Ok, son. Let's do some problem solving and brainstorming because right now, you don't even know where Sasha is, verdad?"

"Yes Dad. That's true. I have no idea where she is. I tried

an internet search but I guess either her new information hasn't been updated or she's unlisted."

"And you don't want to ask this friend, por que`...

"Because I really don't want her to know I lied. I don't want her to know that I'm interested in Sasha because I don't want any rumors flying around at work. She's a gossip, Dad. My business would be all over the office within thirty seconds."

"Ok. I see. Well, were you doing any important work with Sasha? Could you possibly have any questions for her that only she could answer?"

"Well, no."

"Are you sure…?"

"She was on a special projects team with me, but nothing I couldn't handle alone."

"You're positive there isn't something you need to contact her about? Something that only she would know?"

"Ohhh. I see where you're going. I could use that as an excuse to get the number from her friend. I could use a professional reason instead of a personal one. Good thinking, Dad. Thanks."

"De nada, mijo. Call me when you have some good news."

"I will. Tell mom to say a special prayer for confidence for me okay."

"Ok, son. Talk to you soon."

Tyson hung up the phone with his father and began to come up with his story. He needed something believable and true. Prayer had worked for him so he figured he wouldn't stop now.

CHAPTER 31

After the Session

RANDALL PULLED INTO the garage and Brandy met him at the door. By the look on his face she decided not to ask him about it and to just let him come to her when he was ready. He'd called when he was leaving the church so she had already run a hot bath and would have his dinner ready by the time he was out of the tub. Now, this isn't something she did for him on a daily basis, but she felt it might help tonight.

"I ran you a bath and your dinner will be ready in about fifteen minutes" she told him.

"You ran me a bath?" he asked.

"Well, I thought you might need to relax after the session."

"Well, you would be right but I want to tell you about it. Do you want to hear?"

"Of course I do. Why don't you get your bath first and I'll sit and talk with you while we eat."

"Sounds good" Randall agreed and went off to soak.

Aggie got home and couldn't unwind. She was upset. She didn't know exactly what she expected. She even got the answers she needed but it just hurt so bad and she couldn't understand why. She'd known for a long time that her mother didn't want children. She guessed it just felt worse to actually hear it come out of her mouth.

"Bea" Aggie said as her sister picked up the phone on the second ring.

"Hey, Aggie. Give me a minute to put my things down. I just walked in the door. Hold on." Bea put the phone down and Aggie could hear her keys jingling and doors opening and closing. Bea picked up the phone.

"Ok, Aggie. I'm back. What's up?"

"How do you feel about what happened tonight?"

Bea didn't really know what to say because she didn't quite know what Aggie was thinking. She was sure her sister wasn't happy but just didn't know what answer she was fishing for.

"Honestly, I don't really know how I feel about the meeting" Bea admitted. "How do you feel about it?" Bea figured it would just be safer to be honest about her own feelings and just ask Aggie about hers.

"I'm ticked off" Aggie stated adamantly.

"But, why? Didn't you get the answer you already knew you would get? Ain't you glad she was honest?" Bea was confused.

"In a way I'm glad she was honest. But, Bea…didn't it bother you at all that her honest answer was that she never wanted any of us? What kind of mother doesn't want her kids but won't let anyone else take care of them? Don't you think that's the ultimate in selfishness?"

"Well yes, Aggie. But, she admitted that too. She said it was selfish. What do you really want from her?

"Bea, what I want she can't provide."

Bea was really confused now. She had no idea what Aggie was talking about or where this conversation was going. She wanted to help her sister but it was beginning to sound like she wouldn't be able to. But, she had to ask.

"Aggie, what is it that you want?"

"I want peace."

CHAPTER 32

Showdown Do-Over

THE SECOND SESSION began on time. Mrs. Warren opened with prayer and set the gavel on the podium leaving the floor open to anyone who wanted it. She had told Randall and Bea last night that they would definitely have their opportunity to speak tonight if they wanted to. I didn't know if Bea would speak or not because she had been so against bashing their mother but I knew Randall would take his turn. He just might not be as confrontational as his sisters had been.

He moved toward the front of the room to take the gavel after looking at each of his sisters to see if they wanted to go first. Since no one else moved, he did. He didn't appear nervous but I guess he was because he stood there for what seemed like forever before he spoke. When he finally opened his mouth no one could help but listen.

"I never felt like I belonged in this family. Since I could remember, I felt like I was different. I think my sisters did everything they could to help me feel a part, but it just didn't work. To have a mother who treats you like she's ashamed of you…well, I don't think that's something you ever get over." He didn't appear to be speaking to anyone in particular but at the same time he seemed to be talking to everyone. "I don't really know my father. I've only heard things from other people." He finally addressed Arlene. "Why do I not know my father? Why would you keep something that important from me? Can you imagine what it was like for me? I don't know if you care but this has been weighing on me since I was school age. All the other kids talking about their parents. Talking about their fathers' important jobs. Can you imagine me sitting there listening to all of them not having a clue of who my father was?

"I never really talked to you about any of this because I didn't want to make you mad. We knew all too well what might happen if we made you angry or got in your way. Especially me or Amber." He was making Arlene sound more like the incredible Hulk than a mother. "It seemed like you mistreated the two us more than the other two. I don't know. Maybe it just feels that way. Maybe you treated all of us the same. All I know is that it was awful. Haven't you ever wondered or cared why all four of your children left home and never really looked back?"

I saw tears in my mother's eyes. I could tell this was really hard on her but at the same time I think she was happy. Maybe just happy the day had finally come when her siblings would have the courage to stand up for themselves without fear of being hurt physically and/or emotionally. Maybe she was just proud of her brother for searching for the answers he needed to move on with his life.

Randall didn't force his mother to answer even though he ended with a lot of questions. He simply set the gavel back in its place and returned to his seat. When Arlene didn't move Aggie hopped up. She didn't say a word but she took the gavel from the podium and held it out toward Arlene. Apparently, Mrs. Warren didn't have a problem with that because she said nothing, nor did she move from her seat.

Aggie was all over Arlene. She had been the aggressive one from the beginning and she was not about to let her get away with anything! Even though she wasn't the one asking the questions this time, she wanted Arlene to be held accountable. Arlene accepted the gavel because she was given no choice. She walked toward Aggie shaking her head. She might have to struggle through this one but she was going to have to respond.

"I don't know what else I can say 'cept dat I done all them thangs and I'm sorry. Yes, Randall I treated you like dirt and I'm sorry. I don't know what else I can say." Arlene turned around to face Mrs. Warren as if asking for help. Mrs. Warren stood to speak. Arlene thought she had gotten off the hook until she heard what Mrs. Warren had to say.

"Ms. Cameron, I know this is hard on you. I know that

each one of your children are looking for answers from you that you may not have. I know it's tempting for you to give the same answers to what seem like the same questions they're asking. But, if you listen to each of them, they have something different they're inquiring about. They're not all the same and they have some different grievances with you. You have to answer each of them individually. You cannot just lump them all in together because each child has a different set of emotions and feelings. They each think about things differently. Each of their lives was impacted differently.

"I want you to really think about what Randall said to you. Think about the specific questions he asked. Answer his questions right now and only his. Answer his questions as if he were the first one to speak. Each one of your children needs to feel like they've been heard and that their feelings are special and that they mean something to you. You have to understand that none of them have ever heard you apologize to them before. They really need to hear it from you and if you want your family back you may be apologizing to them for years to come. You're going to have to do whatever it takes."

Arlene looked defeated but she turned to face her jury anyway. I understood how difficult this must be for her because she was already guilty in this courtroom. She looked at her only son with regret. At least, that's what it looked like to me. What she regretted, I don't know, but I was beginning to wonder if she was having second thoughts about wanting to have a relationship with her children. Is it even worth it? I'm sure her children felt it was worth it and for everything they had gone through they were really letting her off easy.

"You right Randall" Arlene began. "I was shame of you but I shouldn'ta took it out on you. It was my shame. Yo' daddy was someone I shouldn'ta been with and every time I looked at you I seen him. I took my guilt out on you and I was wrong. "I didn't wanna tell you who yo' daddy was.

I didn't wanna tell nobody who he was. I was thankin' if I kep' it secret I didn't have to be shame. I didn't thank about what that was gon' mean for you. I didn't really care. You aint' never say nothin' 'bout it. You ain't never ask me who it was so I didn't think you cared either."

Randall walked to the front. I don't think he could resist responding to that last statement. Arlene willingly handed over the gavel but instead of taking it from her Randall grabbed onto her hand which was still holding the gavel.

"I did care" he said. "It was very important to me and I guess you just don't remember me ever asking you because I did. It was just that you always ignored me. You either told me to get out yo' face, I didn't have no daddy, or that Riley was my daddy. You never answered me and when I pressed too hard you would hurt me. So, what was I supposed to do? Eventually I just stopped asking you. Now, I did ask other people like Grandma and she told me the truth. She always told the truth. So, I've known for a long time who he is. I guess I just wanted you to admit it." You should have heard the gasps in the room!

Arlene and everyone else in the room were stunned! But even more than that...Arlene was angry! To hear that he already knew seemed to tick her off. She almost let the old, fleshy Arlene come out instead of the one who was trying her best to be the good Christian. She couldn't intimidate Randall anymore but I didn't know if that would stop her from trying. She gathered herself quickly and spoke evenly and calmly.

"Yo' daddy was a sweet man, Randall. It was just that I wasn't supposed to be with him. And yes, he was the blackest man I ever laid eyes on but honey lemme tell you... He was a good-lookin' man. Arlene's eyes lit up like the fourth of July. She lifted her knee and slapped it while shaking her head from side to side all at the same time.

"I knows you always thought I didn't like you 'cause of yo' color. But, it wasn't that. It was 'cause you dark, like him. You look just like him and like I said, every time I looked at you it was like lookin' at my shame. You still look like him. Only, I don't feel shame no more. God took that away from me and he'll take it away from you too, if you let him."

Randall just stood there and stared at his mother. Aggie's face showed what she was feeling. It was pure disgust and I had a feeling she was about to let us know just how disgusted she was. She couldn't wait to get her hands on that gavel!

"I have a question for you" Aggie said to her mother. "Why now are you acting like such a Christian? Supposedly you've been a Christian my whole life. Of course, you never acted like it so, why now? Who are you to tell Randall what God will do for him? God may have forgiven you but I haven't."

"Well, Aggie really, I'm nobody. I just knows what God done for me. I'm glad he ain't like us. He forgives." "For your sake I'm glad He's not like us either because if God were like me He would have taken you out years ago!"

Whoa Nelly! Aggie was ticked off and she wasn't holding anything back. I hoped Bea hadn't planned to say anything tonight because it didn't look like she was gonna get to. Randall was standing between Aggie and Arlene. He turned toward Aggie to try and calm her down. The funny thing is that she was very calm. She was just launching a verbal attack on her mother and she was winning! This time, Mrs. Warren did step in.

"This is good" she said. "I know some of you think Aggie is a bit aggressive but she's showing her true emotion. This is not to say that no one else is being truthful but if this is who Aggie is then she's being honest. She's not holding anything back and I wouldn't want her to. This time is too important for anyone to play around with it. If it's what you feel then I want you to say it. I'll say it again. This is a time to heal. You guys have allowed pain, anger and bitterness to fester for years. It has driven you apart. You're going to have to let all those emotions out. It's not healthy to hold them in like most of you have. I appreciate Aggie's honesty about her true feelings.

"Our time is up for tonight but I want you each to really think about how you really feel. Think about how your life has been all these years. Think about how your lives might have been different if you hadn't gone through some of the things you went through. I'm going to give each of you a homework assignment. I want you all to write a story telling me about your life if you had the perfect mother. And by that I mean for you to think of your personal opinion of the perfect mother.

Tell me what she's like and what you feel your life might have been like if your mother had been like this perfect mother. Bea, we will definitely be waiting to hear from you tomorrow night. Let's close with prayer and adjourn for the evening."

"Oooweee! That was crazy Mom! If Randall hadn't been in between Arlene and Aggie it might have been some *Mortal Combat* up in there!

"Yea baby I know…I haven't been around them in a very long time. I would like to think that Aggie wouldn't have physically attacked her mother. But, I'm not so sure…"

All I knew was that tomorrow was going to be quite interesting. My assignment was going to be easy. My mom is great, except for the keeping things from me. So, I'll just get to tell all the great things about her, but I'll definitely let her know how I feel about not being kept in her loop. Now don't get me wrong. I know that parents shouldn't tell their kids everything because it's not their business. It's just that when important things are kept it'll eventually come out and be painful. That old saying about 'what you don't know won't hurt you' is stupid! Sure, for the moment they don't know I guess it won't hurt. But, the truth is, whatever is done in the dark will come to the light. And believe me, when it hits that light it will hurt.

I was really interested in what everyone would to have to say with their individual assignments. I didn't expect anyone's idea of the perfect mother to sound anything like Arlene. Well, Bea's idea might but no one else's would. Bea was a different character all together. I was aware of something about Bea that she wasn't yet aware of herself. Now, she would have to allow another therapist to walk through it with her. I could only pray that she would continue with her treatment after this whole family ordeal. If anyone needed it, it was Bea.

CHAPTER 33

Take III

BEA WAS ASKED to begin the session since she was the only one who had yet to speak. She got up with confidence and her notebook in hand. I knew she'd been keeping a notebook because she'd brought it to our sessions. It was where she kept her notes on the 'blackouts' she could remember. She had done her brainstorming in it before writing the letter to my mother. I hoped she was journaling as well because she wasn't very good at expressing her feelings verbally. I expected her *perfect mother* letter to be syrupy sweet.

And it was. "My perfect mother would be a sweet woman" she read. "She would have an heir about her that was inviting to even the lowest of people. She would smell great all the time and she would be the best at everything she did. Not to say that she would be absolutely perfect because no one could accomplish that. I just mean that everything she set out to do would be done well.

"She would love her children and take care of them as best she knew how. She would never allow anyone to hurt them. Not even herself. She would be respected by her children, husband and community and would be kind, giving and always available. She would give her children little, pet names and would enjoy spending her time doing things with us. She would always tell us, even if she thought we knew it, that she loved us. And that's pretty much it." Bea ended her reading and took her seat.

Mrs. Warren asked Aggie to be next. She walked to the front of the room without anything in her hand. I guessed she was just going to speak from the heart and *that* she did.

"My perfect mother would basically be everything my biological mother is not" Aggie jumped straight out the gate with an insult. She was just baiting Arlene to see how long she could stand up to this abuse. But, I guess Aggie figured she owed it to her after the many years of abuse she endured at her mother's hands.

"My perfect mother would be a kind, generous giver. Not a taker. She would love and honor her children and treat them as blessings and not hindrances. She would be more concerned about their welfare than what they could do for her. A perfect mother would never try to harm her children and would definitely never stand by and watch someone else harm them. She would be a mother every day in every way and not just on the days she felt like it. She would remember that she gave birth to them and that they never asked to be brought into this ugly world. So, she would spend her days trying to make an ugly world beautiful for them. And, I may have said this already, but most of all, she would love them."

Aggie took her seat, crossed her arms and poked out her lips. She was acting more like a kid than the adolescents I see in my practice. Maybe it's because she never really got to be a kid. She could never rebel. She was too busy taking care of the other children and too afraid her mother would punish her for speaking her mind. I guess now that she's grown and not afraid, she can say whatever she wants. Even if it wasn't what she was thinking, she most certainly was acting as if that's what was on her mind.

Randall took his turn next. Brandy hadn't been attending the family sessions and I wondered why. I thought maybe she was just allowing the family to iron out their differences. I knew it wasn't because he didn't ask her to. Randall would never ask her not to come. She was too important to him. I respected Brandy and Randall's relationship a great deal. I didn't know a lot about them but what I'd seen was refreshing. It was nice to see a couple work together and communicate well with one another. I could only assume she helped him with his thoughts because she was always helping him.

"I hope you don't mind Mrs. Warren, my wife helped me with this" he admitted. I just smiled. "I kind of combined the things she thinks makes a good mother and the things I would like to have seen in my own mother. I asked Brandy to help because I think she's a great mother." Randall blushed a little. *Yes, even dark skinned people blush.*

"Anyway, this is what we came up with… A perfect mother is someone who is always there even when a father isn't. She acts as the mother and the father if she has to because that's just what a good mother does. She always encourages and if she has to criticize, she does it with love and kindness. She always explains things to you the best way she can. If she doesn't know the answers she admits to that but she tries her best to find out for you. She most definitely loves you and she always tells you. A perfect mother knows that she's not perfect and admits her mistakes."

Randall looked up from his paper and directly at Arlene. "But, out of all the things we wrote down, the most important thing was and is love." With a tremble in his voice he said, "I don't believe you could consider anyone near perfect if they don't know how to love." Randall took his seat with tears in his eyes.

I thought I would go up next. I felt like I might be a good introduction for my mom. She was sitting still, looking at her brother with tenderness. I knew she could feel his pain. I touched her hand as I got up to talk about her. Maybe I would be able to say something to make her feel better. After all, she is a great mother. She may have made some mistakes but no one is perfect.

"I know that our assignment was to write about our idea of the perfect mother but no one is perfect. So, I wrote about my mother because I believe she's as close as it gets. I thank God every day that He chose my mom for me. I don't think I could have done any better in life with another mother. She may not be perfect but she's perfect for me.

"1 Corinthians 13:4-7 says *'Love is patient and kind; love does not envy or boast; it is not arrogant or rude. It does not insist on its own way; it is not irritable or resentful; it does not rejoice at wrongdoing, but rejoices with the truth. Love bears all things, believes all things, hopes all things, endures all things.'*

"My mother didn't always say she loved me but I knew she did. It was always in her actions. She did her best to always give me the things I desired and even when I was a brat she loved me anyway. She always offered me the things she didn't have growing up. Sometimes she gave it to me whether I wanted it or not." I laughed and so did everyone else. "But, now I even appreciate her making me at least try the things I didn't like.

"She always wanted to shield me from pain and I appreciate that as well. A good mother will always protect her children. Even from themselves. A good mother disciplines with love and respect and never degrades her children. She spends time with her children and never neglects them.

"I had the opportunity to grow up with a mother who was there for me, but my mother didn't have that. For that, I am truly sorry. I guess I'm grateful that she did the total opposite of what her mother did. I think a good mother learns from her own mistakes and the mistakes of others. And finally, I have to agree with my new aunts an uncle and say that love is the most important thing that a perfect mother would give. If love was all that made a mother perfect then I am looking at perfection when I look at mine." I smiled at my mom and of course she returned the gesture. As I took my seat she reached out her arms to hug me.

That's when it hit me. I had seen my mother's family together several times over the past week and not a single time had one of them hugged another. I hadn't really thought about that until now. I know my mom isn't close to her siblings and none of them are close to their mother, but the other siblings don't seem very close either.

I was surprised when Arlene got up. I thought she would be the last one to speak but she was making her way to the front. I was interested to know what she would say since she hadn't been a good mother. What did she think a good mother was supposed to be like? Per her children, she actually had a good role model. Their grandmother, her mother, was a loving and kind woman. After hearing that, I wondered how Arlene could be the total opposite. Then it hit me again. My mother was the total opposite of Arlene. I guess things can go either way.

Arlene's first set of statements were known to be true. She spoke generously about her mother but what we heard after that was unbelievable. Even as a therapist it was a hard pill to swallow, but it did explain a lot of things to me. It even made me feel a little sorry for my grandmother.

"My mama is a good woman. She did her best to raise me right. I wouldn't trade her for the world. So, as for the lesson, I got to say that my mama was pretty close to perfect."

Arlene paused as if she were catching her breath and reaching for words at the same time. When she began speaking again I wished she had never opened her mouth. "It was her husband that was the problem" she said. "He was the most hateful creature that coulda walked the Earth. He was more like Satan than Satan himself." Arlene's voice went ice cold.

"See, he used to come to my room at night. It was a lot of us girls and we all had the same room so he would make up a reason to git me out the bed. He would tell me I didn't sweep the flo' right or all the dishes wasn't done. He would say anythang so's he could git me by myself. Then…"

Arlene seemed to trail off in thought. It looked as if she was trying as hard as she could to keep her emotions in check. This wasn't something she even shared during our therapy sessions. Now either she was a good liar, which her children would probably agree with, or this was an actual account of an abusive past.

"…He would do thangs to me. Nasty thangs. Oh, it didn't start out that way. At first he would just come git me so's we could talk. I thought I was just his favorite. I thought maybe he didn't know how to talk to Mama. Or maybe he just didn't want to talk to her. He did dat for a while. Then the touchin' started and then other thangs. It got so I couldn't sleep at night 'cause I knew he was comin' for me. It got so I seed him in my dreams and wake up and he be standin' over my bed. I never told nobody 'cause he say they wouldn't believe me no way. He say he would just tell 'em I was being fast. Said they'd believe him 'cause I was just a li'l gal. Little girls was supposed to be seen and not heard and you was just supposed to do what yo' daddy or yo' uncles or your brothers say. So, I keep my mouth shut. Until I found out somethin' dat helped me.

"One day I was at my auntie house and me and two of my girl cousins was talkin'. They start tellin' me how my daddy wasn't my daddy. They say my mama was already pregnant with me when she met him. I didn't know if I should believe 'em or not so I asked Mama. It shocked me when she told me they was right! Like Randall said, she always tells it like it is. She say he wasn't my daddy and that my real daddy died befo' I was born. She say her and the man I thought was my daddy was friends for a long time. Said he didn't want her to have to raise a baby by herself with no man 'round. So, she married him. He told her he loved her even befo' she married my real daddy. He was just waitin' fo' the right time.

"When I found dat out, I sang like a bird! I told my mama everythang and she believed me. We both went after him. He tried to lie and say everythang he told me he was gon' say. Told my mama I was fresh-tailed and dat he caught me with boys and I was just mad at him. She still believed me. She put him out and stopped him from messin' with me but it was too late. I ain't never looked at a man or boy the same way since.

"From dat day, all a boy or man could do for me was buy me thangs or give me money. You see, dat's what my daddy use to do. Every time he do them nasty thangs to me he buy me somethin'. Like he was payin' me for my body. So, when them other boys wanted to be my boyfriend I let 'em. I got lots of thangs from 'em. Yea, I went to bed with 'em for it but dat wasn't nothin'. Sex didn't mean nothing to me. It was just somethin' to do so's I could get what I wanted. See, my daddy, well the man I thought was my daddy, start messin' with me when I was eight years old. When my mama finally put a stop to it, after I told, I was seventeen. I was already ruined.

"Shortly after he lef' we found out somethin' else..." Arlene paused again and wouldn't make eye contact with anyone.

"I was fixin' to have a baby" Arlene said. "I was carryin' a child fo' my own father. Well, of course I knowed then he wasn't my real daddy but he was the onliest one I knowed."

"I had dat baby and named her Sally Agnes."

Aggie just sat there staring at Arlene like she was the Bride of Chucky. "I treated my baby like a burden 'cause she was" Arlene continued. "She was a burden on my heart. I couldn't get away from my daddy 'cause now he was following me 'round. I carried him inside me and then I had to labor for him and take care of him. I couldn't help it but dat was how I thought of my baby. It wasn't no abortion back then. At least I didn't know 'bout it. And if it was it cost money I didn't have. I shoulda gave up my baby instead of treatin' her the way I did. But, I didn't thank nobody else would want her either if they found out how she was made."

The entire room went silent. Now it made sense! Every time she looked at Aggie she couldn't help but remember how and with whom she'd been conceived.

"But, what it done to my mama was worse then what it done to me. After she found out what happened to me she felt so bad. Like it was her fault. She blame herself. She wore so much shame. She was a right woman and she knowed God forgave her but she just couldn't forgive herself. After dat, all she did was take care of us. She smother my sisters. She helped me with the baby. She knowed how I felt about Aggie but she didn't feel dat away 'bout her at all. My mama figured a blessin' had come out of dat evil. I just couldn't brang myself to thank of it dat away. Her husband stole my childhood and I just didn't thank a baby coming out of dat was a blessin' of no kind."

"Aggie, I can't say I'm sorry enough to you. I knows hearing all this is probably a shock. I ain't never wanted any of this to come out. I didn't brang it up in counselin' 'cause I didn't thank I needed to. I didn't want to git into all dat. But, Sally Agnes, and my other chil'en, is all lookin' fo' answers. Well, I don't know if this help you any but it's the truth. This wasn't quite what the lesson was 'bout but this was all I could thank about when I tried to come up with my perfect mother. My mama was wonderful but she couldn't save me. Dat messed her up somethin' awful! She loved her children so much it hurt. I thought if I loved my chil'en like dat I be settin' myself up for nothin' but mo' pain. I'm sorry you suffered fo' thangs dat didn't have nothing to do with you. I hope you can forgive me."

Arlene took her seat and I believe everyone in the room was speechless. I know I was. But, of course, the therapist in me had so much to say. She was kicking and screaming to get out! She wanted to know if and how this new information changed the children's opinion of their mother. But, I was not a therapist at the moment. I was a family member. I needed to stay in my proper role.

But, Mrs. Warren…good old Mrs. Warren asked the question for me. "Does anyone want to respond to your mother? Does what you now know change your thoughts and feelings about your upbringing?" She had opened the floor. I knew I shouldn't speak but I was hoping someone would.

That's when Bea got up again. She was sitting next to her mother so as she got up she touched Arlene gently on the shoulder. "I know you guys have already heard from me but I thought of more to say" she admitted. "I've been pretty quiet throughout these sessions because I've been dealing with issues of my own. I believe they stem from my childhood but right now I'm still not sure of anything.

Bea stopped, turned and looked at Mrs. Warren. "Since I've already read my perfect mother thoughts I want to move on to something that's been troubling me. Mrs. Warren, even though it's off the subject, I have something else I want to talk about. Would that be alright with you?"

"Bea, this is your family's session. Ask them if it would be alright" Mrs. Warren suggested.

"Okay, guys. Would it be alright if I brought up a different subject?" Bea addressed the family.

Everyone expressed their consent. We needed a change of subject after what Arlene had just dropped on us! However, I had a horrible feeling Bea was about to drop an even bigger bomb. She pulled out that piece of paper with the child's handwriting…

One day they'll know
I'm leaving a paper trail
Who the mother really is
Why she should go to hell

Who will tell
How long will it take
She's evil on Earth
Filled with hate

Christian…whatever
Lies upon lies
She doesn't know Jesus
I hope she fries!

Right now I'll do my job
For her I'll protect and serve
Hopefully one day she'll have the courage
But today, she doesn't have the nerve.

Bea finished reading the poem and looked around at each family member finally stopping and letting her eyes rest upon my mother. She could only assume that was who had written the poem since her other siblings denied it.

"This is just one of several poems I've found like this. I'd like to know who wrote them and what the heck they mean."

No one said anything but everyone except Arlene and me looked at my mother. "Well, Bea…I'm not sure why everyone is looking at me because the only person who can answer those questions is you" my mom announced. "I watched you write several of those things."

CHAPTER 34

Monday

THAT WAS SOME family meeting the other night! We decided to take a break after that last session. I hoped Bea wouldn't bring those letters up at the family meeting. I wished she had assumed that my mother wrote them and dropped it. I didn't want her to find out the way she did. I still don't think she quite understands the severity of her issues. That's why she'll definitely need to continue with some intense, individual therapy, possible medication and most importantly prayer.

We're all scheduled to meet again tonight. My mother never got her opportunity to share her perfect mother assignment. I don't know what she's going to say. We didn't really talk about it but I'm sure it won't be as dramatic as what we've already experienced. She was scheduled to return home soon and I kind of wished she didn't have to go. On one hand, I'm worried that if she leaves she won't keep in touch with her family and things will go back to the way they were. On the other hand, I just want her to stay for me. I miss her. I know that's selfish but I'm an only child. I grew up only having her around and now I don't even have that.

All this loneliness just makes me think about Tyson. It really doesn't matter to me that he's with this Jamie person because in my heart he's mine. I don't know what God has to say about it though. That's why I try not to dwell on it but it doesn't change the way I feel. Maybe one day He'll change the way I feel if I'm not right. I thought it would be easier once I left. I thought that if I couldn't see him the feelings would go away. They haven't. Sometimes I think they've diminished but it only takes me thinking about him to bring everything right back. Some days it brings me down. Then, it gets better. Some days I just fly right through the day. The week days seem a little easier because I'm busy. The weekends are usually hard because I don't really have much to do and if I'm doing something I'm by myself. That's when I really feel the pain. When I'm by myself.

It's not like I have to be alone. Guys ask me out all the time. It's just that I don't want them. I know who I want and what I want and if I can't have him then I would rather be by myself. There's no sense in just going through the motions of a relationship if my heart isn't in it. And right now, my heart is taken. If God wants me to do something different He's going to have to hit me over the head with it because I can't see it. But then again, I'm not trying to either.

I had only taken a couple of days off to hang out with my mom and now I was back in the office. I had seen three clients and was ready for a break. I didn't have anyone else scheduled until two o'clock because my one o'clock appointment cancelled. As I sat at my desk thinking about what I wanted to eat for lunch Gabrielle buzzed me.

"Your mother's on line #1" she informed.

"Thank you, Gabby." I picked up line #1. "Hi mom!"

"Hey, do you have time to break for lunch or do you have back-to-back clients?"

"As a matter of fact, I was just thinking about what I should eat. I'll come and pick you up. I had a cancellation for this afternoon so I actually have a little extra time."

I went to pick my mom up from my place. When she got to the car she had already decided what she wanted to eat. That was fine with me because I like to eat but I'm not all that picky. As long as it's not raw, seafood or raw seafood I'll probably eat it.

She wanted to go to *Luby's*. She loved that place and I didn't know why but we went there anyway. She ordered fried catfish fillets and I ordered Salisbury steak. Even though she seemed okay I had a feeling she was struggling with something. Maybe she wanted to take me out to lunch so we'd have a chance to talk before our family session tonight.

I guess I was right because as soon as we finished blessing the table she jumped right into talking about Bea. "What on Earth is wrong with Bea? Now, you're not her therapist right now. You're her niece. Why wouldn't she remember that she wrote those poems? Why would she think I wrote them?"

My mom was throwing all these questions at me that I couldn't answer. It wasn't that I didn't know the answers. It was just that I couldn't talk about it with her because of confidentiality. I couldn't divulge any personal information about my client. When I found out what I know about Bea she wasn't my aunt, she was my client.

I wondered why she hadn't brought this up until now. It had been a couple of days since our last session. Why didn't she ask me about it days ago? Why didn't she just call and talk to Bea? I know they haven't been close but they are sisters. Regardless of what any of those answers were, I couldn't tell her.

"Mom, you know I can't tell you anything. Bea was my client and technically she still is."

"Well, what if we talked hypothetically? Could you tell me then?" she asked.

"Why don't we just wait until tonight during our session? Bring it up then and maybe we can talk about it in that context. That'll be about family and as her niece I can say anything I want. She can't be my client and my aunt at the same time" I said.

I think she understood where I was coming from because she agreed to wait. We had a pleasant lunch and talked about her staying a while longer and then going back home. Of course, we talked about her coming back soon for another visit. She really needed to get back to work and I understood that but it didn't change the fact that I didn't want her to go. She was going to stay until Sunday afternoon so I had her for at least another week. I wanted her to go to church with me and meet my pastor. She had met his wife, of course, but she hadn't met him yet. I wanted her to take comfort in the fact that I was being well taken care of.

I took her back to my place after lunch and told her I would pick her up right after I got off so we could make it to our session on time. Getting back to work I found out that my two o'clock appointment had cancelled as well. Now, I had even more free time than I wanted because whenever my mind was idle guess who popped up?

Tyson had prayed and received his answer. He didn't know how this would turn out but he trusted God. He now knew he had to be honest with this entire situation. After all, he was in this predicament because he hadn't been honest. He simply needed to ask Andrea for the number. Maybe he would be able to get it without telling her anything, but if he had to he would tell her the truth. He needed to speak with Sasha so he could make things right. He was no longer going to operate out of fear. So…Monday at work he would just do it. He'd walk up to Andrea, when no one else was around, and just ask her for Sasha's number.

He needed to be honest with Jamie as well. Tyson had been using Jamie as a diversion from what he really should have been doing and it was time he came clean. It may hurt Jamie's feelings but it had to be done. He couldn't allow anything or anyone to stop him from doing what he knew was right. Especially not someone with a dark spirit following them. Tyson didn't understand why he hadn't seen this before.

He had noticed the feelings he had whenever Jamie was around but he'd contributed everything to stress and life's difficulties. He never put two-and two together to figure out that the actual problem was with Jamie. Jamie was a fun person that most people liked being around but Tyson had been given a revelation. He knew that if he didn't do something about it he was going to miss out on a blessing. So, there was no other choice. Jamie had to go and Monday would have to be the day.

He woke up early Monday morning. This was it! He would take his first step in obedience. He needed to make every effort to contact Sasha but he had to get that phone number from her friend. He also had to have a serious talk with Jamie about their relationship and why it wouldn't work for him anymore.

Tyson began to pray before he even put his feet on the floor to get out of bed. "Lord, I need you to be with me today. Of course, I need you with me every day but today I need an extra dose of your courage. I'm getting ready to tackle two things that may backfire if I attempt them without you. But, I know that if you speak for me it'll work out."

He got out of bed, got ready for work and hopped in the car. He was actually going to be early for work today rather than right on time. Arriving at the parking garage fifteen minutes earlier than usual, he even got a good parking space. Starting to get the feeling that today would be a good day he walked into the building and on to his office to put his things down. While he walked down to the break room to get a cup of coffee he began to go over his plan of action out loud.

"First, I'll get Sasha's number from Andrea. I'll answer any questions she has, honestly, without giving up too much information. Then, I'll have lunch with Jamie, as usual, but this'll be a serious lunch talk. Maybe we'll even have an out of office lunch in case there's a scene. I would much rather have Jamie act a fool in public than in the office! Maybe a public setting will contain some of the foolishness if there is to be any."

Tyson was now on his third cup of coffee waiting for Andrea to get to work. That woman was always late. He was just about to go for his fourth cup when his assistant buzzed him to let him know Andrea was at her desk. Showtime! He put his coffee mug down and headed in Andrea's direction. He wasn't coming back without that number.

"Good morning, Andrea" Tyson greeted, as he arrived at her desk.

"Good morning, Tyson. How are you?" Andrea said as she returned the greeting.

"I hope to be better real soon and that's why I've come to see you."

Now she was intrigued. She wondered what in the world she could do for him to make his life better. All she knew was that it better not be something freaky! She was not about to go there with a co-worker.

"Well, what can I do to help?" she asked.

"I need Sasha's phone number."

Andrea's eyes brightened. "Why?"

"I just need to talk with her about something really important. Look Andrea, I really don't want to get into it. Do you think she would mind me having her number?”

“I don’t think she would mind. As long as you’re not going to hurt her feelings.”

“I’m not, Andrea. I promise. Would you tell me the number so I can save it to my phone?”

“Sure.”

Andrea gave Sasha’s cell, home and work numbers. Although he would never use the home number without her permission, he took all three. Now he had another decision to make. Would he call her at work or her cell? He thanked Andrea for the information and headed back to his office. He’d already sent Jamie an e-mail about lunch and was just waiting for a reply.

Jamie accepted Tyson’s lunch plans and met him there. But, the lunch date, if you want to call it that, had not gone well at all. Jamie was thoroughly upset and didn’t understand why their relationship had to end. Tyson held his ground no matter what. He knew what he felt in his heart and he was sticking to it. Jamie would just have to understand that his relationship with God was much more important than what they had. He needed Jamie to know who came first in his life. Tyson knew he had to put God first or nothing in his world would be right. If Jamie never wanted to talk to him again he would have to live with that. His pastor always said that ‘sometimes you have to cut off some dead weight or dead people if you’re going to move forward.’ He had finally figured out that Jamie was part of the walking dead.

He felt good about his decision. Of course, he never wanted anyone to get hurt but he knew he would rather hurt someone’s feelings than go to hell trying to please them. Tyson told Jamie the truth. He’d said that their relationship was holding him back from something he really had to do. Of course, he hadn’t really wanted to get into all of that during the conversation, but he got his point across. The dynamics of the relationship had to change or there would be no relationship at all.

On the Cusp

TYSON HAD BEEN sitting at home staring at his phone for an hour. He couldn't bring himself to make the call. He couldn't understand why he was so nervous. He had gone through getting the number from Andrea and breaking things off with Jamie. Why couldn't he just pick up the phone and dial?

He started thinking of the easy way out. Maybe he would call her work number and leave a message. That way, she would know he called and she could call him back. If he did it that way he would be putting the ball in her court. Then, it would be on her to make the next move. But, as he sat and thought about it, the first thing that came to his mind was his favorite scene from *School Daze. When I say Tyson you say punk. Tyson. Punk. Tyson. Punk. Tyson, Tyson. Punk, punk. Tyson, Tyson, Tyson, Tyson. Punk, punk, punk, punk.* Leaving her a voicemail to put the ball in her court was a punk move. He should just be a man, admit he was wrong and call the woman. What woman wouldn't accept a sincere apology? He really was sorry for what happened. He was even more sorry he didn't get the chance to correct it before she left town. He knew and felt all of this yet, he still sat staring at the phone, not dialing. *Punk!*

What did he have to be afraid of? She was in another state. She couldn't even see his face. She couldn't see him sweating. All she would be able to do was hear his voice. Maybe she would be happy to hear from him. He couldn't understand why he was thinking the worst. The Sasha he knew was a sweetheart. He had watched her smile even when people talked bad about her, within earshot. She was a gentle soul and he never saw her reject anyone. What was bothering him? He couldn't figure it out so, he decided to ask God.

Tyson was getting off his knees and wasn't too thrilled

with what he was hearing. He wasn't ready for a relationship but who said calling the woman would lead to a relationship? Why had he settled for the relationship with Jamie? Why would he choose something he knew would never amount to anything productive when what he needed was right in front of him?

Question, questions. Too many questions. Why wasn't he ready? What was he waiting for? Did he need to get a house first? Was he trying to build up his savings account so far? How many cars does he have to have? Did he need to go back to school first? My goodness! Did he think his life wouldn't be his own anymore if he had a serious relationship with Sasha?

That was it! It was Sasha! He knew he wouldn't be with Jamie forever, but Sasha… She was different. She was special. Was she the one? If he finally made the commitment to her, that might be the last relationship commitment he would ever make. This might be the one he committed to before God. He was running!

How could he feel this way about someone he barely knew? This revelation was too much. He needed to go to bed! He didn't want to think about it anymore. He would have to deal with this another day. He now knew he couldn't continue to run. He would have to face this head on. Now that he knew, he was going to be held accountable. Running was no longer an option. He went to bed with Sasha on his mind.

Here I was again with my "family." We were all just sitting and looking at one another. Since they were acting like strangers I didn't figure anyone had talked since the last session. I didn't know how Mrs. Warren was going to open this up but hopefully she had a plan. We needed one. No one was talking and everyone looked tense. Especially Bea.

Mrs. Warren didn't ask anyone to pray. She opened up herself. "Lord, we are coming to you once again. You said that wherever two or three are gathered in your name, there you would be. We need you in our midst tonight. We are dealing with some extraordinary issues and you are the only one who can heal this family. Open our hearts and minds so that we may receive what you have to say. Anoint our tongues, so that we would only speak words of peace and not condemnation on one another. Give to us your words, your courage and your power. In the most precious name of Jesus, we pray. Amen."

Everyone said Amen and looked directly at Mrs. Warren. I don't know if they were just being attentive or if they just couldn't bear to look at each other. She was the only one in the room that wasn't a family member. Of course, there was me. Sure, by blood, I'm related but we've only known that for about a week. And, I am the counselor who tried to help them all.

"I want to begin with Aubrey today since she never got the opportunity to tell us her thoughts on the perfect mother. Aubrey." Mrs. Warren stretched the gavel out toward my mom and she stood to receive it.

"Honestly," mom said "I really don't know what the perfect mother would be like. I just know that it's what I tried to be for my child. But, I messed that up so now, I'm not sure. So, I'll just tell you what I used to think. I tried to protect my daughter from anything that might hurt her physically and/or emotionally. She was and is my world. I lived for her. My life wasn't good until I gave birth to her. Sure, I believed in God before but my life was so hard that I started to wonder what I really knew or believed about Him. And then, He gave me Sasha. He gave me someone who would love me. Someone who would need me and depend on me. That's when my relationship with Him became stronger. There was no way I wanted to mess up the precious gift He had given me so I tried my best to learn to trust Him. Sometimes I did and sometimes I didn't. But, I tried to be the perfect mother because…well you guys already know why. Because our mother wasn't." She looked at Arlene after that statement as if to apologize for telling the truth.

"I needed my child to know I loved her and that no one, I mean no one would come before her. But, that's also where I went wrong. He needed to be first. I stopped listening to God and let my past guide me instead of Him. I followed my emotions instead of His wisdom. I was so busy trying to protect myself from the past that I forgot to listen to what He was telling me about the future. I heard Him saying I needed to be honest with Sasha. That she needed to know everything. But, I felt it would hurt me too badly to have to tell her. And well, look at what happened when she found out. She ended up in the hospital! I could have avoided all of that by listening to God when I should have. But, one thing I have learned is that He is a merciful God. I still have my daughter and I can attempt to make things up to her and go forward in a different manner. That's what I think a good mother would do. She would admit when she's wrong, acknowledge it and God and do her best to correct it."

My mother addressed my grandmother. "That is exactly what you have an opportunity to do starting now and going forward. God has given you another chance to make things right. I hope you're listening." She took her seat and no one else moved.

Now what? Everyone had already completed their assignments. What else was left? How would we continue the healing process? I sat and wondered what everyone was thinking and the thing that came to my mind was 'what did each child expect from their mother now?' Did they even want a relationship with her? If so, how did they plan to make it happen? I had all these questions running through my mind yet, I said nothing.

The Cameron family session was at a standstill tonight. No one wanted to talk. Mrs. Warren would ask questions and no one would answer. Finally, she decided she would make us do another assignment. This time she wanted the four children to write about what it would take to make things better between them and their mother. What could their mother do to have a better relationship with them.

Arlene had the most difficult assignment of all. She had to take what she knew about each of her children, individually, and come up with a plan of what she could do to make them smile. That meant she would actually have to take the time to consider who they are and what they like. And, she couldn't ask them. She simply had to go off what she knew of them from the past and/or what she had learned during our time in counseling.

This is going to be great, I thought. This would be a very useful tool if everyone did a good job with it. We would definitely be able to learn a great deal about one another through an assignment like this. They all need to know what each other likes.

My assignment was to try and figure out each person from what I knew of them. I basically had the same assignment Arlene did. Since Aubrey is my mother and I actually counseled with the rest of the family, Mrs. Warren wanted to see how well I knew my former clients, present family. I didn't have a problem with that at all. I felt I knew enough about each of them to figure out how I could make each of them smile.

We ended the session on a good note. Everyone seemed to be pleased with our homework assignment. We were scheduled to return to session the following evening. We were doing intensive therapy because of the time frame and because of the extraordinary conditions this family had been under. This wouldn't normally happen, but this was special. Mrs. Warren was doing this for me. She knew how important it was to me because it was important to my mother. I wanted, so badly, for her to have a family. She had been alone for so many years. Of course, she has plenty of friends, but it's not the same. Family is different. You love them and sometimes you can't stand them, but they're yours. We have to find a way to develop and strengthen the relationships and if it takes intensive therapy to make it happen, then so be it. Desperate times call for desperate measures!

CHAPTER 36

Tuesday

WHEN WE WALKED into the office Mrs. Warren had the room set up in such a way that I knew what was going to happen. If anyone thought the previous sessions had been intense, they had no idea. The heat was about to be turned up a few notches!

"I hope everyone has their assignments completed" Mrs. Warren began. "You're going to need them for what we're about to do. Some of you may get lucky and not have to take your turns today, but Arlene you're on for the rest of the week. This week is not going to be easy, but it's necessary. And before we begin, I want you all to know how serious this is. I want you to be as honest as possible. I know some of you have no problem with that" she said as she glanced at Aggie. "For others of you this is going to be difficult. But, I pray that when it's over you will all be much better for having done it."

With that said, she began her prayer and then asked Arlene to come up. There were two chairs facing each other. The rest of the chairs were in a semicircle facing the two. The people who would sit in the chairs facing each other would be close enough for their knees to touch. That was the idea. I had done this experiment several times. It works!

Arlene was asked to sit in one of the chairs and Mrs. Warren asked her to choose one of her children to sit in the opposing chair. I thought to myself, if *Arlene is smart she'll choose Bea first since she has no idea what's about to happen.* Evidently, she wasn't thinking like I was because she chose my mom. My mom was a sweet soul but she had her moments and Arlene had just opened the door for her to have one of those moments. My mom was going to have the chance to confront her mother with whatever she wanted and Arlene was going to have to take it.

So, there they were. A face-off between mother and

daughter. Mrs. Warren gave the rules of the exercise. The child was to begin with telling Arlene what it would take to mend and make their relationship better. My mom had her paper because she didn't want to leave anything out. So, she began.

"First of all, I want an apology. I need a sincere apology for the way you treated me. And not just me. I want to hear an apology for all of your children. It was hell living with you and you at least, owe me that." She stopped and stared at Arlene. She wasn't going to continue until she got that apology.

"Aubrey, I knows I done you wrong" Arlene said. "For what I done, I shoulda and coulda been locked away. I ain't have no right to do what I done to you or your brother and sisters and for all them years of bad times I'm sorry."

I guess my mom accepted that apology, for now, because she kept going. "You need to get to know me. The real me. I want you to learn to love me as I am now. I don't think you did or ever could love Amber. That's why I refuse to be called by that name. Amber was a little girl who was hurt. She was hated by her own family and I don't want to ever feel that way again. I'm Aubrey now and I want you to learn to love Aubrey. Do you want to do that?"

"I want it with all my heart, baby."

"Can I trust you with my feelings? Can I trust you with my life?"

Those were serious questions being asked because those are the very things Arlene had tried to destroy when my mom was a child. She treated her with malice and even allowed the other children to hurt and attempt to kill her. These were not questions to be taken lightly. There was a lack of trust on my mother's part. I didn't know how I was feeling about this whole reunification thing really. I mean, the family does need to make amends and at least get to know each other, but trust... That's another issue.

"You gon' be able to trust my everythang. I'll show you" Arlene said. "I don't deserve it and I knows I have to earn it. I'm just askin' for a chance."

"What are you willing to do?" Mom asked.

"Anythang. I knows I got to go slow 'cause I knows you

aint sho'."

"You're right about that. I don't trust you and I don't know if I ever completely will, but I would like to see if I can."

"Thank you" Arlene said.

"Don't thank me yet because this is going to be difficult for you. I have many years of things I haven't forgotten that you're going to have to make up for. I have forgiven some of them but I haven't forgotten. I'll probably throw some things up in your face. Are you willing to handle anything thrown at you?"

I wondered if my mom had meant that literally. I had never really known her to be violent or vindictive but this experience was bringing out things I didn't know about her. She might need to clarify that statement because my aunt Aggie would probably be the first one to take her up on it. I'm sure she would love to throw something at Arlene. Literally!

"Ain't no other way, Aubrey" Arlene said. "I want my family. I want the family I never had."

"Well, I'm willing to try, but I have to call the shots. I don't trust you yet. Even though I'm an adult now, I still have some of those feelings of fear that you put into me when I was a child. I'm working on that with God but I haven't gotten there yet."

"I understand."

My mom looked at Mrs. Warren and said she was finished with what she had. Mrs. Warren looked at Arlene and said "it's your turn. I know you only knew Amber as a young person but is there anything you remember about her that would make her smile? If there's nothing you remember about Amber, you should think of something that you know about Aubrey that you could draw from."

Arlene sat there for a moment. I hoped she was going to use her seventy something years to draw some wisdom because if she said the wrong thing, she was about to set herself back a few paces. She was still sitting there, saying nothing, when she turned to look at me. *I know she ain't thinking I'm gon' help her!* When that huge smile came across her face I thought to myself... "bingo!"

"My grandbaby" she said. "She is one of the loveliest young women I done met in a long time. You done a fine job brangin' her up. Thank you for lettin' me meet her. Thank you for thankin' enough 'bout me that you let her be my counselor even when you figured out who I was. I don't thank thangs coulda come out no better. She's somethin' to look at and a kind soul, just like you."

"Thank you" my mom said with a smile on her face. Arlene had succeeded! Of course, she used me to do it, but hey…you gotta do what you gotta do.

CHAPTER 37

Wednesday

TYSON HAD GONE through his whole day and hadn't been able to call Sasha. He tried once, but he was unpleasantly interrupted by Jamie. He had been sitting at his desk with the door closed. He had dialed four of the seven digits to Sasha's work number when Jamie burst into his office unannounced and uninvited!

"Are we not going to lunch?" Jamie asked with attitude.

"No, Jamie. I don't think it's a good idea. Maybe we need some time apart."

"Oh, so since you ended our 'relationship' we can't go to lunch anymore?"

"That's not what I'm saying Jamie. What I'm saying is that maybe we should let things die down a little. You know, so the emotions aren't so raw. Maybe, after that, we can be friends."

"Whatever, Tyson!" Jamie slammed the door to his office so hard the walls rattled. Great. Tyson thought to himself. Just great. Part of the reason he'd said what he said to Sasha was to appease Jamie, but he'd hurt Sasha. Now, his true feelings for Sasha have caused him to hurt Jamie. Instead of making things right he'd hurt two people.

Great. Just great. He replayed his day several times on his way home. And several more times over dinner, during his shower, while playing his Wii® and while getting ready for bed. He wouldn't be able to handle it tonight if he called Sasha and she rejected him. *I'll do it tomorrow*, he thought. Maybe things will look better and different tomorrow. Even though he knew tomorrow wasn't promised, he couldn't bring himself to make that call. Even though he knew he was going to have a restless sleep, he couldn't bring himself to make that call. Tomorrow he'd do it. Tomorrow.

Tomorrow came way too soon for Tyson. He rolled over and looked at his alarm buzzing at six o'clock. He didn't sleep a wink! This was going to be a long day. He got up to get ready for the work day. He even decided to pack his lunch so he would have a good excuse not to go to lunch with Jamie. He had a good enough excuse already, but it didn't go over too well yesterday so, he thought he should have a backup plan in place.

He got to work and the first thing he did was call Sasha's work number. He guessed it was too early for her to be in because the answering service picked up. *You have reached the confidential voice mail of Dr. Sasha Wade Payce. If this is an emergency please hang up and dial 911. If you are calling to cancel your appointment please press two. If you are a new client please press one to leave a detailed message and your call will be returned by the end of the next business day. For all other inquiries press three and your call will be returned as soon as business permits. Have a blessed day!*

Tyson already knew what he would say if he had to leave a message. "Hi, Dr. Payce this is Tyson Juarez. Please give me a call as soon as business permits. This is not an emergency. You can reach me at …"

He left his number at home and work. He didn't know if Sasha had an assistant or if she would personally listen to the voicemail. He tried to sound as general and professional as possible. He would have to wait to see if she called him back. The ball was in her court. Yes, he took the easy way out but at least he made the call.

My office work and clients would have to get along without me for the next few days because I decided to take off to hang out with my mom before she had to leave town. This family business was getting interesting and whenever we got home from our sessions we were always so tired. Everything was such a mess when she first arrived that we really hadn't spent any time together.

We decided we would go to the mall today. Gabby volunteered to hold down the office for a half a day, each day, the rest of the week. I told her to let me know if we had any emergency calls that I needed to take care of. Everything else would have to wait until Monday.

"So, baby girl" my mom started "what's the love life looking like?"

"Mom, I would rather not get into that" I said dryly.

"Why, not? You're a good catch. Why aren't you seeing anyone?" I lied. "Well, it's just too soon. I haven't been here long and I'm trying to make sure my business is in the black before I add anything else to my plate." "I understand that. But, don't make me wait too much longer for my grandbabies. I want to be young enough to be able to do things with them."

Oh, no. The dreaded "grandbabies" talk. I know how old I am! I know I should have started having babies years ago but…it just didn't work out like that for me. I'm not going to marry someone who I know is wrong for me just to have babies and get a divorce! So, maybe I'll just be alone. I don't know. I'd made too many mistakes choosing the ones I wanted. The ones I thought were right. I have horrible taste! So, my mom is gonna have to wait on God for those grandbabies.

We hung out until it was time to go to session. We went home to freshen up and drop off our packages before we headed to the church. When we got there the chairs were still set up just like they had been the night before. Of course, that was no surprise. Mrs. Warren was going to let everyone have their chance at this. She was right when she told Arlene she would be on the spot for the rest of the week. She should be. She's the cause of all this drama!

Arlene took her seat and chose Randall to be her next prosecutor. They waited for Mrs. Warren to give them permission to begin. Randall had his notes but he didn't look at them once he started. "My family is really important to me" he said. "You don't even know them. That hurts. I know it's partially my fault for not bringing them around but can you blame me? One of my children is light-skinned and the other one is darker. I know how you treated me because of my skin color. I purposely married the lightest woman I could find. Yes, I love Brandy, but I didn't want my children to look like me because of the way you acted toward me. If I brought my family around you, how would you treat them?" Randall asked that question with so much hurt and seriousness in his eyes that I wanted to cry.

"Son, I want a chance to know yo' family."

"Those are nice words but my question was 'how would you treat them'?"

"Like I said befo' Randall, yo' skin wasn't the problem. It was my shame."

"So, you took your shame and hurt out on me?"

"Yep. I'm sorry but that's what happened. That's the honest truth." Arlene admitted.

"So, let me ask you this… Are you still ashamed of me?"

Oooh. Good one Uncle Randall! Grandmommy Dearest was gon' have to step lightly around that one! Man, this was getting good. I wished I had a video camera and something to eat!

"No" she stated. "I ain't shame of you. I made a mistake but you wasn't the mistake."

"I don't really believe you and I definitely don't trust you but I guess I'll have to start somewhere" Randall said.

Arlene had seen Randall's family on several occasions. It was just that they never stayed long enough to really let the children get to know her. He had wanted it that way. He didn't want his children to know the kind of mother he had.

Randall had completed his assignment and it was now Arlene's chance to make him smile. Now, Randall was not a hard person to get along with, but he was not too cool with Arlene. I didn't know if she could make him smile or not. She knew it was her time to speak but just like before, she had to think about it. None of his children were in the room so she couldn't use the trick she used with my mom. She was going to have to dig deep.

"Well, since we bein' honest, I always did thank you was handsome. And, when you got to high school all them little fresh-tailed girls was always after you. I knowed then you was gon' make somebody a good husband one day. I'm real proud you got a nice family. I'm proud of you too 'cause you done so good even though I treated you so bad."

She did it. She actually made him blush a little. She figured it out. She actually listened to him. He wanted to be seen by her. Good old Arlene. I wasn't fooled though. The Lord was helping her. When I realized that, I knew she was going to be able to make each one of her children smile before this week was over. If that was His plan.

CHAPTER 38

Thursday

I WOKE UP with Tyson on my mind. I guess it was because of the conversation my mom started trying to have with me yesterday. The one about dating and grandbabies. I lied to her because she didn't know about Tyson. No one really knew how I felt about him except me and God and I didn't want anyone to know. That way I could pretend I wasn't in so much pain.

Not that my mother didn't give good advice. It was just that I knew the pain would be intensified for me if anyone else knew how humiliated I was when everything went down at work that day. Andrea doesn't even know how strong my feelings are for Tyson and he definitely doesn't know and never will! That's another reason why I keep things to myself. If no one knows I can always deny, deny, deny. *Tyson who? Please, he was just this guy I used to work with. I barely knew him.* That's the kind of stuff you can get away with as long as nobody knows the truth. It's okay if God knows. He'll never tell. He would never gossip. He would never try to make a fool of me. But people? Especially co-workers and church folk? They will throw you under a bus in a minute!

Today was going to be a rough day if I didn't keep myself busy. Whenever I wake up with Tyson on my mind I have a hard day. Those thoughts of rejection allow the enemy to work on me. My self-esteem, self-confidence, self-worth and self-everything else took a big hit with just that one rejection. It doesn't matter how many complements I get, they still don't take away the sting of that one rejection. Why? Because I don't have feelings for those other people so their words don't weigh as much. The ones we care the most about are the ones that hurt us the most. That's why my family is having such a hard time getting along. Hurtful words coming from someone you love or who you thought loved you, hurt so much more than those same words coming from an acquaintance or a stranger.

I was so caught up in my thoughts that I didn't hear my mother calling me.

"Girl, what are you doing? I called you three times" she said.

"Sorry, mom. I was thinking about something. I didn't hear you. Whassup?"

"You wanna go to the movies today?" she asked.

"Sure. That sounds good. What do you want to see?"

"Let's see that new love story that came out yesterday."

"Okay. Whatever you want."

"Well, you know I'm not watching any of that deranged stuff you like to look at."

"I know Mom. Pick out the movie and the time and we'll do it" I agreed.

Great. She wanted to watch some gag-me-with-a-fork love story. Just great. Like I don't have enough love issues already!

Session time rolled around again and all were present. Arlene was making her way to the hot seat and she had just invited Aggie to join her. I guess she wanted to end on a good note, with Bea, so she thought she would get Aggie out of the way. All I could think was that it was about to get hot in here!

Aggie jumped right in without Mrs. Warren having to prompt her. "Well, I guess I've pretty much said all I have to say to you about growing up. Now, I want to know how you plan to turn years of torture into something good?" But, Mrs. Warren stopped Aggie before she could get going.

"Aggie, I want you to concentrate on telling your mother what you need in order to have any kind of relationship together" she directed.

Aggie took a breath, looked down at her hands and shook her head. I didn't know if she was at a loss for words or what. I don't know if she really knew either. She was definitely going to have to change gears from where she was just heading. Even though she mentioned that she'd said all she needed to say, it seemed she was going to let Arlene have a little more.

I don't think this family session will be enough for most of Arlene's children. I think they all really need some one-on-one counseling and then joint sessions with Arlene. She'd really done them harm. I know she's saying now that she never meant for any of this to happen but the truth is…they all got issues! Correction… We all got issues!

Aggie was finally ready to speak. "I need for you to acknowledge me for the person I am" she said. "You acted like you didn't even know I existed unless you wanted me to do something for you. I wasn't Sally Agnes to you. I was more like your personal servant. You never once told me you appreciated anything I did. Never once told me you had any sort of feelings for me. Do you realize that I grew up wishing anybody else's mother was mine but you? When my friends would talk about what they were doing with their mother's when they got home or over the weekend, I would just melt away into the background. I knew I would never do any of those things with my mother.

"I need to know who I am to you. The only identity I had was that I was the oldest girl. That's how you always saw me. As just your oldest girl. It was almost as if I didn't have a name." Aggie paused again as if to collect her thoughts "I guess," she said, "what I really want is to feel like I'm important to you."

She stopped talking. Her face softened. She looked at her mother as if she was begging for love with her eyes. That was the first time I had ever seen Aggie look so vulnerable. I started to say a silent prayer rooting for God to speak through Arlene. I wanted to see more of this softer side of Aggie, but if Arlene failed at this moment Aggie was going to put her guard back up. This time she might build a wall so thick and high that we never get back in.

Arlene reached over and touched Aggie. She took her hand and Aggie didn't pull away. This was the first time I had seen Arlene touch any of her children. She looked into her daughter's eyes without saying a word. Neither one looked away or pulled away from the others touch. Then came three words from Arlene's mouth that sent both of them into tears. "I need you."

Arlene continued to talk through the tears which made the

rest of us tear up. She told Aggie "I always needed you. Just thank about what woulda happened to the kids without you? I wasn't no mama. You was they mama. You took good care of all us. You shouldn'ta had to do it. You was just a girl yo'self. And you wasn't crazy neither. It wasn't never nothin' wrong with you. That was somethin' I put on you for my own good. I was the one needed help. But, it wasn't you Sally Agnes. Never. I'm sorry. Forgive me."

Those last two short sentences nearly sent Aggie into her mother's lap. They embraced and just held each other. I just sat there smiling through my own tears. I knew it was God. To make Aggie break down? It had to be. That woman was tough as nails on the outside but inside…she was still that little girl desperately seeking recognition from her mother. And today, she finally got what she had been searching for. This wouldn't be the end of it. This was only the beginning, but I would have to say this was a really good start.

CHAPTER 39

Friday

ANDREA HAD WAITED as long as she could. She was expecting Sasha to give her a call and tell her she talked to Tyson but that hadn't happened. She really wanted to know what was going on. Would she have to call Sasha to get the scoop? She definitely couldn't ask Tyson because he gave her the stone-face when he got the number from her. She knew he wouldn't be giving up any information. But, she would have to wait until this evening. She needed to catch Sasha at home so she could really talk to her. Work conversations always had to be short because she had her clients coming in and out. But, she was definitely going to call tonight. Especially since it appeared that Tyson had broken things off with Jamie.

As Andrea was thinking about what she might say to Sasha when she called later, she saw Jamie walk by her desk on the way to Tyson's office. She hadn't noticed them going to lunch together for the past few days as she normally did. That had everyone in the office talking. Gossip. It never did anything except get people hurt, but it sure was fun to be on the side that was doing the gossiping.

The rumor going around the office for the week was that Jamie had caught Tyson cheating and broke up with him. Of course, there was never any real evidence that they had even been dating. Jamie was still trying to be friends with Tyson but Tyson was so embarrassed about being caught that he had been avoiding Jamie like the plague! Jamie was still trying to go to lunch and maybe work things out but Tyson was having none of that.

That was some pretty juicy stuff but no one could confirm it. Gossip. No one could ever confirm it. That's usually why someone always ended up getting hurt. Gossip is never the whole truth. It's either a partial truth or a straight-up lie!

Andrea was wondering if that was the reason why Tyson had been trying to contact Sasha. Maybe he wanted counseling. Maybe he wanted someone to give him some advice on what he should do. Andrea wasn't sure what his reason for getting the number was but she intended to find out. For now, she would just have to keep an eye on Tyson…

He had succeeded in getting Jamie to leave his office without things getting ugly. Maybe this would be okay after all. He had a lot of work to do and he had a lot of things on his mind. Namely, Sasha. He decided he would give her until Saturday evening to call. If she hadn't called by then he would cut his losses and keep going. He knew he wouldn't go back to Jamie though. He had always known that relationship was wrong for him. It was just that after Sasha was gone it was easy for him to remain in it.

Well, Sasha or no Sasha, he knew that if he went back to the way things were with Jamie he would suffer spiritually. That relationship wasn't right and wasn't going to be right no matter what he did. There was nothing wrong with being a platonic friend to Jamie but that was as far as it could go. Tyson just thought it best to stay completely out of any type of relationship with Jamie so he wouldn't be tempted. He knew God would never put any more on him than he could handle but he knew, all too well, that he could get himself into some sticky situations.

It was going on the third morning since Tyson had left Sasha that message and she hadn't called back. He was beginning to wonder but he had promised himself he would give her until Saturday evening. Nevertheless, the fact that she hadn't called yet was torturing him. He thought she liked him. She hadn't been gone that long, but maybe she had already forgotten about him. Maybe she had met some new guy that would be better for her than he would. All sorts of thoughts flooded his mind. He was so deep in thought that he didn't notice Andrea standing in his office doorway. He startled when he realized she was staring at him.

"What is it Andrea?" He asked. Kind of in a rude tone.

"Nothing, Tyson. I just wanted to see if you called Sasha

yet."

"Look Andrea, I really don't want to get into that with you right now. I have some projects due soon and I need to get busy, if you don't mind."

"No problem" Andrea said, as she walked out of the room closing the door behind her. She wondered what was going on. She could only assume they hadn't spoken yet because Sasha hadn't called her and Tyson seemed so tense she thought he would break the pen he was holding in his hand. Maybe Jamie was just getting on his nerves. Office break-ups could be a mess!

She went back to her desk to call Sasha, at work, to see if she could get any information. She had run out of time last night and hadn't been able to call like she planned. She picked up her phone, dialed Sasha's direct line at work and got her personal voicemail. Andrea looked at her watch. It was five to two where Sasha was. Andrea had purposely called during Sasha's usual paperwork time, in between clients. Sasha was always prompt. She would end each session at exactly ten to the hour and begin the next session on the hour. She would leave herself with ten minutes to do her session notes from the previous session before she moved on to the next client. Maybe she had gotten on the phone or gone to the bathroom. Andrea decided to try her again in an hour.

I was so glad I decided not to go to work because I don't think I would have been able to enjoy today as much. After last night's session I was feeling really good! Aggie and Arlene had experienced a break through. I wouldn't say that everything was great but it was getting better.

I was more excited for my mom. She had always been a pretty happy person but now it was more than happy. I think it was actually joy.

I was looking forward to our last session tonight with Arlene and Bea. Things had started to look up for the family. My only concern about Bea was finding out what was really happening to her during the blackouts. The family had successfully avoided her questions each time she brought them up. I honestly believed they had no idea but I had suspicion that my mother knew more than she let on. But, we would soon find out.

Bea had beaten Arlene to the chairs at the front of the room. Naturally, she knew she was up. She was the only one left. Arlene came in shortly after Bea and took her seat. I could tell that Arlene was confident that tonight's session would be a piece of cake. But, I was feeling a little uneasy. Bea was going to have the opportunity to confront her mother and tell her what she needed from her. The key, for Bea, was going to be to remain in control of her emotions because if she didn't…

"Good evening everyone" Mrs. Warren greeted. "I just want to let you all know how well you have done these past few days. I know this hasn't been easy but I am proud that all of you are hanging in there.

"We have our last full session tonight and then we'll set some future goals. I hope and pray that this family won't stop here. That you will continue to do whatever it takes to heal these deep wounds. What we've started is just the beginning. And with that said, let's get started." Mrs. Warren turned to Bea and signaled "You're on."

"I have to say that I am so happy to finally have all of the family back together" Bea said. "I realize it's been rough on most of you and I'm having a real issue with myself. Throughout this whole ordeal I seem to have come out unscathed again. I don't feel as if I'm in touch with my emotions at all.

"Thinking back over my life, every time I should have been emotional about something…the blackouts. I feel like I've missed out on some things and now I realize that you…" Bea looked at Arlene "…are at the bottom of it all. So, I need for you tell me what happened to me. For a while, I thought that when I had the 'blackouts' I was actually passing out. Like I was going to sleep or something. But, thanks to Aubrey, I know I was still functioning. I just don't remember what I was doing. I've heard stories about me doing terrible things that I don't remember. You must have noticed. You should be able to tell me something. What would make our relationship better and closer is the truth. I feel like you're hiding something from me and it's time you tell me what it is."

I didn't know how much Arlene knew about Bea's illness but I did know that if we opened this can of worms we were in for a long night. I was wrong about wanting Arlene to pick Bea first. If she had done that we may have never gotten to anyone else!

I got Mrs. Warren's attention and motioned, with my eyes, for her to come to me. I hadn't really talked to her about this but I felt like I needed to let her know what I knew about Bea. She came over to sit by me and I tried to be as discreet as possible. I told Mrs. Warren of my suspicions and the look on her face told me she already had an idea of what was going on. Of course, she was more seasoned than I. Boy, was I glad she had things under control. I could relax a little, but only a little.

"Bea, you was always meek. I wanted to keep you safe" Arlene said.

"Keep me safe from what? You? You never protected any of the other children.

Why me?"

"I was tryin' to keep you safe from yo'self."

"What on Earth are you talking about? You really thought I would try to hurt myself?"

"Yes."

"I don't believe you. I'm finding out you was never really concerned about us. It was always about you. So, tell me…what were you trying to protect yourself from?"

Whoa. Bea was coming for her mother! That worried me. This was a change from her usual behavior and from what I had discovered about Bea, this wasn't a good thing.

"From yo'self Molly Bea, honest" Arlene said.

Arlene started fidgeting and blinking her eyes.

"What did you think I would do to myself?" Bea asked.

"Well, when you was a young'n you was so mild mannered. You didn't care 'bout nothin' goin' on 'round you. But, then you got sass to you. Like the time you put Amber in the trash can and the time you pulled the knife on me. I was gittin' 'fraid of you so, I tried my best to keep you happy. When you wasn't happy you done them terrible thangs."

"Oh. Why didn't you get me any help?" Bea asked.

I wanted to know the answer to that question too. She had the money...

Arlene looked down at the floor... "That was what them govament checks was fo', but I didn't never take you" she admitted.

"See, that's what I'm talking about. You spent money that was supposed to help me. Help us. And you just blew it!"

"Bea, I didn't really know then. I thought you was just throwin' little hissy fits. By time I figure you was really in trouble it was too late!"

Bea was squinting her eyes and pursing her lips in Arlene's direction. I could see her chest expanding and contracting. I was looking at both of them and getting a little anxious. *Let it out Bea*, I said to myself. *You have to release that anger or...*

"I should have killed you when I had the chance!"

Before she even finished that statement Bea's hands were wrapped around her mother's throat! Everyone was stunned for just a split second and then Randall was up! He was trying to pry Bea's hands from Arlene's throat. I sat, paralyzed. Randall pounded on Bea's hands and then he tried weaving his fingers through hers in an attempt to unlace them from Arlene's neck. My mom and Aggie pulled Arlene in the opposite direction of Bea's vice grip. Bea was screaming obscenities! Mrs. Warren was the only one who was calm. She motioned for me to come to help her. She whispered in my ear and told me what needed to be done. I was now in therapist mode. I began to talk.

"Bea. Can you hear me? If you can hear me I need you to answer me. Bea." I used the calmest voice I could. To myself, I sounded like the "dry eyes" guy.

"Bea this is Mrs. Warren. If you can hear me please answer your niece."

That was a strange request. I wondered why Mrs. Warren had referred to me as Bea's niece. Sure, technically that was true but it was still strange. I touched Bea's leg and repeated. "Bea, if you can hear me answer me. I'm waiting for you to speak."

The grip on Arlene's neck finally loosened enough for her

to break free. Aggie and mom moved Arlene away from Bea as quickly as they could while they had the chance. I continued to attempt to get Bea to answer my question.

"If you can hear me Bea, say yes."

Finally, Bea blinked and looked at me "yes, I hear you."

The car ride home was silent. We had taken Bea to the psychiatric ER just to have her checked out. They were going to keep her overnight for observation and we would go back to pick her up later today. It was now two o'clock Saturday morning. What a night! Arlene got the shock of her life! Actually, we all did. I had never experienced anything like that before in my entire career! I don't care how long you go to school. I don't care how many hours of crisis training you have. I don't know if anyone is ever prepared to handle something like what happened tonight. Man, was I glad that Mrs. Warren was there! God was definitely on her side.

She wanted us to come back for a final session tomorrow. I didn't know if we could take anymore. After tonight, I'd had enough. But, I trusted Mrs. Warren. If she felt we needed to come back, then that's what I was going to do.

CHAPTER 40

Saturday

"GOOD MORNING MOM…how did you sleep?"

"Not too good. I couldn't get Bea off my mind."

"Yea…me too."

"What happened to Bea? What in the world would make her snap like that?"

I had an idea but since I wasn't sure I just said, "I don't know…"

Before leaving the hospital this morning the family decided to go back to see her as soon as visiting hours started. That would be at eight o'clock. We all felt bad about even leaving her there because she was fine by the time we got her to the hospital. She had calmed down and was back to herself. She didn't even remember what happened! She didn't understand why we wanted her to be checked out. None of us really had the heart to tell her that she had physically assaulted her mother! But, we did tell the doctors. We didn't know what time they were going to release her so we decided to visit and just wait to see what the hospital staff had to say.

The only thing Bea knew was that she had "a blackout" during the session. She remembered that she got angry with Arlene and her next recollection was me asking if she could hear me the very last time I asked. We didn't tell her what really happened. Mrs. Warren felt like she was too fragile for us to tell her and of course, I agreed.

By the time all of the family arrived at the hospital they were ready to release Bea. The staff psychiatrist informed us that he gave Bea some sleep aids just in case she needed them for tonight. He also prescribed something that Arlene would have considered a "nerve" pill, and recommended that she seek therapeutic services. Luckily, we already had that under control. None of it came as a shock.

We gathered Bea and went to the church. Mrs. Warren promised the last session would be nothing intense. After last night, everyone was a little fried. We had all come in separate cars except Mom and me. Bea decided she would ride with us. Her car was still at the church. We had left it there last night when we took her to the hospital. I offered to stop off and get her prescription filled but she told me there was no way she would be needing that medication. The way I felt, I started to tell her to get it filled for me.

We got to the church and the chairs had all been moved back into original formation. A semi-circle. Everyone took a seat and Mrs. Warren began with prayer. The way she prayed was so intense. She was determined and desperate. She wanted our family to be healed. And if she had any favor with God, He was going to do it just because she asked so fervently.

After talking to God, she began to talk to us. "I want you all to be blessed. I want you all to bless one another. There is so much hurt in this room and it will not all be healed at once. And God is not going to just do it for you. You are going to have to work for it. You are going to have to show Him that you want it.

"I'll get you started and then you're going to have to do the rest on your own. You'll definitely need to continue counseling. I know that Aubrey is returning home so you will have to make it work. There are some assignments you can begin with that will be very important to your healing and reunification. I would suggest that you complete the assignments and then allow them to evolve. Come up with other creative ideas. Sasha can help you. She won't be your counselor anymore, but as a member of the family, she can make suggestions.

"Your first assignment is to communicate. Everyone needs to write a personal letter to the other. That means each of you will have to write five letters. Then you will need to answer the letters you receive. So, not only will you write five letters but you will receive five letters and you will respond to five letters. After the letters, you need to begin making at least one phone call a month. That will be each of you making one call a month but you will actually talk to the same person twice. For instance, Aubrey will call Arlene once but then Arlene will have to call Aubrey once as well. This is not going to be an easy task but it needs to happen. You guys have to get to know each other again. You have to learn what is important in the lives of your family members. That's the only way you can reconnect.

"Bea, I have someone special in mind to counsel with you. Aubrey, I would suggest that you find someone in your area to begin individual counseling with. As for the rest of you, Sasha and I would be more than willing to recommend other counselors for you. But, the bottom line is, you all need this. You cannot forget about the last two weeks. You've made some progress. Please don't throw it away and go back to the way things were before. And, if you haven't learned anything else from all of this…please stop the secrets! Be honest. The lies do nothing but hurt. And whether you want to believe it or not, there are lies of omission. By that I mean, withholding the truth from someone is the same as lying to them.

"You guys need to become aware of the things people do to distance themselves from one another. You have to do everything you can to start building bridges to each other. And, I want you to start today. I want you guys to get dressed and go out for dinner tonight. My treat. Aubrey is leaving tomorrow and I don't believe you have all been in one place together since the reunion. The family sessions and the hospital don't count." Everyone had to chuckle about that comment.

"I also want to invite you all to service in the morning. I don't know what my husband is going to preach about but I know he'll have an awesome word for you! He would love to have all of you there. Bring the rest of your family along. We want to see you all!

"Before I dismiss you I just want you all to know that I believe in you. I know that you can be healed. I believe in Him. I know that He is everything. But, you have to believe. If you don't it won't happen. He can do anything. Always remember that. He brought you all here. And like I said before, if you think this thing is a coincidence you're wrong. Nothing that

God does is luck. It's divine. I'll see you all in the morning. Have a great dinner!"

Mrs. Warren hugged each one of us and whispered blessings and encouragement to each. She made us hug one another as well. That was kind of weird because I don't think our family is the hugging kind. But, it was therapeutic. Touch is therapeutic. Right then, I couldn't help but think of Tyson. Ugghhh! His touch was something I had never felt, only dreamed about. The touch I wanted from him had no filth about it either. Just warmth. When I think about him wrapping his arms around me I just feel so safe and loved. But, that's only in my dream. That's the only place where it's safe to love him. He wouldn't reject me there.

Tyson wanted to keep himself busy all day. This was the day he had chosen to let the Sasha thing go if she hadn't called by this evening. He didn't know if that was fair or not but he didn't want to keep himself in limbo. He hated the feeling of not knowing what to do because he was a person who always liked to be in control. He understood that a relationship couldn't survive if one person needed to be in control of everything but that had never stopped him from trying.

He decided he would take himself to the movies. He didn't see anything wrong with going to the movies alone. He was sure other people saw it as desperate but he didn't. He was a very confident man, on the outside.

Just as he was getting his plans together his phone rang. He had barely gotten out of bed. Who could be calling this early? He started to ignore the ring but figured maybe it was important. Whoever it was, had to know him. The bill collectors and solicitors didn't normally start calling until after ten o'clock.

He grabbed the cordless to look at the caller ID. Jamie. Unbelievable! Then he remembered they had made a date for tonight before the "break up." Aw man, he thought. He just let the voicemail pick up because he really didn't feel like dealing with that at the moment. Taking that phone call might put a damper on his day! The voicemail clicked on. Good. He would just check the messages later.

He headed for the bathroom to shower and shave but before he reached the shower door his cell phone rang. No way! It better not be Jamie! This time he decided to ignore it. He hopped in the shower and started singing. Trying to drown out any negative thoughts or unwanted phone calls. Maybe he would take himself to lunch too and just make a date of it. A date with himself. Why not? *Women do that kind of stuff all the time. Why shouldn't guys do it too?* Sure, it wasn't considered manly but so what? It was what he felt like doing.

Tyson jumped out of the shower still singing and before he could get dressed his doorbell rang. Now he was mad! If this was Jamie…Tyson was ready to go off! Why couldn't the relationship just be over? Why couldn't Jamie give him some time to himself? They didn't have anything that belonged to the other so there was no need to keep in contact. There was definitely not a reason for either of them to show up at the home of the other!

He finished getting dressed and took his time. Showing up at his house, unannounced was not a good move if Jamie had any hope of them being friends. He grabbed his keys and his wallet and went through the garage. He started his car and pulled out. Jamie came around the corner flagging him down. Tyson stopped, simply to avoid a hit-and-run! Jamie was getting on his nerves now and for a split second he thought about committing a crime.

But, he rolled down his window instead. "Whassup Jamie? Why are you at my house so early and without…" Tyson stopped in mid-sentence because he was about to say without calling but realized that Jamie had called. Twice. "…unannounced. I was on my way out. Is there an emergency?"

Jamie looked confused. "I thought we had a date today."

"We did, but after our conversations on Monday and Tuesday I assumed you knew we wouldn't be hanging out today" Tyson was annoyed. "And anyway, even if we did have a date, why would it be this early?" "Well, you didn't answer either of your phones so, I just thought I would come by to make sure you were alright".

"Oh, Okay. Thanks for your concern. That's sweet, but did

you ever think that I was still asleep?"

"Well, no. You're always up early."

"Yeah. You have a point. But, everything is okay. I was on my way out. I don't think it's a good idea if we hang out today. I apologize if I wasn't clear on that. Take care and I'll see you on Monday."

Tyson's garage door was already down. He rolled his window up and backed away from his house leaving Jamie standing in the driveway. He didn't want to be so rude but he knew that if the conversation had gone on any longer it would have become unpleasant.

Tyson spent the entire day by himself. He ate twice, went to the movies and shopped. Now he was home. Alone. A sadness fell over him and he began to wonder if maybe he should call Jamie. What would it hurt for them to be friends? After all, Sasha hadn't called and by now he figured she didn't plan to. It had been five days since he left her that message.

He knew it was no one's fault but his own. He started it when he rejected her at the office. Why would she call him? He was a jerk to her. Now, he was paying for it. You reap what you sow, he thought. If you give rejection you get rejection. Tyson lay in bed and threw himself a pity party. After he finished with that he threw himself a guilt party. Then he sang, when I say Tyson you say punk... He partied until he dozed off to sleep. He had given up on Sasha, but he still drifted off to sleep thinking about her.

The family had chosen Red Lobster's for dinner and we were having a really good time. Eating is one of my favorite hobbies so, I would have had a good time whether they did or not! No one was really talking about themselves but they were talking about their families. Everyone had children except me. I was hoping my mother wouldn't jump on that and start talking about grandbabies again.

I watched the siblings as they ate and talked. I also noticed that Arlene was sitting as far away from Bea as she could but she was seated right next to Aggie. Now that was a miracle! I thought Aggie would have been the one that ended up with her fingers attached to Arlene's throat. It turns out that their little

Ms. Sunshine, Bea, was the violent one. Who would have thought? Well, actually, they'd seen it before. She just didn't know she had it in her.

We all agreed to go to the eleven o'clock service in the morning because the church was closer to the airport than my house. My mom's plane was scheduled to depart at three. I figured we'd get out of church by one, grab a quick bite to eat and take Mom to meet her plane. I didn't want her to go and now everyone in the family shared my feelings. She was the reason we were all together. Sure, Arlene had come up with the idea, but most of the family had decided they wouldn't attend if my mom didn't agree to come. Well, I sure am glad she did. The visit started off rocky but it was beginning to smooth out nicely.

We paid the check with the gift card Mrs. Warren purchased for us. We planned to meet at the front doors of the church at 10:30am. Mom and I couldn't stand being late so we said 10:30 so the family would all be there by 10:45am. That way we wouldn't be walking in after service had already started.

It was time for bed and after the last couple of days I was ready for a good night's sleep. Mom stayed up and packed to make sure she wouldn't have to do any last minute running around in the morning. I jumped in the shower, brushed and flossed my teeth, said my prayers, and of course… thought about Tyson.

CHAPTER 41

Sunday

TYSON WOKE UP with a hangover even though he'd had nothing to drink. He needed to get up and go to church. He was hurt that Sasha didn't call him so he knew he needed to get out of the house. No use in sitting around sulking all day. The best place for him to be on a Sunday morning was at the altar, especially since he had a broken heart. He didn't want to admit that to anyone but God. He already knew anyway...

He was all ready for church except he couldn't find his cell phone. He looked all over for it. The last time he actually remembered having it was yesterday before he left the house. When Jamie was calling. He headed back to his room to look on the dresser. On his way passed the sliding glass door leading to the patio, he noticed a small crack. There was glass on the floor and the door was unlocked. He ran to his room. The cell phone wasn't on the dresser. He picked up his home phone to call the cell. If it was in the house that was the best way to find it. But, he knew he wouldn't find it. He went into his den to check his computer. Nothing else appeared to be missing but he had a feeling his home had been invaded. He had driven away yesterday and left Jamie standing in the driveway...

Tyson arrived at the church right as the choir was beginning praise and worship. He didn't even get a chance to sit before everyone was asked to stand up and join in. He didn't mind though. This was one of his favorite parts of the service. He loved music. He couldn't play any instruments or sing a lick but he loved music. He enjoyed a variety of styles too. Partly due to his upbringing.

Even though he couldn't sing he did have rhythm. How could he not? His father was Latino and his mother was the double A. African-American. Whenever anyone asked him about his heritage he would always acknowledge both. He felt that if he didn't he would be sacrificing a part of himself. He had the utmost respect for both his parents and their respective families. He was proud of his bi-racial, bi-lingual, bi-cultural heritage. It made him unique.

The church that he was a member of helped him embrace everything he was. They had people of all races to either visit, attend or become members. He had even been asked to utilize his first language during Bible studies. He was fluent in Spanish. His father and paternal grandmother would only speak Spanish to him when he was a child. He didn't like it because it embarrassed him in front of his English-speaking friends. Mr. Juarez spoke English fluently but he wanted to be sure that Tyson would be able to communicate with everyone in his family. He also knew that since he wasn't going to raise him in Puerto Rico he would have to instill the heritage and language in him somehow. Tyson appreciated his father for that. It had helped him a great deal in many areas of his life. It made him so happy to feel needed. Especially at church.

Tyson was getting lost in his worship. He was beginning to forget all about the pain he'd felt this morning. The angry, suspicious thoughts that had started to develop for Jamie were dissipating. He was where he needed to be.

The sermon began with "Forgiveness! Forgiveness is not always for the other person. Forgiveness is often about releasing someone or something so you can have peace for yourself."

This was a message that Tyson definitely needed to hear. He had so much guilt about the things he had said about Sasha. About the way he broke things off with Jamie. Even though he knew it was the right thing to do, Jamie wasn't happy about it at all. Maybe he could have done things differently. Maybe he could have taken the time to soften things a bit. Explain a little more than he had. Maybe then Jamie wouldn't have reacted so negatively and so harshly. Not that it didn't need to happen. Just maybe not the way it happened.

"Now, I'm not saying you have to like everyone and be friends with them" Tyson's pastor continued "but, you do have to love them. You may have to love them from a distance but you have to love them. Jesus loved even those who crucified him and we have the nerve to be mad and hateful toward people for stealing a parking space! Give people a chance. And after you give them a chance, give them another one. We're not perfect. We're just trying to be. If you forgive others God will forgive you. You want to be forgiven, don't you? Well, so do they.

Maybe the same person you want forgiveness from needs forgiveness from you. Why don't you, as a Christian, take the first step. Call them. Apologize to them. Ask them for forgiveness. Even if they don't accept it, you know you tried. But, don't stop there. Try again. They may never forgive you. But, don't allow their unwillingness to forgive to mess with your walk. You go on forgiving."

Tyson knew what he needed to do. He had just been given a boost of confidence! He didn't really feel like being a punk right now. He wanted to do the right thing. He was listening to his heart. He needed to forgive but most of all he needed to be forgiven. He knew that God had forgiven him and he was working on forgiving himself. He wanted to ask Sasha for her forgiveness. Whether she accepted his apology or not he needed to do this for himself.

That was a great service and Tyson was feeling good! He was so glad he went. He had a challenge in front of him. But, he couldn't find his cell phone and all of Sasha's numbers were in the phone. If he didn't make that call today he might punk out again! He would have to figure out how to get in touch with her. This meant he might have to beat Jamie down to get his phone back or suck it up and call Andrea and ask for the numbers again! Ugghhh!

He was really, seriously thinking about beating Jamie down regardless! He just knew God wouldn't be pleased with that so, he tried to come up with an alternate plan. After all, he couldn't be positive that Jamie had the phone anyway. All he had were his suspicions. And the cracked patio door! He suspected that after he left his house yesterday, Jamie went in to find something to hold on to and lucked up on the cell phone. Now there would be a reason for Tyson to come over or call.

The anger was coming over him again until he realized... He had a tracking system on his phone. All he had to do was pull up the locater and he could find out the exact location of his phone and the person and/or place holding it hostage.

Um-hump. He recognized the address and location of the phone immediately because he had been there several times. Now he would have to get himself together so he could come up with a plan that didn't involve bringing physical harm to the captor of his phone. Tyson wasn't a violent person but Jamie was taking things too far! Breaking into his house? If Jamie had any hopes of them being friends it had been ruined with this one stupid act of desperation. Tyson headed for his car determined not to allow his day to be ruined.

With each step I took toward my trunk I became saddened. I was putting my mom's bags in so we could take her to the airport after church. It was starting to feel like the day I left home all over again. My mom was buzzing around singing as she normally did. Going to church always made her sing. I used to pretend not to like her singing but it was actually pretty good. I joined in with her and sang in my head. It did make me feel a little better.

We hopped in the car to make sure we weren't late. "Hey Mom…do you need to stop by store to get souvenirs for your friends back home?"

"I might look when I get back to the airport, but I really don't intend to spend too much money on that. Maybe I'll get some stuff on my next trip."

That made me feel a lot better. She was already thinking about her next trip. I couldn't wait to see her again and she hadn't even left yet.

We arrived at the church promptly. To our surprise the whole family was already there! Arlene, Aggie, Bea and Randall were present and there were several others with them. I didn't really know any of them but I thought I recognized some of them. Probably from the minute at the family reunion that I was coherent. As we got out of the car and walked toward everyone I started to smile. I began to recognize people from their descriptions.

I had already met Brandy. His daughter looked exactly like him except her complexion was lighter than his. It reminded me of a vanilla wafer. She was gorgeous. So was his son. He was a nice mix of both his mom and dad. He walked like his dad, smiled like his mom and his complexion bore a strong resemblance to a smoked almond. These are my cousins. Wow! I actually have cousins!

I was introduced to Aggie's children as well. We were closer to the same age. There were four of them. Three girls and a boy. Just like Arlene's children and in the same birth order too! Two girls, a boy then a baby girl. Interesting. I began to wonder if they'd gone through any of the same experiences. I wondered what my mom was thinking. This was the first time I had met my cousins and her first time meeting her nieces and nephews. She was grinning from ear to ear. So, I think it would be safe to guess she was pretty happy.

We all went inside the church to try and get seats that would hold the entire family. We took up two pews. It was kind of neat. I'd never had family before and now I had enough to take up two pews! Everyone sat and appeared to be happy that we were all here together. I wondered how well any of them new each other. Had the cousins seen much of one another before this morning? The magnitude of what was happening here was overwhelming.

Aubrey thought she was going to have to excuse herself. She couldn't catch her breath. She was hoping no one around her was watching. Hoping they were too caught up in the message to notice. She was definitely praying that he wouldn't see her and that if he did, he wouldn't recognize her. She started planning her escape route.

Was Pastor Warren in my head or did Mrs. Warren talk to him about me? His message was right on target. I mean, it usually hit on something I needed but I didn't recall it ever being this close! I was almost paranoid. Who did I tell my business to? He couldn't possibly know all this information about me unless... I knew Mrs. Warren wouldn't do such a thing. Plus, the part of my business he was all up in, she didn't even know about! Nobody did. Of course, God knows how to touch the heart of any person. It was up to us whether we would listen or not. And right now, I was definitely listening!

"Relationships are difficult but they're worth it" Pastor Warren told us. "Relationships are important to God. If they weren't he wouldn't have focused so much on us loving one another. He would just allow us to do whatever we wanted to whomever we wanted without consequence. But as you all know, that's not how He works. We cannot just treat each other any, ole kinda way. We need to stop putting conditions on people and just love them the way He does. Give people another chance. Stop holding grudges. Stop getting your feelings hurt so easily. Try and put yourselves in the other person's place sometime. Try and think about how you would handle situations. Think about someone besides yourself for a change."

Pastor was so right. We were selfish people, for the most part. We did things according to how it would make us feel and not according to how our actions might affect another person. I couldn't help but think of how things had gone down before I left home. What if Andrea had kept her mouth closed about my feelings for Tyson? She didn't really think about how she was putting him on the spot. But, I have to take some of the blame myself. I could have reacted differently as well. I didn't have to just run off. When I made that decision I wasn't thinking about anyone but myself. I was just trying to spare my feelings and save face. I didn't really think about how my mother would feel about me leaving or how my job might be affected. I didn't even give them any notice! I left all my friends behind and have barely talked to anyone besides my mom since I left. I may have severed some important relationships by handling the situation the way I did.

Unbelievable! The voice was a little bit different but the face was the same. Aubrey was beginning to realize that the longer she remained in this town the less control she had over her life. First, her daughter had found out about her family before she planned to tell her and now this. How was she going to get out of this one? She needed to get out of this church undetected. She hadn't heard much of the message because she couldn't concentrate. So, she didn't notice that Pastor Warren had finished his sermon. Still planning her escape route she was jarred back to reality by the announcements.

"Would all of our first time visitors please stand" Mrs. Warren asked.

Oh, no! She was going to have to stand up for everyone to see. Maybe she could get away with not standing since they had two rows of family members who were already standing. And then, it happened.

"Aubrey, would you stand please. Sasha does so much for the church and the community. I want everyone to know who her mother is!"

She had no choice after that. She stood and the congregation applauded her for having such a lovely daughter. She tried not to make eye contact with him but he had seen her. He nodded and smiled. But, didn't look as if he recognized her. Maybe it had been that long. Maybe he'd forgotten about her. But, how could he? Forgetting that she had asked God to make her invisible to him, now she was angry! She didn't see any recognition in his expression. Was he that cold or was he that forgetful? He didn't even look twice at his first love!

After service, everyone rushed up to talk to the pastor. That was Aubrey's chance to get lost in the crowd and head for the back door. Before anyone could turn around she was in the parking lot! Her daughter and the rest of the family followed looking confused. Her plan was to get out the church and out of the state before her emotions got the best of her.

"Mom, I wanted you to meet Pastor".

"I know honey but there were so many people around. You know I'll be back to visit before too long so I'll just meet him then".

I knew something wasn't quite right but I had no idea what it was. Mom looked like she was having some sort of mini meltdown. I decided I would wait until we got to the car to see if she would talk to me about it. Then, I remembered that Bea, along with everyone else, had planned to accompany us to the airport. She was definitely not going to open up with everyone there. I then decided to just wait until she got back home.

Maybe over the phone she might be more inclined to tell me the truth. But, I would wait for her.

CHAPTER 42

Now What?

MOM WAS ON her way back home and I had a long drive ahead of me. I started thinking about how these last two weeks of my life had gone. I just started to praise God in the car as I drove. He had orchestrated this entire thing! Before all this happened I had been asking him to reveal things about my life to me. Never, in a million years, would I have thought of anything like this. I have a family!

I definitely started to wonder what else was ahead for me but I was afraid to ask. Be careful what you ask for is a cliché. Be careful what you ask God for is the truth! He just might give it to you. So, if you ask you better be ready for the answer. I wasn't quite ready for the answer I got. But, it was worth it.

God is good! He wants good things for us. He wants to see us healed. I like what Mrs. Warren said to my family. She said 'it's time to heal'. And, she is right. This family has been estranged and in pain far too long. My only prayer now is that we continue the healing process. I say "we" now because I have become a part of the process. I actually became a part of the process when they came to me for counseling. That was some of His handy work too. And, it's awesome. I can't wait to see the finished product. I can feel him molding us. He knew we would never have done this on our own.

Oh! I know Arlene might want to take credit for this because she was the one who came up with the idea of the family reunion. But, what she may or may not understand is that He put the idea in her spirit. She was just being obedient when she followed through with it. And of course, I would hope that everyone would remember that had God not put it on my mother's heart to come, there would have been no reunion. The siblings had either not wanted to attend or only attended because she was coming.

What would happen next nobody knew. We all had a lot to

think about but my concern was that my mom came through this experience unharmed. I was watching the clock and her plane was supposed to land in two hours and fifteen minutes. In my mind, I was giving her three hours to call me. My heart was heavy about what happened with her at church today. She seemed to be fine until Pastor Warren got up to preach. She looked as if she'd seen a ghost! I'm sure she didn't know I was watching her. I just couldn't figure out what was going on. But, I was starting to piece some things together.

She shot out of that church for a reason. She didn't even want to meet Pastor or speak to Mrs. Warren. Was she attracted to him or something? Was the message that bad? Maybe I shouldn't be so concerned about it. My mom acts strange like that sometimes. I'll just wait for her to call me. I needed to check my voicemails and maybe catch up on other stuff for work. I could do that while I waited. Having been out of the office for three days, there was no telling how many missed calls I had.

After locating his phone, Tyson decided to drop by Jamie's house. He prayed as he drove.

Lord, you know I need to discontinue my relationship with Jamie. I need your help to make sure I do what I need to do. I thought that breaking it off would be the end of it, but it looks like I was wrong. I never meant to hurt anyone in this whole thing, but I have. Help me make it right. I don't want to have anger or resentment toward Jamie and I definitely don't want those feelings coming back at me. Help me, Lord. I can't figure this out. I can't fix this on my own. Give me the words to say.

Tyson continued praying earnestly until Jamie opened the front door. "Hey, Jamie. Sorry for dropping by unannounced but I couldn't call you. I don't have my cell phone. When I tracked it I realized it was here. Just came by to pick it up. Would you get it for me please?"

The smile on Jamie's face slid to the floor. "Don't you want to come in?"

"No, thank you. I'm just leaving church and really want to get home. Thanks for the offer though."

Tyson saw the defeat in Jamie's eyes but stood his ground.

Jamie turned toward the living room, leaving the door open and retrieved the cell phone off the coffee table. Jamie simply handed the phone over to Tyson and closed the door.

Thank you, Lord.

Tyson hopped back in his car without having to go "Hulk smash" on Jamie or get into anything unnecessary. *Won't He do it!* He had only one more thing to do before he went to bed tonight.

Why is it taking her so long to answer?

What is that girl doing? She knew I was going to call when I got home.

My phone was ringing. I guess I fell asleep. Must be Mom.

I don't want her voicemail. I want her.

I need to talk to her about this before someone else does.

I can't find the stupid phone and I turned my tracker off.

I don't want to lose my nerve.

I hope she doesn't have to go to the hospital after she finds out about this.

Both of my phones are ringing and I can't find either one of them!

Answer the phone Sasha.

Answer the phone Sasha.

There it is! "Hello? Ooops, hold on, I dropped the phone! Hello?"

"Hi Sasha."

Instead of the phone, my heart dropped this time. Whoever was calling on the other line would have to wait. The sound of that voice sent chills down my spine and I started to sweat.

"Hi, Tyson."

Aubrey tried to call her daughter at home, but she didn't get an answer. She wasn't sure why she was in panic mode, but she was. The voicemail picked up. She hung up, dialed her cell phone and got that voicemail too. Frustrated, she had no choice but to leave a message.

"Sasha, this is your mother. Please call me when you get this message. I don't care what time it is. I have something very important to tell you and it cannot wait. Call me back. Tonight! No matter what time it is."

Aubrey hung up the phone feeling like she was about to explode. Of all the secrets she had kept from her daughter, this one might be the one to break her. But, she could not wait a moment longer. She needed to tell Sasha that the pastor she so adores is her father…

IT'S TIME OUT for "what goes on at home stays at home" because it's not true. What goes on at home goes everywhere you go because you carry it. What this phrase really means is… don't talk about it. If life and death are in the power of the tongue, what happens to your power if you don't speak? From reading this book I hope you learned another incorrect phrase. "What you don't know won't hurt you." The lies! What you don't know can and will eventually hurt you because nothing remains a secret forever. It's time to start dealing with our stuff and getting rid of it so it's not passed down to the next generation. The help you need is available if you want it. Are you ready? A Time to Heal is just the beginning...

Get Connected

Facebook.com/AttheTableCounseling
Instagram.com/atthetablecounseling
Twitter.com/ATC_Counseling

Author Soneakqua J. White has created an online course to assist you in your healing process. This course is designed to help you deal with a mother who makes it difficult for you to care *for* and/or care *about* her. If you have ever asked yourself "why does my mother treat me the way she does" this course is for you. If you have found yourself wanting to scream out "Help! My mom doesn't like me" this course is for you. If you spent the majority of your life trying to make your mother proud of you or just trying to survive being raised by her and you still have not succeeded…this course is for you. You will learn how to love yourself even though she didn't like you. You will learn to stop compromising your mental, physical, emotional and spiritual health to get someone to love you who does not acknowledge your effort. Take your power out of her hands and live! Copy the link below in your url to receive the coupon code for this course.

https://www.udemy.com/working-through-mommy-issues/?couponCode=DOTHEWORK